# When All Hell

# Breaks LoOse

A NOVEL

## Camika Spencer

ST. MARTIN'S GRIFFIN ✖ NEW YORK

Book design by JoAnn Metsch

www.stmartins.com

Library of Congress Cataloging-in-Publication Data

Spencer, Camika.
    When all hell breaks loose / Camika Spencer.
        p.   cm.
    ISBN 0-312-26793-2
    1. Afro-American Fiction.    I. Title.
PS3569.P4459W47    1999
813'.54—dc21                                                    99-20832
                                                                    CIP

First published in the United States by Akimac Publishing
Published in the United States by Random House, Inc., New York, and
simultaneously in Canada by Random House of Canada Limited, Toronto

First St. Martin's Griffin Edition: October 2000

10 9 8 7 6 5 4 3 2 1

**In memory of**
brady gray
adolphus spencer
christina l nolan
edna lee gray


**Dedicated to**
christopher j spencer
bridgette clay (spencer)
bertha gray
john & louise lemmons
mr & mrs cephus williams

# Acknowledgments

THANKS TO: GOD for speaking me into this existence. Virginia and Charles Williams for being the coolest parents on this planet. My dad, Calvin Spencer, for learning a few lessons the hard way and then telling me about it. My brothers Rawland and Troy. My Aunt Dorothy and cousin Keisha for having books everywhere and allowing me to forage inside the bookshelves. Black Images Bookstore for hiring me, molding me, and teaching me how to treat an author and how to be one. Toni Patterson and Irish Smith Burch for loving my made-up stories so much I decided to publish them. Omar Tyree for allowing me to run inside his head about this business. All black bookstores and book clubs who sold and supported the book before the acquisition. Sederrick Raphiel and the Design Factory (when you come to the door, just tell them your name is on the list). Lushena Book Distribution for hustling the paperback. Carrie Coles of Dygnati Books for telling Manie about me. Manie Barron (my BP!!!) who is waaaay too giggly sometimes. And finally, to my future agent . . . get ready!

I would be remiss if I didn't mention those who have supported me since I was scooped. . . . My Random House/Villard staff . . . y'all are bubbly too! The Spencers, the Grays, the Hayneses, Cherish Greer, Melissa Clay, Kyndal Robertson, Pervis Taylor III, Kandace Barnett, Sonja Gray, Teresa McGilbray, Tyra X (Yelder), the Roque-mores, the Fullyloves, Kendralyn Lewis, David Farmer, Raylene Sullivan, Simeon and Opal Robertson, the Sankofa family, the Reci-procity Family, Heather Douglas VanDuan, Jordan Rechis and the WTS EDS Team, Jimmy Porch, Raymond Mbala, Haji Akhigbade, Dwight Aziz Roseman (*what if?*), James Mardis, Kalamu ya Salaam, Janie Williams, Jacqueline Jones Harvey, JLove, Quaraysh A. Lan-sana, Demetria Cobb, Charmaine Jefferson, Sam Bowie, Deep Ellum Poets, SDCC, Ron Kavanaugh, Troy Johnson, Kirdrik Hill, the FAM, Christopher "Nike 30" Jones, Ronda R. Penrice, Michael Peguese (the best attorney in Dallas), Thomas Green, Shandra Hill, DeIra Lacy, my line sisters (ETSU F'91), Traci McKinley, Nichole Shields, Tony Carter, Linda Jones, Soul Rep Theatre, Cedric Bailey, Deborah Curry, TNT Escort Service, degriot space, Ramon Mc-Cowan, Simone Jackson-Rogers, and the Wilkins family. Finally, to the ancestors, who were nice enough to send me reference points in the essence of Pearl Cleage, Emma Rodgers, Evelyn Palfrey, Brenda Robertson, Angela Bassett, Oprah Winfrey, Erykah Badu, Sonia Sanchez, and N'bushe Wright. In the spirit of continual growth, change, love, thoughts, words, and deeds, I cannot say it enough: Thank you! Thank you! Thank you!

# When All Hell Breaks Loose

# Sunday Morning—6 A.M.

**W**ITH THE SMALL black velvet box covertly in my hand, I nudge her out of her morning slumber. She looks like a brown angel. Quiet. Restful. I've never felt this way about any woman, and what I'm about to do will be my first and last time.

"What is it, baby? Is something wrong?" she asks as she looks at me. On her side of the bed, I get on my knees. I'm so close to her face, I can smell last night's dinner of pizza and Coke. Foul as it is, this is what love is about. Right here. This moment, in the peace and quiet of the morning. I lean in silently, not sure where to begin. The daybreak is making itself known. The room has taken on a deep blue-gray color as if the sun can't get through the clouds. I feel my heart beating. I wonder if she can hear it.

"Adrian Jenkins, I just wanted to take this opportunity to tell you I love you."

Adrian smiles a sleepy smile, telling me she understands. Her hand glides from the bed and touches mine. Her touch is warm, and it makes my Willie stir out of its sleep.

"Gregory, baby, I love you too. Now and forever."

"I want to know if you can love me in the cold," I say. My home-boy J gave me this idea and the script. I have it memorized to a T and I'm serious about every word.

"Yes," she says, cracking the singing of the birds outside the window with her chalky morning voice.

"I want to know if you can love me when I'm old."

"Baby, you know I can. Stop being silly and come to bed."

"I want to know if you will feed me when I'm sick."

"Gregory, isn't it a bit too early to be playing Twenty Questions? You know I will feed you when you're sick. Remember last winter when you had the flu?"

"Will you always let me know what's bothering you and give me the opportunity to help?"

"Yes. Now come to bed, baby. I miss you over here." She pats the empty spot next to her.

"One last question."

"You are so silly and so romantic." She giggles. "What's the last question?"

I pull the box from behind my back and place it, opened, on the edge of the bed near her nose. The blue-gray morning goes well against the diamond. Twenty-two-carat total weight. Gold and diamond band. It shines like the moon at midnight.

"Adrian Jenkins, will you marry me?"

She rises out of the bed, her hair matted to the back of her head. Tears fill her eyes. "Gregory Alston, it's too early in the morning for this! Look at me! I look a mess!" There's a smile on her face as the ring goes on her finger. Tears fall from her eyes. It looks pretty good against her naked hand and body. Instead of telling me, she pulls me into bed and shows me her answer. It's a big yes! At this time, nothing can come between us . . . nothing!

## 1

'M FEELING REAL good right about now. A brother don't have many days when he's on cloud nine. I mean, just last week my car had a flat, the hot water in my apartment was off for two days, and our company basketball games had been canceled. If I didn't know better, I would think it just wasn't meant for a black man to be happy at all. But this morning, before some serious lovemaking with my girl, Adrian, I did it. I asked her to marry me. I believe, in my heart of hearts, she's the one thing in this world that makes me smile in spite of all the bad, and she has been for the past three years.

Let me tell you about my Adrian. She's a self-employed beautician with no children. She's caring, supportive, intelligent, and fine. The one thing that really attracted me to her was, after our second year of dating, she promised to never leave me. It wasn't just what she said, but how she said it. There was conviction behind it, as if that was what she was living for. That counts for a lot with me, and that's why I love Adrian Jenkins and want to spend the rest of my life with her. No woman has ever made me feel this way, and I trust my feelings.

We've been dating steady for the past three years. I know that's a long time, but I had to make sure she was my type. I'll admit, when I first met her I thought she was wild and unsettled. She just had that wild and unsettled look. Most beauticians have it. I see them all the time at the clubs looking like Lil' Kim video hopefuls and rejects. They wear fake nails that are a million colors, platinum blond highlights in the hair, and the Big T Bazaar designer Versace, Dolce, and Donna Karan imposter clothing. I don't know what they teach our sisters in hair school, but with some of 'em, it's a wonder Mary Kay, Flori Roberts, and Avon haven't taken over the White House and painted it mauve with gold highlights, posting Patti LaBelle up as their trademark.

When I first met Adrian, the only thing that turned me off was her nails. On both hands, they were long and blue with constellation symbols on them. She had the moon on her thumbnails, the sun on her pinkie nails, and planets and stars on her six middle finger nails, which just about covered everything I learned about outer space in grade school. I was turned off because it reminded me too much of this chick I used to date back in the day named Deidre, who used her nails wickedly in bed. Makes me shudder at the thought. But aside from the nails, I was totally attracted to Adrian. She didn't have a lot of makeup on. It was just enough to make her facial features stand out and make a brother like me take notice. She had on a brown leather-and-suede pants suit. Fitted like a glove and her booty was talking to me. For real! I could hear it going, "Yo Greg baby! I'm over here waiting for you! Come on, sweetie!" Her physical was popping off in tongues. Now, let me remind you, my woman is fine. I'm talking about five foot four, one hundred ten pounds, firm, and brown-skinned. Not that skin color matters. I've been with women who were so black they looked purple at night. And then I've been with those of the light, bright, damn near white persuasion. But Adrian is a creamy brown. She has the skin tone that falls somewhere between hazelnuts and dark honey. If you ever met her, she would remind you of Chili from the three-female group TLC. Although Adrian doesn't have naturally curly hair like Chili, she keeps her short style kept up. Like I said, she's a beautician.

Back to how I met Adrian. I was at Players, a local club for the twenty-to-thirty-something crowd, and she was sitting at the bar with two of her friends. One of them was kind of thick. Healthy arms and a booty that could have walked through the crowd on its own. She wasn't fat, just big-boned, while the other friend was fine like Adrian, but her haircut was all wrong. She had one of those asymmetrical-to-the-fifth-power-with-honey-blond-highlights things going on. Her head looked like a cutting board, but I assume that's what the sisters are into because she wasn't the only one that night sporting the hairdo. They were laughing and you could tell they were talking about other people in the club. Going through their girlfriend motions as they sipped their drinks. Look, point, talk, giggle.

At first, I was reluctant to go over to Adrian because she had one of those looks that sisters sometimes give in a club. It was that look that says, *I'm looking good, I'm feeling good, I want to dance, but not with you!* If it hadn't been for the way she smiled at me, I would have never approached her. Not in this lifetime. I don't wear rejection well. It isn't my color. The DJ was spinning a nice remix of a song that had the crowd hyped, so I told myself, *What the hell,* and walked over and asked her to dance. At first she hesitated and had me standing there like I was Joe Fool or somebody. I got kind of pissed because her girls were checking me out, looking me up and down like I was yo-yo. I knew they would probably have something to say once I walked away from the bar. Look, point, talk, giggle. Women always do. Adrian looked over at them and smiled. The one with the bad haircut smacked her rose-colored lips and said, "Girl, go on, I'll watch your drink." I held my hand out and she took it. I still remember how soft her hands were the first time I touched her. Man! Every time I think about my baby, I feel good! Anyway, we danced the rest of the night. Before the club closed, we did the man-and-woman thang by exchanging phone numbers and ever since then it's been heaven on earth. Man, I love my lady!

So here I sit, Sunday morning, getting ready for church. Adrian just left. She was ecstatic. The ring cost me a pretty penny and I'm glad I got a college education and a damn good job working with computer systems. Otherwise, I would have been at the Dollar General store trying to get the Cinderella cubic zirconium special without the pumpkin. Those hairdressers make nice money, especially if they're good. Adrian is the best. Her salon is called AJ's Getaway. It is the only black-owned and black-run shop here in Dallas where sisters can go and get a free massage if they get a perm, cut, and color. Adrian is working on getting a business-improvement loan so she can add to the shop. She wants reading and day care rooms. She believes that hair salons should be an escape where black women don't mind giving their money. They can't mind much now, because she's driving an LS400 fully loaded Lexus. I'm telling you, my lady is bad! Dammit! I better hurry up.

I'm supposed to go to church today with my sister, Shreese. She's my baby sister by three years, but we're close. She's all into the church scene and it affects everything she does. She goes four nights a week and all day on Sunday. I mean all day, from sunrise to sunset. She's on the usher board, in the women's chorus, and head of the Pastor and Staff Relations Committee. She is the only woman I know who cried and fasted for two weeks when she found out gospel artist Kirk Franklin married Tammy. She also has a framed, blown-up, action-sized photo of her and T. D. Jakes hanging in her living room like it's a Brenda Joysmith original. That wouldn't be so bad, but the picture is in a frame that cost her a good ninety-seven bucks! She professes that Mr. Jakes is worth every penny spent on the frame.

My sister has some serious religious issues that need to be resolved, is what I think! I believe she's more into the practice of church than the purpose of church. She's always been that way. Back when I was a senior in high school and she was a freshman, she would carry her Bible to school with her every day. Other students used to tease the hell out of her. By the time she graduated, she had been voted "Most Likely to Achieve Immaculate Conception." But it was cool, because I never had to fight the boys off her like most big brothers had to do. Shreese didn't go out on dates and she didn't allow any guys to call her after six. She's always been a little weird, but I love her and she's good people. Telling her about my engagement is going to be tough, because Shreese takes nothing lightly.

Oh, hell! Where's my watch? Oh, I left it in the kitchen. Got my keys, Bible, wallet, cool . . . I'm out. I better watch my swearing, too. Last time I visited, I almost let one slip out.

## 2

MOUNT CANNON BAPTIST Church is packed when I arrive. Luckily my sister saved a spot next to her. One of the ushers looks at me crazy because I'm late by ten minutes. She's an old, wrinkled-looking woman with pouty lips, gloved hands clutched tightly together, and several noticeable chin hairs. Probably drove her one and only husband to an early grave and hasn't had companionship in her life since, except a half-blind dog the size of my shoe. She cuts her beady eyes at me and tightens her lips as if I'm forcing her to do her job. I ignore her and straighten my tie. She leads me in and takes me directly to where Shreese is sitting. When my sister sees me, she beams. She pats the empty spot and I cross over a few people and sit down.

"Greg, you're late," she whispers. "You missed Reverend Dixon's welcome to the visitors."

I lean in and kiss my sister on the cheek. "It's good to see you too, li'l sister."

"You didn't bring Adrian?" she asks, looking past me.

"No, she rushed home this morning. She told me to tell you she's sorry she hasn't gotten around to visiting church with you, but she will soon."

"She needs to be in church with you right now. I know y'all can't see the error in your ways, but Sundays are for repentance."

"Reese, don't start."

The pastor has said something we both missed and the congregation says, "Amen," in unison. Shreese picks up her program and fans herself. The church is stuffy and I can barely stand the tie being around my neck already.

The choir gets up to do a song. As the director announces the "A" selection, an upbeat version of "Down at the Cross," my mind begins to drift to Adrian's answer to my proposal and how we celebrated. The lovemaking is so fresh on my mind, I have to cross my legs and adjust on the pew, in order to keep my Willie under control. I'm slightly ashamed that I could think about sex in the middle of church service, but I know I'm not alone.

The choir immediately starts jamming the song and my sister jumps up on her feet, clapping her hands and singing along. I look at the choir and shake my head in disbelief. They're rocking intensely, and some of them are blatantly dancing! I'm talking about the Friday night stuff! One sister with a short bob haircut with gold highlights is doing a dance I know I was just doing last week down at the Prime Times club near downtown. Then there's this brother who is doing a grand rendition of a slide step, reminiscent of James Brown! Mount Cannon is jamming like it's New Year's Eve in Times Square. I suppose they can since the church has a full band of brothers who I grew up with, most of whom still play Saturday night gigs at local jazz spots around Dallas. They even have a Caribbean drummer. Now I know what they mean by, "It's on when the club close." I can't tell if they're jamming for Jesus or auditioning for a role in the next Janet Jackson video. They're rocking this song, but where do you draw the line? See, I'm from the old school, where gospel music was more humble, without all the glitter and pretentious behavior. This music definitely moves me because the musicians know what they're doing and they understand what the right amount of bass and keys can do to the human spirit, but it appears no different than being at a play or some put-on show. Shreese is even cutting the holy rug a little, with a small two-step, jitterbug-type dance. I've never seen her groove before, and looking at her do her small step, jump, and bounce is causing me to wonder what she does in her spare time.

I almost jump out of my skin when some woman in the back gets the Holy Ghost and starts screaming and flinging her arms about as she falls over a pew and catches another sister square in the back of her head. Several ushers rush over and surround her, making sure she doesn't hurt anybody else, including herself. She's a big woman, who is catering to at least two hundred and sixty pounds! I can see why they pick those plump women as ushers. They all look like courteous football linebackers.

Half the church congregation is on its feet. I stand up too, envying the small children who are sleeping through all this praising and hollering. I don't want these people to think I'm not having a good time, so I clap along like a robot. I keep my eyes darting around in case someone near me gets the spirit, because I don't want to be in their way. The heat rises in the sanctuary and I take my program and fan my face. Three women and one brother in the choir stand have fainted and have been carried out, but the choir is still bouncin'.

The pastor is sitting in his chair like an emperor. I've always wondered what it was like to sit in one of those big chairs that all big-time pastors have. Reverend Dixon must have skills because he has gold knobs at the ends of the armrests—at least, they look gold, probably just brass or gold-plated. I'm not doubting that this man has a blessing on his head, but in my experience, preachers who carry themselves like Dixon have come across as professional hustlers and this man is no exception to the rule. Shreese told me that Dixon isn't like that. She said he has an anointing that was placed on him when he was twelve and ever since has been on a mission from Jesus. Hmph, Shreese is naive. The only thing placed on this brother's head at twelve years of age was a hair relaxer that he obviously hasn't the will to let go of. He's sitting up there like a black Adonis, smiling and waving to some of the congregation members. He randomly shouts out praises, which cause some of the members to go wild with the music. Shreese told me he's single and on many occasions he has talked about how he's waiting on the Lord to send him a virtuous helpmate, which cancels out about eighty-five percent of the women in his congregation. Shreese practically brags about how he is always complimenting her on her kind ways and beautiful voice. I can see that she's hopeful something will blossom with him, and being a pastor's wife would be right up her alley. If he was anything other than a pastor, I know my sister wouldn't give him the time of day, but he's not and I have to keep a watch on him. He's older than my sister by six or seven years, and that is enough for me to make sure his intentions with her, if there are any, are pure. All the other women in the congregation seem just as eager to be the next Mrs. Dixon. As I stare at the brother, I can almost see what they like in him. If I were a woman, I would say he's handsome on that street level, but I'm not a woman. If you can imagine a young pimp in the pulpit, then that suggests a good concept of Reverend Dixon. A real ladies' man of God. He was also recently elected to a seat on the city council, which moved him up a notch on the status belt. I never believed in mixing church and politics, so I have strong doubts about this brother and his ministry. I just hope nothing pops off between him and my little sister, 'cause then I'd have to act a real fool.

My legs get tired, so I take my seat, hoping the song will end soon. Lucky for me, the choir begins to wind down. I guess it's because half of them have been carried out due to heat exhaustion or the Holy Ghost. The bass player even took off his guitar and shouted into a silent submission. Reverend Dixon gets up and stands at the podium, stretching out his hands to silence the church. As the congregation and the choir take their seats, a few of the fainted return, looking like they've been through some bad weather. The ushers case the congregation and then return to the back of the church to take their seats. Dixon puts his hands down and closes his eyes and everyone bows their heads and waits for the prayer. He begins to pray in song.

"Most merciful and gra-a-acious God. We ask for your anointing sp-i-i-irit right now. . . ."

I lift my head and look around. No one else, with the exception of a little girl in front of me, has their head up. She smiles at me and waves. I wave back, causing her to giggle. Her mother taps her and makes her turn back around. Pastor Dixon still has his arms stretched out and the words seem to flow from his mouth like liquid. Liquid smoke, to me. But I must admit, he's got his method down and exact, with the outfit to top it off. Designer cuff links, manicured nails, and designer dress shoes to complete his look. Most of the younger sisters in the congregation are fanning their low-cut blouses, causing the fabric to sway away from their perfume-coated skin, revealing the roundness of their push-up-bra-enhanced breasts. I'm sure they're praying that Reverend Dixon is looking. I put my head back down to concentrate on his words because I know Shreese is going to quiz me later. She always does.

". . . and let eve-r-r-ry person within the sound of my voice receive your blessed spi-i-i-i-rit, O God. Lead your sheep to the pasture of everlasting life! These and other blessings I ask in the name of your only son, Jesus, Amen."

Shoot! I missed the main part of the prayer. I say another pointless "Amen." We raise our heads and take our seats as the pastor begins his sermon. Shreese pulls out her Bible like she's about to be drilled. Her fingers wait anxiously near the pages and she's staring straight at the pulpit, directly at Dixon. He straightens his lapel—it's made of Kente cloth—and begins to speak.

"Today's sermon isn't for the faint of heart nor the weak in spirit. I come to y'all today to bring the message of God. My sermon today is entitled, 'The Right Love Comes from Above.' "

The women in the audience give a hearty "Amen."

From their response, I can tell they are single, bitter, and probably big supporters of the Lifetime cable channel. The I-don't-need-a-man-but-Lord-send-me-a-man kind of women. The player-hating kind of women. The few brothers in the congregation, including myself, sit quiet. One of them is already nodding off to sleep. Shreese just nods her head in agreement as she jots the topic down on the back of her program.

The pastor repeats the topic and begins his sermon. By the time he finishes, I'm out of my blazer and sleepy as hell. Shreese has had to nudge me twice because I started nodding, doing that sleepy head-roll that can hurt you if you don't have a headrest. I know she let me get some shuteye at some point, because when I woke up, her program had writing all over it and I couldn't tell where she began. I dip into my blazer pocket for my wallet and prepare for the offering. As the donation bucket comes around, I drop in two dollars and Shreese looks at me like I did something wrong.

"What?" I whisper to her.

"Gregory Alston, that's not ten percent of your earnings."

"I know," I say to her as I put my wallet back into my pocket. "My bills got to get paid too, you know."

"Ecclesiastes five and ten reads, 'He who loves money is not satisfied with money,' " she replies, as if I am being stingy with my givings.

"And my bills say, 'If you don't pay us our money, we're going to take more of your money.' It's called interest, and I'm interested in paying my bills too."

Shreese hits me on the arm and shakes her head. "That's a shame. A pure shame."

I can't believe she tried to front me about two dollars. I've never given any church ten percent of my earnings. That's well over six hundred dollars a month. Besides, this church looks fine to me, and Pastor Dixon doesn't look like he's hurting for much.

Now I'm really ready to go. My sister has insulted me and I'm sleepy, starving, and sweating like a bullfrog in a snakepit. Once the collections are taken up, there are announcements and the benediction. Thank God! I'm ready to go!

I still end up waiting an additional forty-five minutes for my sister after service. She yaps away with some woman in a green polka-dot dress and matching hat. I'm tempted to blow my horn, but just as I get ready to, Shreese flounces over and hops in. "I have to be back at three," she says. "We have a planning meeting for our Women's Day program."

I look at my watch. "It's only one-thirty, we have time. Is Chili's Restaurant okay?"

"Sure." She looks over at me and smiles. She reminds me of how our mother used to look in her younger days. They have the same small lips and the same dimpled right cheek.

"So what did you and Adrian do this weekend?" Shreese asks.

"She came over after she closed the shop and we rented movies."

"Did she stay the night?"

"Shreese, does it matter?"

"Greg, I'm just asking, you don't have to be so irritated with me. I guess the devil must have been welcoming you to the floor when you stepped out of bed."

"There was no devil in my room this morning, okay? Anyway, I wanted to tell you that I asked Adrian to marry me and she said yes."

Shreese gets loud. "What?! Marriage! Oh Lord Jesus help."

"Yeah. Quit tripping."

"Did you pray about this decision?"

"Time told me she was the one," I reply smartly. "I've known her long enough to realize I want to marry her."

"Three years ain't diddly-squat, Gregory." Shreese looks out the window. "Lord have mercy on us all." Her fingers tap lightly on the Bible that is lying on her lap. "The Bible says that fornication is an impurity and a work of the flesh. How do you think you got a good woman from this kind of behavior?"

"Shreese, it's no secret to you that I'm not a virgin. And it's no secret to you that my fiancée is not a virgin, but that don't make us impure or less loving."

"You haven't read your Bible lately, have you, big brother? Because if you had you wouldn't be saying such devilment."

I switched on the radio to interrupt our conversation as I whip onto Camp Wisdom Road, less than a mile from the restaurant.

Shreese begins humming along with the gospel tune that's playing. I can feel her staring at me again, so I look back at her.

"Now what?"

"Have you told Daddy?"

"Not yet. I was planning on stopping by the house this afternoon to tell him."

"You should have told us you were at least thinking about getting married," she mumbled. "You didn't even consider your own family for something this serious."

"Shreese, it was a last-minute thing. I bought the ring just two weeks ago."

"We should have known you were buying it," she snapped. "Two weeks is hardly last-minute, Greg."

"What's with you? Why do you seem to be having such a hard time with me marrying Adrian?"

"Because, Greg, you two have been fornicating and Lord only knows what kind of living Adrian does. She's too worldly." Shreese pushes a loose strand of hair back up into the neat bun on her head.

I'm annoyed at my sister's badgering and accusations. "What is that supposed to mean?"

"She's a hairdresser, for crying out loud. Pastor Dixon says the salons are full of wild, worldly women. You need to make sure you're not fooling yourself."

"So when you go get your hair done, you aren't being worldly either?" I challenge.

Shreese looks at me as if I have insulted her. "No, I am not a worldly woman. I don't sit in there and gossip. I talk about the goodness of Jesus and I try to share with those women the true walk of a virtuous woman. As soon as my stylist is finished, I pay her and walk out of the fires of damnation untouched, like Shadrach, Meshach, and Abednego! Thank you Jesus!" Shreese throws her hands up and closes her eyes like it hurts to think about getting her hair done.

"Shreese, Pastor Dixon is not in a position to tell you what worldly is, because it seems he hasn't looked in the mirror lately. While he runs around keeping his congregation from having nice things, like a church with proper air-conditioning, you-all dig deep every Sunday and have managed to put him in a big church, fancy clothes, and a Mercedes. Sounds like he's worldly to me. A worldly fool at that."

"Watch how you talk about a man of God, Gregory!" Shreese slams her hand on her Bible as if that alone will protect Dixon. "And let me tell you something. Loving a woman of the world is damnation on your soul. Blessed not is the man who walks in the company of sinners."

I pull my car into the parking lot at Chili's. It screeches to a halt. Shreese is still looking at me. I have to set her straight. "Look, I love Adrian, and I'm ready for this. This is *my* decision," I say, pointing to myself. "When you meet the man you've prayed for and are in my shoes, then you can tell me what you think, but right now, just be happy for me, that is all I ask."

"Okay, but you remember, Gregory Louis Alston, I'm your sister and it's my job to look out for you, just like you look out for me." She snaps her fingers in my face. "I don't feel good about this announcement you've made, but I won't let that interfere with *your* happiness." She puts her Bible in her purse and steps out of the car. She begins humming some church tune as if our conversation never happened.

I stare over at my baby sister, wondering why I have to be the one to put up with a sister like her. When I have to deal with her religious thrashings, I get mad because I know that Shreese is knee-deep into this because our mother left. She's been faithful to the Bible because she has always believed that God would bring Louise back, and I know that's just not going to happen. Shreese looks so much like our mother it's amazing. They have the exact same features, except Shreese never wears her hair down like our mother used to. I'm sure it's way past her shoulders by now. The last time I can recall Shreese's hair being down was when she was still sporting pigtails. Mom used to wear her hair down all the time before she left. I'll have to tell you about my mother later. That's another story for another time, but I promise to tell you about it. Meanwhile, it's time to get my grub on.

I DROP SHREESE back at church and head over to our dad's house. I like driving through the old neighborhood. It's classic: lots of trees, big front yards, children playing, and neighbors who've known each other a lifetime. When I drive up, Pops is outside mowing the yard. He has on a pair of overalls with no shirt on beneath. Sweat is dripping from his face, but as always, he's smiling from ear to ear. He turns off the mower and waves as I get out.

"Hey, son!" He grips my hand tightly and pats my back.

"Hey, Pops. What's going on?"

"Hell, the usual. I was out here trying to get some of this yard work done before it gets too late."

We walk into the house where it's cool. Immediately, I'm nostalgic, as always. This is the house Shreese and I grew up in. Pops still has our pictures plastered everywhere. The same furniture, even the same 1979 General Electric refrigerator that hums loudly in the kitchen. Pops goes into the bathroom and comes out with a towel. He wipes his sweaty face and arms as he sits in his favorite La-Z-Boy recliner.

"So, whatcha know good?"

I lean back on the couch. "Just working." I loosen my tie and un-button the top of my shirt.

"How's Adrian? She doin' all right?"

"Yeah, we saw each other this morning."

"Oh?"

"Pops, I asked her to marry me and she accepted."

"Congratulations, son!" He leans over and slaps my knee with a big grin on his face. "You sure you ready for that kind of responsibility?"

"Yeah."

"Taking care of a woman is hard work." Pops leans back against the chair. "Like a car. If you treat it bad, don't take care of it, nine times outa ten it will embarrass you in front of folks."

"I'm ready to try." I grin. "I think I know how to take care of a car."

"Sure you do, son." He laughed. "Did you tell your sister?"

"Yeah, I told her."

He chuckles a little. "What'd she have to say?"

"The same old stuff. 'God is going to send his wrath on you for fornicating. It ain't right,' " I say, imitating my sister in a high-pitched voice. It must have been a good one, because Pops breaks out in laughter.

"That girl is something else. You sound just like her."

"She said she was happy for me even though we weren't living right."

"Yup. That's Shreese." He wipes his face again. "So, has a date been set?"

"No, she just accepted this morning. She was too excited to do much else besides run home and call her parents. I'm going to let Adrian decide on the date, so when I know, you'll know."

"I guess I can look forward to having me some grandbabies to help take up some of the space I have here, huh?"

"I don't know about that, Pops, because we're not in a rush to have kids. Adrian talks about it all the time, and I know she wants a family, but she and I really want to be settled in good and have a secure place to raise kids. You may have to keep spending time with old Corduroy out back." I'm referring to our twelve-year-old Doberman. *Old Corduroy,* I think. *One good eye, deaf, and has a bark that sounds like a turkey's gobble but faithful to the end.*

"Whatever, I'm expecting to see some little Alstons runnin' around here. Our family is going to end if you and Shreese don't buckle down and start acting like regular folk and bring me some grandchildren."

"There's always Uncle Bennie's kids and their children, your greatnieces and -nephews."

"I ain't talking about my brother and his family. I'm talking about the Adolphus Roosevelt Alston family. My name has got to go on."

I look at my dad and let out a nervous laugh.

"Aretha already done had two and she got a third on the way, while you and Shreese running around here working yourselves to death with no one to share or leave your valuables to. Son, it's important to have a family to come home to and to trust that your name will go on once you leave this place."

I'm still sitting speechless as he rambles. Lately, Pops has been hell-bent on having grandchildren.

"And B.J.'s girlfriend is expecting too. Even B.J. is contributing to the Alston name surviving."

"Pops, Bennie Junior don't count. We all know Stephanie is pregnant by another man."

"Bennie Junior said he's going to adopt that child when it's born."

"Then I think you should wait and see."

"Gregory, that's beside the whole point, which is, when am *I* going to have some grandchildren?"

"Pops, you'll have to talk to Adrian about that. Or better yet"—I laugh—"talk to Shreese."

We both break out in laughter.

I END UP changing clothes and helping my father finish the yard. When I get back to my place, I'm sweaty, tired, and funky. Sundays are always long days and I anticipate going back to work, where I know there will be something for me to do. When I press the review button on my answering machine, there are four messages:

*Beep!*

"Greg yo, this Tim. Bring some workout clothes tomorrow. There's a basketball game at the recreation center and I managed to get a few of us from Data Tech in on it. See you tomorrow."

*Beep!*

"Greg honey, this is Adrian. I was just calling to say I love you."

"I love you too, baby," I say to the machine.

*Beep!*

"This call is for Gregory Alston. Please call Citibank at 800-555-4021."

*Beep!*

"Gregory Bean! This is your Uncle Bennie! I was calling to tell you congrats on your engagement!" He's laughing like a little kid. "Your daddy sure is a happy camper about this one 'cause you know this will bring some action in his life. Call me, so I can lay down the laws of being head of the household." Uncle Bennie's wild laugh rings through the answering machine. "Anyway, keep me up on everything, and if you need me, you know you can call your unc. 'Bye."

The tape stops and resets itself for new calls. I pull off my shirt and head to the shower. I got to get to work tomorrow and tell my best friend, Tim Johnson, about the engagement. This is almost as scary as telling Shreese.

## 3

I WORK FOR DATA Tech. It's a computer consulting firm. It's been in business for twenty-seven years and it's a good company to work for. Basically, this company designs private databases for small to medium-sized companies. We just went global last year, and that's when I got my big promotion to senior corporate recruiter. I design the database presentations and send my teams out to bring in new business. I supervise four groups. When I first started working here, after graduating with a master's degree in computer information systems from East Texas State University, I was the only African American in my division and there were only six blacks in the building. The company started expanding four years back, and now more than seventy-five percent of the staff are people of color. (I hate to use the word "minority," because I never viewed people of color and women as minorities.)

Most of the brothers here are cool, but Timothy Johnson is my road dawg. He struts into my office every Monday morning to tell me about his weekend. This time, I got something to share as well.

"Say man, what's up?" Tim is looking at me like he's expecting something. He's standing in the doorway to my office, as usual. I'm checking out the tie he's wearing. It's an ocean-blue silk with yellow and green checks. Goes perfect with his ash-gray suit. He works in accounting and makes good money.

"Nada cool breeze. A long weekend, is all."

"I hear ya. I went out on a date with Simone Lacy and it was wild."

"You mean Simone from the finance department upstairs?"

"Yeah, that's her." Tim comes in and closes my office door. He sits confidently in one of my guest chairs and starts in about his date with Simone. I listen eagerly, as if he's telling me something I don't already know. Most of Tim's stories about women start and end the same: He checks her body out and they end up in the bed.

"Greg, first off, this woman meets me at the Velvet Elvis on McKinney, and she is looking good. Not corporate at all. Black suede skirt that was hugging her ass, low-cut blouse, and pumps that had about a three-inch heel. I'm talking about looking so good that during the entire date, I couldn't stop thinking about what positions I was going to put her in."

I chuckled.

"We have some drinks and go back to my place and talk. She holds some cool conversation, too. You know, we go through the usual questions: 'Are you from Dallas? Where'd you go to school? Do you know such and such and what do you like to do' kind of stuff, right?"

"Mmnn." I nod my head in agreement.

"Next thang I know, man, we're in my bed bumpin' and grindin'! She was riding the hell out of me! Greg, I have never in my life been turned out like that! It was wild!" Tim has a dazed look on his face and for a brief moment I can tell he's thinking about specifics and it doesn't matter if I'm sitting here listening to him or not.

He continues, going on and on about how he had Simone on the edge of the bed screaming his name and then they moved to the hallway and did it on the floor. He pulled up his shirtsleeve to show me the carpet burn on his dark brown forearm and the bite mark on his shoulder. Tim always has some wild and crazy story to share with me after the weekends, and so far this one takes the cake.

"So Simone gets down like that, huh?"

"Supafreak! I had to set another date with her. We're supposed to go out again on Wednesday."

"You betta go work out at the gym. Sounds to me like she's playing to win. You two were doing it rough reggae-style."

"For real! But yo, check this out. After we did it, she said she had a homegirl—"

I interrupt my friend. "Tim, you know I'm seeing somebody. Speaking of which, I just asked Adrian—"

"Nigga, this ain't about you." He laughs. "Simone is talking about a threesome! She's down with the supernasty dawg! I'm going to have my first ménage à trois!" Tim has raised up out of the chair and is standing before me like he's the man. His chest is out and his head is up. "I've been trying to get to this point since I left grad school."

"Yo dawg! You've finally arrived at the freak nasty phase!" I say to boost his already huge ego. "Congratulations, my man."

We slap palms two times.

"Greg, I'm about to be Mr. Freak Nasty to the rest of y'all."

"Hey," I say in all honesty, "you the man."

Tim sits on the edge of my desk and looks at me. "So, what did you and Adrian do this weekend?"

"The usual."

"Greg man, you're starting to act like my parents used to and it's scaring me."

"What do you mean?"

"Renting movies, miniature golf, walks in the park. You and Adrian are too young to be acting like Ma and Pa Kettle."

"Being with Adrian on a Saturday night is all I need. Tim, I'm ready to settle down. I've been where you are, and I'm here to tell you that it becomes lonely after a while."

Tim looks at me in disbelief. "Man, loneliness is a state of mind. There are too many women in the world to be locked down to just one."

"Well, aside from all that, I asked Adrian to marry me."

"Are you serious, bro?" Tim's eyes widen in disbelief.

"As a heart attack." I lean back in my chair.

Tim slides off the desk and sits back down. He looks like a bolt of electricity just zapped him. "I knew you would pull some old crazy shit like this." He looks at me and shakes his head. "You sure you ready for marriage? Greg, this is your prime time. Why settle now? Are you sure you're sure?"

"Positive."

"This means no more nights out with me watching ass walk by, making passes and getting those digits."

"Tim, we haven't done that in over two years."

He relaxes and exhales a deep breath. His face calms from the hysterical look he showed just seconds before. "Cool, here's some dap for the proposal and some more for the wedding night." Tim daps me another two times. "It's actually about time. You and Adrian been kicking it kind of strong these past three years."

"Yeah."

"Does this make me . . . ?" he asks, pointing to himself.

"Best man," I say. "Of course."

"You know the last time I wore a tux I was in high school, right?" he jokes.

"Tim, there's a second time for everything, bro."

He looks at me one last time before leaving to go to his office. "My road dawg is finally hitching the old mule to the cart. I can't believe it. Congratulations, man." He smiles and walks out.

"Thanks, Tim."

TIM AND I started at Data Tech together as interns. He graduated from Huston-Tillotson College in Austin. We used to compete against each other back in the day at black Greek step-shows in college, but we never formally met until we both moved to Dallas. He's a Kappa. I'm an Alpha. Our situation is cool, though, because our being in two different fraternities has never interfered with our relationship as friends. We've known each other for six years, and Tim is the only person who has seen me get buck wild with a woman. Let me tell you that story right quick before I go to my meeting.

The second summer we interned at Data Tech was in '90. I had just pledged Alpha Phi Alpha that spring and Tim was gearing for the Kappa Alpha Psi line at HT that was coming up that fall. Being a fresh Alpha man and all, I wanted to kick it, so I asked him to come hang with me one Friday night.

Back then, niggas were hanging out all over Dallas. This was before the gangs and random acts of violence got bad in the city. The most terrible thing going on for middle-class blacks back then was car theft. You could go to Kiest Park and the Venue was still open. There was Camp Wisdom Road, which had become a strip for people to ride up and down all night, and then of course there was a few places in Arlington and Grand Prairie you could hang.

Well, Tim and I optioned for Greek night at the Venue. The place was packed and we had to wait damn near twenty minutes before they let us in. We got in and immediately girls started checking me out. It had to be the Alpha pin on my shirt, because honeys were coming at me left and right—reactions foreign to me before I pledged. Tim was sitting back in the cut, trying to be cool, but he has that Kappa look, so sisters just assumed he was one. Tim is one of those chocolate pretty boys. Dark curly hair and piercing slanted eyes. His face is smooth and he has an innocent, perfect smile. He's built, too. Every time we'd go out together, sisters would be on his ass. This particular night, he was wearing a red polo shirt and some khakis. We were lucky none of the real members of K-A-Psi tried to give him the secret handshake or else Tim would have gotten his ass beat down for perpetrating.

These two AKAs came up to us from out of nowhere. One of them just hugged me. She pressed her firm body against mine and wouldn't let go.

"Hey, frat!" she said excitedly.

I played it cool and greeted her. She was a beautiful dark-skinned girl. The color of molasses. She had medium-length hair and chestnut-colored eyes, and she wore a black-and-pink dress that fitted like a glove. Her homegirl was all on Tim's jock, but it was cool because my big brothers had told me that at some schools the AKAs and Kappas hang tight together. Her homegirl was fine too, except she had on this army-green pants suit with a salmon-pink shirt that wasn't exactly color coordinated. I guess her yellow skin and long hair made up for it, because Tim was checking her out. We introduced ourselves. Dark and Lovely's name was Danielle, and her friend's name was Evan, short for Evangeline. They were from Dallas but attended Hampton University in Virginia. Both neophytes of their chapter.

We ended up hanging together most of the night and we all left the club together.

Danielle invited us over to her sister's place, who just so happened to be out of town. We got over there and Danielle pulls out some B&J wine coolers, rum-and-Cokes, and a bottle of Boone's Farm Strawberry Wine. We got loaded playing this drinking game. I can't remember all the details of us playing the game, but every time you stuttered over the beginning letter for your sentence you had to take a big drink of alcohol.

"Arthur ate absolute butter." Danielle giggled.

"Butter breeds big children," Tim said.

"Children catch cold . . . cold . . . damn!" Evangeline took a swig of the Boone's straight from the bottle. We all laughed. Then I came in:

"Children catch colds daily."

"Daily Daddy done dropped eggs." Danielle giggled at her abuse of the English language.

"Eggs exterminate everything freaky!" Tim yelled.

"Freaky families finger goats." Evangeline got it right that time.

"Goats gobble grass . . . I mean . . . Shit!" I took a swig of the liquor, and the game continued for the next two hours.

As it turned out, we all ended up drunk, laid out on the living room floor. Danielle retrieved some blankets and she and I lay in front of the couch, while Tim and Evan found a cozy spot near the fireplace.

Danielle asked me to hold her and I did. Her body was soft and warm against my legs and chest. She snuggled in tight and the more she snuggled the more Willie started talking to me. I tried to control it, but I knew she could feel it moving against her butt. Then she moaned. It wasn't loud, just real low and restful. Sexy. She wiggled her butt enough to tease me, but Willie was up by then and he knew what time it was. I was reluctant at first, because I didn't like the idea of having sex with Danielle while Tim and Evan were only a few feet away from us in the same room.

The tripped-out part was that, when I looked over to see if they were asleep, I could tell they were already getting busy. The cover was over their heads, but it didn't take a rocket scientist to tell the position they were using. Let me put it this way: they looked like a human coffee table! Bow-wow! Ruff-ruff!

So, Danielle and I went at it. We were kissing and touching places on each other, and she told me when she was ready. I was thrown off a bit, because I wasn't used to any girl telling me when she was ready and talking to me during sex. Danielle was definitely talking to me, and I know Tim and Evan heard her. She reached down and grabbed Willie and said, "Give it to me, baby!" She began some heavy stroking. I could feel myself throbbing with anticipation. Her voice sounded like it was in full stereo. Dolby! As uncomfortable as the situation was for me, I realized a brother only lives once. I thought to myself, *Fuck it, she wants it, I'm going to give it to her.* I put on a condom and as soon as I got inside her good, she started making noises and talking real loud. I wanted to join her in the conversation, but I couldn't—I didn't want the others to hear me. But I was the last thing on Tim's and Evan's minds. They were moaning passionately under their covers.

For the next ten minutes, I was lost in everyone's voices. Each pant and moan enforced my self-inflicted silence. I held my breath as I pumped Danielle, concentrating on getting it done as quietly as possible. I was the only one who wasn't saying anything until I felt my nut coming. My stomach tightened with butterflies and sweat broke out on my forehead. Danielle's hands had gripped my lower back and buttocks. Her eyes were closed and she was cheering me on.

"Come on baby! Come on Greg baby! I know you can do it baby!"

I started pumping for real. I'm talking about crossing time lines and seeing my childhood pass in front of me. Sweat broke out on my forehead. I held it as long as I could, but I damn near blacked out from the strain. I now believe that trying to hold a nut should have a Surgeon General's Warning attached to it. But when I let loose, it was like the Fourth of July. All I remember was screaming, "YEAH BABY! OH YEAH! GODDAMMIT YES!"

Scared the hell out of everybody in the room. I was drenched in sweat, and Danielle held me against her the way a brother needs to be held after coming the way I did.

The Energizer Bunnies, Tim and Evangeline, giggled beneath their covers and continued their secret party. I don't know what those fools were into, because they did it again before we left that morning. The next day, we exchanged numbers with the girls and left.

Tim talked about that night for the next two weeks! He kept saying shit to me like, "Greg, you's a wild boy! I don't know why you pledged Alpha, 'cause you's a dawg," or, "Greg, when you hollered out like that my nuts froze up!"

He tripped for a long time about that, but it was cool, because I still score on his ass about Evan's no-fashion-sense-having ass. He takes it all in stride and never makes me feel bad about being the gentleman that I am.

That's why Tim is my best man.

That was a long time ago. My view on women is totally different now. I don't just take them for granted anymore. I don't play games with them, either. I realized that having one-night stands is not only dangerous but makes you feel cheap and lonely in the long run. Adrian has come into my life and made me realize a lot of things. Up until I met her, Shreese was the only woman I could honestly respect, and that was because she is my sister. I still haven't forgotten to tell you the story about my mom, but now is not the time because I have a meeting to get to.

"MR. ALSTON, IS the Dillinger Construction account going to set up another presentation date?" LaShawn Denton is looking at me with eager anticipation, as are the others.

"Yes, Miss Denton, they were duly impressed with the presentation you did and they were eager to have you come out and do another presentation for the CEO."

Everyone in the room claps. LaShawn and her group are all smiles. Right now, they're the only group under me that has sold all of their presentations, which this year alone have brought in over $750,000 in revenue for Data Tech—and also increased my pay by three thousand dollars a year. LaShawn Denton is the only intern in Group Three, and she leads the pack. She's a real smart sister who is bright and a quick, accurate thinker.

"Does this mean that their database will change if they go with what we have to sell them?" she asks.

"No. Dillinger is simply looking for an enhancement product. They want more shortcuts, macros, and buttons. Whoever created their database is now out of business, so we are actually going to have to start from scratch with a database for them that will last."

One of my new hires, Miguel, raises his hand.

"What about the programming? If the database was solely created to run on a particular operating system, then won't we have to design a whole new one anyway?"

"No. If they're still running on DOS, God forbid"—people in the meeting room laugh at my remark—"then we'll create DOS-based enhancements for their systems."

The room is quiet.

"Anything else?"

No one says anything.

I passed out agendas for the next week. "Okay, here's the rundown for August. Group One is still working on the Kaiser account. I need to run through that TCP/IP Network information with you. Let's schedule that for Wednesday. Group Two, will you get those Power Point slides in to me this evening and have the Dillinger account slides ready for Group Three by Friday morning? Group Three, you need to have at least three macros and shortcuts programmed into the system and name the program. Group Four, you've got invoices that need to be finished and sent to the finance department. I am working on getting two accounts for September, so gear up and be ready, Groups Two and Four. That's all."

Everyone rises from their seats and leaves the meeting room. I take a deep breath.

When I get to my office, LaShawn is waiting by the door. "Mr. Alston, can I speak with you a moment?"

"Sure." I open the door and allow her inside. She stands at the desk. She looks worried about something, but I can't detect exactly what's bothering her.

LaShawn is the same age as my sister. She got a late start on her education and is a sophomore at Texas Woman's University, which is about an hour's drive from here. All I really know about her personal life is that she has a daughter and is raising her alone. But I think it's great that she overcame all that unwed-young-mother hoopla, and still decided to get back in school.

She stares at the picture of Adrian on my desk; then she looks up at the photo of Adrian and me that sits on my bookshelf. We were in Mexico and we both have on these huge straw hats. It's my favorite photo.

"I . . . I . . . uh, just wanted to say thank you for giving me the opportunity to work with Group Three." Something is bothering her, but she looks like she's going to confide in me, so I wait.

"Miss Denton, you are one of the brightest interns I've seen come through here. You have earned this position. There's no reason to thank me."

She stands in an awkward position, and I notice she's still looking at the picture of Adrian.

"Do you know my girl Adrian?"

"Uh . . . yeah." She looks down at her shoes, a slight smile on her face. "She helped me to see how precious life can be when things are put in their perspective order. This all went down during my pregnancy."

"Oh really?" I say. "So she was a support system for you during troubled times, huh?"

"Something like that. We all get a little confused sometimes, and Adrian was there during my confused time in life. She was able to make me see things for what they are rather than what we want them to be. My boyfriend had just dumped me and left me scared and pregnant. I didn't know what to do. You know what I mean?"

I think about my family situation. "I know exactly what you mean. Adrian has been there for me in good times and bad, too. She makes me think about other things instead of the things that hurt."

LaShawn looks at me as if she wasn't expecting that answer. She straightens her skirt and fixes her collar. "Well . . . I just wanted to say thanks." She smiles and walks out of the office quickly.

I sit semi-stunned for a brief moment, but I figure LaShawn felt uncomfortable when I mentioned my personal situation. I guess she didn't want me to get personal with her and I hope this doesn't change our boss-employee relationship.

I briefly entertain the thought of LaShawn having a private crush on me. I'm not saying that I'm all that, but let's face it, I got the job, the money, and the looks. Who wouldn't fall in lust or love with a five nine, proportioned, brown-skinned brother with dark eyes, an award-winning smile, and hands that love to touch bare skin? I like kissing and nibbling, too. Women always compliment me on my full lips, my well-manicured light mustache, and my smile. I am in the perfect position to cater to a well-deserving woman, and any woman in her right mind would be happy with me . . . as long as she's in her right mind.

LaShawn is young, but she's going to make some brother real happy one day—that is, if she doesn't go through any more heartbreaks or heartaches.

A woman can become hardened after too many damaged and failed relationships. "Faithless" is the word I prefer to use. They quit going out to socialize; they gain weight and start hanging with gay men, and when they're out and about running errands, they'll have on house shoes, with big pink rollers in their hair, and they'll be in sweats. Not the sweats that you go shopping in, either. I'm talking about some sweats they wore in college that are now two sizes too small with a few holes in them. Then, the one time you do see a bitter sister looking good, she's got this look on her face that says, *Don't even try it!* I don't know, maybe I've come across too many bitter women in my lifetime. My point is, young, hopeful, smart girls like LaShawn Denton should never have to face that reality.

Women should know by now that they have to be responsible for themselves. Brothers out here ain't tryin' to act right. And the few who are find themselves constantly being tempted by women I refer to as bitter women who want revenge. These sisters are angry because their man left them for somebody else, so they go out to take someone else's man. Black women can be a trip.

I can't believe Terry McMillan had the audacity to write *Waiting to Exhale,* as if she needs to male-bash with all the loot she has! If the women who read that book were smart, they would have protested her, because she made them all look desperate and conniving. I only read the book after walking into Adrian's salon one day and the customers were gossiping and carrying on about how good the movie was. They all looked up at me with those real beady eyes as if I had left each and every one of them in a bad situation. Mad at the world, and for what? Because Ms. McMillan had put it in writing *and in their heads* that the brothers are the problem.

If you ask me, the *only* problem is that black women haven't taken it upon themselves to handle up on their personal business when they get involved in a relationship. They are the ones who need to provide the condoms, make a non-car-having brother walk or take the bus, take back their apartment keys, stop waiting for the phone to ring, and get off their knees praying for a man. The average brother only has two things on his mind: making money and getting laid. I'm not an average brother; this is why I can say the truth and not be ashamed.

Last note, sisters need to learn how to breathe, too. Because, like my man LL Cool J said, "Waiting to exhale collapses lungs." That statement was funny when I first heard it, but it's true. Besides, *Waiting to Exhale* wasn't nothing compared to *Disappearing Acts.* Now, *that's* the book that should have been put on the big screen. The way Franklin pooped over Zora is what should've had sisters fuming like scarred dragons. Better yet, the way Zora let herself be pooped on! I don't know how I got on this trip about the sisters, but I got mine and I will do whatever it takes to keep her, because Adrian is a good woman, I'm a good man, and we go good together. This evening at the gym, I will tell the fellas about my engagement. I can't wait to hear what they have to say. I'm already expecting at least one of them to be disappointed; the question is, Who?

## 4

B Y THE TIME I get over to the gym after work, Tim, Eric, Jamal, and Phillip are already there. We all work at Data Tech together, except for Jamal. He's self-employed and works from home.

The guys are sitting together in the bleachers while the referees get the gym set up for the game. We're all about the same height except for Phil, who is about five six and the color of manila paper. He's stocky and has calf muscles that look too big for his legs.

Phil went to Jarvis Christian College—a small black college in East Texas. Back in the day, Jarvis was known as Jarvis "Crooked" College because many of its students never matured to the collegiate thinking level and on any given night you could travel down there and catch a good game of dominoes, spades, or dice, and even football and basketball pots went around for the big gamblers. The students were rowdy and full of party back then, and I hear things haven't changed much. Sometimes you can't tell Phil has been a part of the higher education system by the way he talks and acts.

Jamal doesn't have a degree, but he's the exact opposite of Phil.

Well read and highly intellectual, Jamal knows more than most of us about general subjects. He went to trade school and got certified in graphic art. He can talk all day about the history of African life in America, the slave trade, how the human brain works, and even the mating habits of the South American june bug. He reads anything and everything he gets his hands on. Jamal is a friend of mine from high school and part of the crew.

A little Asian woman is walking around with a clipboard. She looks like she's getting everyone's names and phone numbers. I stroll over to the bleachers where the guys are and take a seat next to Eric.

"Greg, what's up, man?" Eric says. He flips his blond hair away from his temples.

"E, how ya doin'?" I spread dap to Eric.

"There he is! The last of the great bachelors. Congratulations, brother," Jamal says. We lock hands and grip. He has his shoulder-length dreadlocks pulled back in a rubber band and has on an old faded shirt that reads, I SURVIVED THE MILLION MAN MARCH. I dap him. "Another good brother is about to help this old world out," he says to me.

"Thanks, man. You-all are going to be my groomsmen, right?"

"As long as the woman you couple me with is single and has a big booty," Phil responds. "It's bad enough you gettin' married, but please don't couple me with no ugly-ass female."

"Forget Phil, Greg. We got your back, man," Eric huffed.

Jamal and Tim nod and voice their agreement.

I pull out my sweat towel and a water bottle, not worried about Phil anyway. He's the youngest of all of us and the one with the most lessons to learn. Eric pats me on the back. He's the only white guy in my clique. Actually, he's cool to be as white as he is. Eric has blond hair and grayish-green eyes that seem to turn every time he blinks. He graduated from Baylor, one of the biggest and whitest schools in Texas. But when you see his mannerisms along with the way he walks and talks, you'd think he's a brother straight from the 'hood somewhere.

"Finally making the big step, I see," he says. "Life gets pretty solid from here, you know."

"Yeah, can't wade in the water forever," I respond.

"Whatever!" Tim yells loudly. He's bouncing a basketball and doing rotating drills between his legs. "I'm going to wade in the water a long time. Too many fish in the sea to be on lockdown with one big trout."

"Tim, when did you ever have a reason to stop being a player?" Phillip asked. "All the women you date are just as selfish and lonely as you are."

Eric points to Tim. "I think you should turn in your Players' Club card. It's about time you found a woman who's going to be around a while."

Jamal laughed. "Ain't no woman alive who'll put up with Tim's shit for a lifetime."

Tim picked up the ball and looked at us sitting on the bleachers. "Man, I was born a player and I'm gonna die a player. If it wasn't for men like me, half of y'all wouldn't have a reason to be good men, but I makes 'em and breaks 'em before they break me."

We all laugh as Tim shoots and misses the basket.

Jamal taps me. "So how did you come to this conclusion?"

"Adrian is my girl and I love her. I figured three years was more than enough time. She's good to me and she's never given me any reason to doubt her love for me."

"That's cool, man. I hope you two have a long, successful life together." Jamal ties his shoes, then leans back on the bleachers.

Eric runs over and starts guarding Tim. They get caught up in a playful game of one on one, leaving me, Jamal, and Phil sitting together.

"Greg man, I don't understand you," Phil says. "You have the finest woman I've ever seen, and you're going to ruin that by marrying her. I mean, don't you still want to ride that ass when you want to and send her home when you don't feel like being bothered?"

Jamal looks at Phil. "Man, what kind of question is that?"

"J, man, I'm just keeping it real. When Greg marries Adrian, she's going to change. All women do. By the way, Greg, does Adrian cook?"

"Yeah, she cooks. Why do you want to know?"

"Shit, if a man is going to marry a woman, the bitch needs to know how to cook."

"Phil, why is every woman a bitch to you?" I ask, disgusted. "Don't you know that term is played out?"

"It's just a figure of speech. Don't get all bent out of shape. Just because I have a degree don't mean I have sold out to being true to the game. I didn't come from humble surroundings like some of us in here." Phil sends his words out toward the court.

"I know you ain't talking about me!" Tim yells. "Women can still be bitches in my book. I just choose not to use the term too loosely. Y'all remember Ronnie Banks, right?"

Some of us shake our heads, recalling the Italian model Tim flaunted around us for three weeks before breaking it off with her. If my memory serves me correctly, she used his credit card to buy a plane ticket for some guy she swore was her manager. Tim cut her loose immediately after that.

"Ronnie used to let me call her my bitch. She loved it but only allowed me to call her that in private. She even called herself a bitch."

I laugh at Tim's remark before getting back to Phil. "Phil, your degree is not a symbol of selling out, but rather a symbol of better positioning. All I'm trying to say is, stop referring to women as bitches."

"Brother, sisters are too precious to be called bitches. Is your mother or sister worthy of such a title?"

I can tell that Jamal is about to start preaching his pro-black talk. He's the only brother I know who can talk endlessly, all day long, about male and female relationships, but prefers to be single. On average, Jamal dates one woman every four or five months. One day he told us his philosophy on dating was simple: "If you don't waste a woman's time, then your time won't be wasted." I think this brother has been through a lot of emotional struggles and is just using that as a very lame excuse. But I have to hand it to him, he definitely knows how to treat a woman. He's always approached by the finest sisters when we go out, and women from his past still hound him.

"The black woman is to be put on a pedestal and not lusted for or prematurely desired. Calling her a bitch is causing within yourself psychological warfare, Phil."

Phil gets up and walks away. "Fuck that Malcolm shit, J, these bitches ain't worth it. These tired-ass women always talking about what can I do for them. Shit, I ain't got time for that. When is a bitch gonna do for me?"

Eric fakes around Tim and shoots. The ball falls gracefully into the net. He throws his hands up and looks at Phil. "You'll get someone to do for you when you grow about five inches."

I can't help but laugh, and Jamal joins me. We all tease Phil about his height, but it never seems to bother him.

"Man, that brother has some critical issues," I say, referring to Phil.

"I feel you," Jamal responds. "I hope you and Adrian plant some beautiful seeds and keep our people going. "We need to create a strong generation of brothers and sisters."

"Now you sound like my old man."

"It's important, man. Young black couples today will spend their life earnings on a wedding and then turn around and say they can't afford children. It's selfish and unfair to the unborn spirits."

"The economy is bad."

"Forget the economy. The economy ain't never stopped them from showing us shit like *The Brady Bunch.* Had us believing you could support that many kids and still manage to vacation every year and wear nice clothes at a time when our country was at war. Surely, you don't believe that 'economy is bad' shit, brother." He leaned back. "When I find my queen, we're having a whole tribe like our grandparents used to swing it back in the day. My grandmother had nine, her sister had thirteen, my mother's sister even has ten. I think it's cool to have your own village like that."

"Where do you plan on finding a woman who's going to have that many kids in this day and time?"

"They're everywhere. But I want a natural sister. She has to eat right, be spiritually in tune, be humble, and be 'dechemicalized.' "

"Dechemicalized?"

"No perm, no deodorant, and baking soda toothpaste," Jamal says with a serious look on his face. "I could even dig a little hair under her arms. Not an Afro or nothing like that, but I want a woman who isn't afraid to be what she is."

I shake at the thought of a woman with hair under her arms. "To each his own. Right now, my worry is getting past the wedding."

"What? Is she talking about a big wedding?"

"Not yet. I hope not."

The Asian woman comes over and gives us green sleeveless shirts with numbers on them. Four guys from Microsystems come over and join us. We all introduce ourselves and begin stretching for our game. Tim and Eric are already sweating.

The opposing team comes in, and by the looks of them, the game is going to be a good one. We've got them by height, but they got us by speed from the looks of four young brothers on the team.

I stretch my legs, arms, and neck. Last time, I caught a cramp from not stretching good enough and had to be carried out of the gym. Adrian is cooking for me tonight at my place and I don't want to be busted up to a point where we can't get our groove on afterward.

When the game starts, I'm playing guard position. Phil is the point guard and he's running up and down the court like a track star. I think he's trying to show the young dudes that he's still got whatever it was he had eight years ago. The young dudes are hanging with him and box him twice, causing our team to turn the ball over. We call a time-out and huddle up together.

"Man, these young fools are fouling me! Didn't y'all see them foul me!" Phil yells. Nobody responds to his ranting.

"Okay, here's what we'll do," Eric intervenes. "Phil, pass left to Greg. Greg, penetrate the middle, go behind the back to Simon, and Simon to layup. Got it?"

Simon is one of the guys from Microsystems. He's medium height and thin. He doesn't look too sure of his new responsibility. I start to say something, but decide against it. We come out of the huddle and go back onto the court.

Phil gets the ball and looks over to me and Eric. Our other team members are acting as if the ball is coming to them. One of the youngsters is guarding me, and I'm struggling to get by his quick legs. Phil passes me the ball and I'm lucky to have grabbed it. This kid is guarding me as if his life depends on it. I pivot around the youngster and penetrate the middle, and just as the young buck pulls up on me, I pass behind my back to Simon. He grabs the ball and just as he turns to do the layup, he runs smack into one of the opponents. I'm shocked because Simon looked like he was trying to run through the guy. They both hit the floor, and only the opponent returns to his feet. Simon is lying there and blood is oozing from his nose.

"Simon, you all right?" I ask as I kneel beside him.

Simon is dazed. He's looking around at us with an unsure expression on his face. He blinks a few times, then shakes his head. Jamal and Tim pull him up slowly and stand him on his feet. One of his Microsystems co-workers comes over with ice wrapped in a towel and hands it to him. His nose is already starting to swell and I cringe a little. After we get Simon settled, we huddle back together. Eric automatically becomes the lead man again.

"Okay, we need strategy."

"What we need is some Ben-Gay and Gatorade," Phil says. "My shoulders hurt."

"You are what you eat, brother," Jamal replies.

Phil rolls his eyes at Jamal. "Eat a bean pie, Malcolm," he says, sulking.

"Okay, guys, let's focus. Let's do the same move, except Tim will move in to Simon's place." Everyone agrees.

This time we put our hands together and holler, "Win!" Now I'm feeling we're about to run this game. Granted, we are older, but we've watched every NBA game since I can remember and we've got the spirit. I walk back onto the court like Dr. J. Jamal and Tim remind me of Kareem Abdul-Jabbar and Isaiah Thomas. Eric is the image of Larry Bird and Phil is reminding me of Magic Johnson. We walk back on the court, ready to handle our business with these children.

Needless to say, we end up losing the game by thirty points. Those young cats have us running around that court like we're stooges. Most of our plays fail, Eric jams a finger, and they manage to steal the ball from us ten times.

One of the young fellas is coming straight with the moves of Kobe Bryant mixed with Sam Perkins. This kid is amazing. After the game is over, I find out he is Andre Jones, the top point guard in the Southwest Region and a recent graduate of Dallas's W.E.B. Du Bois High School. Should have known. I give the young man his props. He is good. Damn good! Phil is worn out. He's limping and bent over like his back has been thrown out. Jamal has taken off his shoes and is wiggling his cramping toes. Tim and Eric are standing by the water fountain talking to some of our teammates from Microsystems. I grab my bag and water so I can jet out.

"Greg man, you out?" Tim asks.

"Yeah, Adrian's cooking for me tonight."

Phil starts in. "Already got her domesticated, huh? I knew that bitch could cook."

Jamal groans and shakes his head.

"Phil, when you get you a woman like mine, then we'll talk," I respond.

"I got me a woman," he brags. "Y'all remember Darvetta?"

"I know you ain't talking about Darvetta with the chipped front tooth." Tim laughs.

"It's a gap! I've told you niggas a thousand times, Darvetta has a gap!"

"Whatever, man," I say as I walk out. "I'll check y'all tomorrow at work."

"Peace out," Jamal says.

Tim and Eric wave from the fountain. I'm happy to be finally headed home. I'm looking forward to spending time with Adrian and getting my grub and my groove slap on.

When I open the door to my apartment, the smell of lasagna runs up my nose and I feel my stomach growl.

"Hey baby!" It's Adrian and she's sitting on the couch leafing through some kind of business book. She gets up and greets me at the door. I pull back before she grabs me.

"Watch out baby, I'm sweaty."

She pulls me in to her soft body anyway. "I don't care. I haven't seen you all day, and I missed you." She leans in and kisses me. We embrace and I'm loving every minute of it. She releases me and goes back to the couch. She has on a brown silk tank shirt with tan leggings and brown leather open-toe clogs. Her toenails are painted gold and she has on a toe ring. Her skin looks so clean and smooth, I can't wait to get showered so I can hold her. "What are you reading?"

She holds the book up so I can see it. "This is a book about getting business improvement loans."

"Read anything interesting?"

"Not yet. Right now, I'm trying to figure out how to compare interest rates."

"Oh." I retreat back to my room. I grab some fresh clothes and head for the bathroom.

When I finish my shower and come out, Adrian is in the kitchen taking the pan of lasagna out of the oven. It looks good. The three cheeses she used are melted perfectly and she has chopped garlic, basil, onion, and pepper on top. I grab the dishes and silverware to help set the table. We sit down together and dig in. I notice her engagement ring is not on her finger.

"Baby, where's your ring?"

She reaches in her shirt and pulls out a gold chain with the ring dangling neatly from it.

"I can't wear it all the time at work, because of the water and chemicals."

I nod my head in agreement. "Good idea."

"Actually, one of my clients told me to do this."

"Have you set a date?"

"Yes." She smiles. "I want us to be married in March at the Botanical Gardens. March twenty-second."

"Eight months?"

"Greg, a year is too long to be engaged. Eight months is perfect, and March is such a beautiful time of year in Texas."

"But the engagement time seems a little short. Is that going to give us enough time to get everything together?"

"We're having an alternative wedding, Gregory. I'm not doing nothing traditional but saying, 'I do.'" She dips back into her lasagna. "Nontraditional means cheaper, quicker, and different, that's all. It will be wonderful, you'll see." She smiles as she chews. Cute. I melt.

I feel relieved that she is not interested in a big ceremony. It's not that I wouldn't pay for it. I just don't like all the drama of feeding people I don't know. "Well, if it's going to make you happy Adrian, then it's cool with me."

"I would like for your sister to be one of my bridesmaids."

"Are you sure? You know you don't have to do that on my account."

"I know, but it will give Shreese and me a chance to get to know each other before you and I are actually married. I know your sister is churchy and all—"

"Very churchy," I interrupt. "My sister is symbolic of everything church-oriented. She's a walking advertisement for the Holy Club."

Adrian laughs.

"Baby, I'm just telling you. I don't know how she's going to react to this."

"Sounds more like a warning."

"No. Just a word to the wise. You may be asking for more than just having her as a bridesmaid. Did I tell you that my sister used to have tent revivals with her dolls in our backyard when we were little?"

Adrian laughs, almost spitting out her drink.

"Baby, I'm serious. Shreese would line all her dolls up, pitch a tent with a blanket, and stand outside talking to those dolls like they were real. I didn't tell you?" I'm laughing, recalling Shreese's tent meetings.

"No, you didn't, but that was a long time ago. I think Shreese just never hung out with a female she could get to know."

"Yeah, and before it's all over, I'll have two holy rollers on my hands."

"Not."

"We'll see. I'll give you her number and you can call and ask her. I don't want to have nothing to do with it."

"Gregory Alston, I think you're being too cautious."

"We'll see."

We finish up our meals and clean the kitchen together.

That's another thing I love about Adrian. She's clean and loves sharing the responsibilities of household duties. She moves about in the kitchen concentrating on every single detail. She wipes the standing water from around the sink and on the cabinets.

By the time she finishes, my kitchen looks different. It almost has a glow to it. I'm trippin' because it always looks brand-new when she cleans it.

I join Adrian on the couch and flip on the television. We watch *Malcolm & Eddie,* this show on UPN. Eddie Griffin is a fool to his heart. I laugh at his jokes throughout the whole show. Malcolm Jamal Warner isn't as funny, but sometimes his timing gets him a few laughs. They should have gotten Chris Tucker to play Malcolm's role, then the show would be funny as shit. Adrian lays in my arms sucking her teeth at every joke Eddie does. I know she's trying not to laugh.

"Why does he have to be such a clown all the time?" she asks.

"He's a comedian." I laugh. "It's how he makes a living, baby."

"I just think Eddie Griffin is too smart to be doing all this goof-ball antics and talking about people all the time. The same goes for Chris Rock."

"What do you mean?"

I love to hear Adrian voice her opinions. She's smart for someone who graduated from high school and went straight to hair school. Sometimes I wonder where'd she get all of her knowledge. Most beauticians I've met don't have a third of her common sense. Either that, or they hide it very well.

"Chris Rock makes jokes about really serious issues. He's politically intelligent and doesn't realize it. His format doesn't consist of jokes about the average black comedian stuff."

"Like what?"

"Like sex, weed smoking, taking a shit, and stealing. He talks about taking over the White House and the prison systems. So does Eddie Griffin. I just think they're two great, funny black men wasting more potential than they're using."

*Damn, my baby is deep! I like that in a woman. Straight opinionated!*

"Give me an example of a comedian who is doing what you think they should be doing, then?" I challenge.

"Well, Steve Harvey, for one. When he was here in Dallas, he was down with Commissioner John Wiley Price. He had a thriving comedy club, he's had two television shows that dealt with decent issues. He wasn't taking no shit from ABC, so he left."

"But he also wimped out on that radio station in Chicago. Left them hanging."

"Don't tell me you're going to hold that one thing against a good man like Steve Harvey," she huffs.

"You're right. I still wish he would come back and reopen his club. But you must admit, Chris Rock does have his own talk show on HBO."

"Damn, why should we have to pay to hear him talk common sense, though? See, he should have told the network folks that he wanted to be on prime time. Maybe Jay Leno would get canceled with his corny ass."

"Adrian, Chris Rock has to make a living. I'm sure HBO is paying him good money to do what he does."

"Greg, I sit all day listening to black women come in griping about their boyfriends, husbands, sons, uncles, nephews, and even their male bosses, and it makes me sick to hear how stupid some of them are when it comes to dealing with men. But when have we seen any good, positive, aware, bold brothers on regular television. That's where half of the images are coming from. They don't have cable in the ghetto."

"Oh, they have it. It's bootlegged, but they have it."

"You know what I mean, Gregory."

"Well, history has played a big part in the mentalities of both black men and women, honey. You can't just blame it on television."

"But Greg, you can't blame everything on history either. When I see men in today's society like Martin Lawrence, Luke, Master P, Too Short, and all the others who don't make women feel any safer in this world, it pisses me off."

"Adrian, I don't think these brothers mean anything by the things they do. It's just money for them. Shit that sells. It's just entertainment."

She shakes her head. "But what about the security of women? What about us?"

*What about y'all?* I think. *I have enough troubles trying to stay out of jail, out of the drug war, or being viewed as a sellout because of my college degree and love for nice things.*

"You think black men are running around here mad at Adina Howard, Millie Jackson, Lil' Kim, and Foxy Brown?" I ask. "They sure don't give good black men any hope."

"No I don't think that, because men don't think with their brains when encountering those kind of women."

"That's not a true or a fair statement, Adrian."

"Greg, when was the last time I heard you even open your mouth in protest when we sat here on this very couch watching Adina Howard on BET? I've never heard you talking about lost hope. Come on, tell me."

I shrug.

"See what I mean?"

"Adrian, I'm not going to bash those sisters because they're proclaiming their sexuality on the screen. It's their freedom. To get mad and swollen would be like . . . like . . ."

"Too much like *right.* Am I correct, Greg?" She shifts her position in my arms and smiles before returning her attention to the television. "A booty shaking is just too much for you to try to cover up and be mad about."

"I see your point. But baby, men are men. We look because it's pleasing. I hate to be so up-front, but men like looking at women."

"I just think that if the black men, and men in general, took it upon themselves to take their lives and positions in this world a little more seriously, then the women would follow."

"So you're saying that men are the reason why women do what they do?"

"And what do *they* do?"

"You know, wear hootchie outfits, argue in public, talk loud, and disrespect each other."

She looks up at me, amused. "I'm saying that before your kind came along, we were doing just fine." She giggles and rests her head on my stomach. "Hell, yes, the women would follow. Now we act just like men want us to."

I sit quiet while holding her. I can't figure out what she meant by that, but it's too late to be insulted and I'm too horny to go there and start an argument. The last thing I need to do is make her mad at me and cut myself off from getting any love tonight. *God forbid,* I think.

## 5

SEPTEMBER IS ALREADY here. It's still hot as hell and I can't even tell that summer has come to an end. Adrian and I have been ripping and running trying to get our wedding arrangements done. We met with the caterer yesterday. He was some gay brother named Marquis LaSalle. His name even sounded gay to me. He was cool, though, and all about business. We're serving the usual: chicken wings, Swedish meatballs, fruits and vegetables. Adrian also ordered a four-layer French vanilla cake with homemade icing, and it's as expensive as it sounds.

I figured most of the people behind the scenes at this wedding lead alternative lifestyles, because Adrian has more gay friends than I have pairs of socks and that's saying a lot. The limousine driver, our coordinator, and the person singing the Lord's Prayer are all gay too. She used to have a guy working in her shop that was flaming, so I suppose he hooked her up with most of these people. The rest of the folks I knew from around the way. We have a live jazz band playing the reception. Most of them I went to high school with. The one singer I scheduled is an older woman Pops knew from his days in the music world. I already know that Shreese and Jamal are going to trip about the alternative lifestyles, so I've decided to just keep my lips sealed. Maybe they'll never say anything to me.

Tim is coming over in a few, so we can go look at some tuxedos. Adrian picked black and red as the color scheme for the wedding. I figured as much. Red is her favorite color. The walls at her shop are a matte red. I'm game for it. Actually, this wedding thing is a bit overrated. The only things I'm excited about are the bachelor party, the ceremony, and the reception. Everything else is pretty much for the woman's enjoyment.

Speaking of the wedding colors, let me call my sister and see if she is going to wear the red dress Adrian selected for her bridesmaids. Shreese doesn't own anything red. She believes that red is a whore's color. Don't ask me where she got it from, but my first guess would be Reverend Dixon. Her phone rings four times before she picks up. Unusual. When she answers her phone, music blares through the receiver. I can hear Kirk Franklin and the Family singing loudly in the background.

"Hello?"

"Hey Shreese. What are you doing?"

"Getting ready to take Pastor Dixon some soup. He has a cold." I can tell my sister is in her kitchen. She's rummaging through silverware.

"Doesn't he have someone to do that for him?" I charge.

"Greg, don't be silly. I love helping the pastor out. It's part of being a disciple for the Lord, and he called me specifically requesting my homemade vegetable soup."

I let her remark slide, too busy trying to talk about the dress. "I was calling to see if you spoke with Adrian."

"Yes. She called me and I accepted her invitation to be a bridesmaid. I was actually kind of surprised, considering we're like night and day. God and Lucifer." She chuckles.

"Give Adrian a chance and you might just end up loving her as much as I do. It was her idea to ask you to be in the wedding. Do you think you can behave long enough to walk down an aisle and stand until your big brother is married?"

"Maybe." Shreese is smiling. I can tell by the inflection in her voice.

"So you don't have a problem wearing red?"

"I do, but Gregory, I told you: This is your wedding. I've prayed about it and God has already forgiven me, since you're my brother."

"So you're really okay with this?" I ask again.

"Sure. Pastor Dixon said I may be able to reach some lost souls at the wedding."

"Shreese, I don't want you trying to save people at my wedding. Your presence is enough."

"Hmph. Lord knows Jezebel will probably be rolling over in her grave while trying to enjoy the wedding at the same time. Satan has a way of coming around and making a situation look like it's okay, when it's not. But the Lord. Alleluia! The Lord has equipped me with the answer. Thank you, Jesus!"

I sit quiet while my sister has her religious moment. She always takes time out to have a personal dramatic shouting session with herself.

"For what it's worth, thanks," I reply.

"You're welcome, but you need to be thanking the Man Upstairs. You marrying Adrian is not the work of He who comes to save."

"Adrian is really a good person."

"I'm sure she is."

"Pops likes her."

"Pops liked all your girlfriends. He's too busy trying to become a grandfather."

We both laugh.

"Have you thought about calling Mom?" she asks.

"No." I frown at my answer. Shreese knows how I feel about the subject of our mother.

"Don't you think you should?"

I exhale. "Not really. And I don't want to talk about her right now."

"Okay, okay. Dang.'Gregory, I don't know why you act like you hate her so much."

"Hey, look, Shreese, I have to go," I lie to rush my sister off the phone. "Tim is at the door."

"I didn't hear him knock."

"You weren't listening."

"A lying tongue is the way of Satan. God is going to get you, Gregory."

"He already has. 'Bye, Shreese."

She hangs up without saying anything. It's cool, though. Shreese is funny that way sometimes. I'm upset that she brought up our mother. Who does she think she is? Now Tim really is knocking at the door.

"Hey Greg! Open up, man!"

I go to the door and let him in. He struts in with some expensive-looking sunshades on to complement his starched and ironed red shorts with matching red-and-white-striped shirt.

"What's happening, cool breeze?"

"You the man, you tell me." We slap each other five.

"You ready to hit the mall?" I ask.

"Yeah, but let me tell you, it's hot out there. I ain't never seen a hot day like this in September."

"This heat ain't no joke."

"So, did you and Adrian find a caterer?" he asks.

"Finally." I grab my car keys and wallet and we head out the door.

"Who did she decide on?"

"LaSalle."

Tim shrugs. He's not familiar with the name.

"Have you and Simone been out anymore?" I ask.

"No. She's supposed to call me, though. That threesome we pulled was all that!" he says excitedly. "Her homegirl's name was Charnelle. She was fine, too! I'm talking about thick legs, long hair, and the softest ass I've ever touched." Tim is smiling and shaking his head. I'm laughing on my side of the car. "Man, I was like a bitch after they were through with me. I was hounding Simone day and night for a little while. I phoned her to give it another go and she wouldn't return my calls. I went by her crib, but no one answered. Shit, eventually I had to start looking elsewhere. I can take a hint. Tonight, I got a date with this chick named Neecy. She's a bus driver."

"School bus driver?"

"City bus. She drives for DART."

I laugh. "Yo, man, how in the hell did you hook up with a woman who drives for DART?" Dallas Area Rapid Transit is our city transportation. We always joke by calling it "Driving Africans 'Round Town."

"You know me, I gets around," he brags.

We climb in Tim's silver Acura Legend and pull out of the parking lot.

"Seriously."

"We met at the barbershop."

"She had her son with her?" I ask, assuming that would be the first reason she was at a barbershop.

"She doesn't have any kids. She was getting her hair cut."

"She wears a natural?"

"Yeah. She has naturally curly hair."

"That's not what I meant," I respond as I put on my own designer sunshades. "So I guess you're about to tell me how non-American she looks."

Tim looks at me. "This woman has it going on!"

"What does she look like?"

"She's originally from El Paso and she has a nice accent. She's mixed with black, Choctaw Indian, and Mexican."

"Tim, when are you going to date a black woman?"

"She is black. We all know that in America the twenty percent of Mexican and thirty percent Indian in her don't count," he states with a laugh.

"No, I mean a woman who has dark skin," I argue.

"What does it matter?"

"Bro, I've just never seen you with a dark-skinned woman, that's all. I'm beginning to think you have a hangup on skin color, and that's hard to believe since you're dark-skinned yourself."

"I've dated across the board, Greg. . . ."

"I know, man, and none of them, since *I've* known you, would have failed the brown bag test."

Tim shifts into fourth as we get on the freeway. "Man, I just haven't come across one I really like. Skin color has never been an issue with me. If a woman is down to be with Tim, and Tim is dig-gin' her, then it's on."

"What about Vanessa Ross? She was dark as a purple grape, beau-tiful, and was diggin' you."

"Vanessa was married. You know I don't get down like that."

"She was separated when you met her."

"And she went back to him after I was through with her. You know I don't get down like that."

"What about that fine sister you met at that Chinese restaurant? What was her name?"

"You're talking about Arlandra."

"Yeah, that's her. She was dark-skinned and unattached."

"Yeah, she was, but her attitude was stank and she didn't have a job."

"Simone has a stank attitude."

"Yeah, but she was exotic in bed."

"And she's also a redbone." I laugh. "Okay, would you go out with Tichina Arnold?" She played the role of Pam on the show *Martin.*

Tim shook his head. "She looks too rough, man. I didn't like the way she acted on the show, either." He frowns up like a bad odor is resting on his top lip. "I like a sister who is feminine at all times re-gardless if she's famous or not. A woman like Chatina or whatever her name is wouldn't last with me."

"That is the finest black woman I've ever seen! Tim, you can't tell me you are letting her acting take over her looks."

Tim ignores my comment. "Try another one," he says, smiling.

"Okay, what about Lauryn Hill?"

"Was she the one who played in that old movie with Whoopi Goldberg?"

"Yeah."

"M-m-m. She's too skinny. I like a meaty woman."

"And Kellie Williams from that show *Family Matters?*"

"Too young."

"Last one. What about Toni Braxton?"

"Toni Braxton ain't dark-skinned," he protested.

"Nigga, you a damn lie. Toni would not pass the brown bag test," I argue.

"Well, for your information, yeah I would fuck Toni."

"I didn't say nothin' about fucking!" I break out in laughter.

"Shit, I did. I'd give it to her good, too. Tim Johnson style. Have her singing all kinds of love songs. I'd give her a Grammy she could be proud of."

I'm cracking up, even though Tim still hasn't convinced me that he would date a woman with dark brown skin. We get to the mall in no time. Gingiss Formal Wear is kind of crowded. There are several groups of men in there looking at tuxes and suits. Jamal is waiting for us when we walk in. His dreadlocks are down, framing his strong facial features. Sometimes, I can't believe that's his hair. My shit would never do that.

Growing dreadlocks was something I never even considered when I was growing up. My mother . . . I mean, my father always kept my hair low to my head. Jamal has been growing his for about five years now, and I think it's tight as shit. I ain't sweating my boy or nothing, but his hair is cool and only Jamal can do that and get away with it.

He's a freelance graphics artist. He has accounts with some of the top advertising firms in Dallas and several others in other cities. You may have seen some of his work in magazines like *Essence, Ebony, Vibe, Esquire,* and *GQ.* He's paid in full all the time, and he works from his house, so he can grow his hair down to his ankles if he wants to.

We walk up to the counter to be helped. A portly man with red hair and freckles looks over at us. When he returns to the counter, small beads of perspiration are formed on his nose and he doesn't look pleased that new customers have walked into the already crowded store.

"How can I help you?"

"I'm here to view some vests and ties for Alston," I say.

The man goes to the back and returns with a list. Once he spots my name he goes into the back again. This time he takes a few minutes before he comes out. He's carrying about ten different vest sets. He takes them over to a nearby table and lays them out.

"When you find what you like, bring it up to the front and fill out the order form." Portly walks away.

"Who ate his breakfast this morning?" Jamal says smartly. "That cracker needs to relax a little. Take some weight off."

"Literally." Tim takes off his shades and helps me sort through the packages. He pulls out a black-and-red-checked silk vest with matching tie.

"This is cool."

I look at it. "I dig the vest, but a checkered cummerbund and tie are whack."

We all begin sifting through the vests. We see everything from polka dots, to stripes, to snowflakes. After getting the selection down to three vests, we finally decide on a red silk vest with black diamonds. I really don't like it, either, but I don't want to make this an all-day event.

I take my selection back up to the desk and the same store attendant is standing there looking more bitter than ever. I give him the vest, fill out the order form and get the hell out of Gingiss Formal Wear.

We decide to get a bite to eat, so Jamal follows Tim and me across town. We end up at Jo Mama's Soul Food Kitchen. We get a booth near the front. A small jazz band is playing and I immediately notice the tune. It's "Lover Man." I know because Diana Ross sang it in *Lady Sings the Blues.* I also have a Sarah Vaughan CD where she blows the hell out of the same song. I love me some Sarah. In my opinion, she is the hottest jazz singer ever. Forget what you've ever heard about Billie, Ella, Abbey, Nancy, Nina, and all the others. I mean, they're great in their own right, but they can't touch Sassy.

When I first heard Sarah Vaughan sing, I was about four or five. We were living in New Jersey and my parents took me and my sister cross state to New York to a jazz festival where Sarah Vaughan, Miles Davis, Coleman Hawkins, and other legends were performing. I still remember how statuesque she was. Tall, thick, and dark. Lovely! I can still see her holding that cigarette while blasting, "It Never Entered My Mind."

I wouldn't be telling you this story if it weren't true, but I have proof that I was there. In my father's house, hanging on the wall, is a picture of me, my sister Shreese, Sarah Vaughan, Lena Horne, and my mother. I have on these high-water purple denim pants with a Disney World T-shirt, and Shreese has on a yellow Winnie the Pooh jumper with matching ribbons on her two long ponytails. It was the last time I saw a live performance before we moved to Dallas. My sister and I grew up on straight old-school jazz all our lives.

Anyway, Sarah's voice was what I heard most of my life after that. I would sit in our study and play her records all the time on my Superfriends record player. The richness in her voice was so warm that it could make you sweat. I was in college when she died in 1990. I got sloppy drunk that night after I found out. Ended up missing classes for two days and my father had to travel down to Commerce, Texas, and beg the school not to throw me out of Hubbell Hall, the all-men's dorm on campus. Needless to say, there has yet to be another like Sarah.

This band playing at the restaurant isn't doing too bad a job. The bass player could use some more skills. He's actually walking a tired dog. No swing in his play at all. Not pulling the strings enough. He's young-looking, so I let it rest.

We all order and have drinks as we wait on our lunch. Tim is sipping on a rum-and-Coke, Jamal has a ginger beer, and I'm gripping a Heineken. As the waitress walks away, Tim stares hard at her ass. When he turns back around, he sees me shaking my head. He shrugs his shoulders in guilt. "What? She has a nice ass," he says innocently.

"But did you have to stare at her like that?"

"Man, her ass had me hypnotized." He laughs slyly.

"What if you walked by a table and a group of women stared at you like that?" Jamal asks.

"I'd fuck 'em all."

We all laugh. Tim's good with comebacks.

"No, seriously," Tim responds. "I think women enjoy being stared at. That's what God put them here for."

"To be looked at?" I ask.

"Yeah. They don't do nothing else but take your money. I haven't met a woman yet who didn't want something materialistic from me. Either my money, my sex, or my car."

I disagree. "Tim, you've been going out with too many gold-diggers and women who are a direct reflection of yourself. Sisters who are caught up in looks, status, and fashion. That's why you think they're just to be looked at. I can't believe you said that."

"Greg, you know it's true, man. We could do without the secretaries, waitresses, manicurists, and teachers, right? These women ain't trying to hear about the bills you got to pay if it's not their bills. All they do is take from you until you can't give no more, then ride your dick until it goes limp."

"Women are simply trying to take back what was originally theirs. They just don't know it," Jamal interrupts. "Women are the mothers of civilization. Surely you don't believe that story about the snake in the garden, do you?"

"Jamal, what are you talking about?" I challenge him.

"Adam and Eve." He takes a drink from his bottle. "That wasn't a snake in the Garden of Eden. That was another man."

"Aw, shit, there you go talking that Malcolm shit again." Tim adjusts the cap on his head. "What's the truth this time, Brother Bilal?" he asks sarcastically. "Enlighten me, my brother."

"The truth is that when the Good Book was rewritten, man was called a snake because he whispered in Eve's ear and it was unlike anything she had heard before. Women had no reason to whisper when they were the only ones walking the face of the earth. Have you ever noticed, when people whisper, it sounds like a snake?"

"So you're saying that there were two men in the Garden of Eden?" Tim laughs.

"There was more than just two people walking the earth at that time, but before then women were here first and they created man. All existence comes from a womb, not a nutsack," Jamal proclaims. "Adam and Eve were a civilization of people, not just a man and a woman. What do you think God meant by 'in *Our* image'?"

I'm listening to Jamal, trying to understand where he gets all this crazy-sounding radical information from. It makes sense to an ex-

tent, as all theories do, but to totally accept it goes against everything I was raised to accept as a Christian. I shake my head at his
question. "I don't get it, Jamal."

"Have you two ever paid any attention to how women react to a
smooth-talking brother when his game is tight?" he asked. "The way
the man slides all up on her and leans in, letting the heat of his
breath tickle her earlobes? The sister gets like butter and will do
damn near anything for that man, that's the truth. Imagine him asking her to close her third eye and use the two on her face to see his
logic and ignore her own innate wisdom. That was the knowledge
right there. Wasn't a tree with apples on it, but rather it was the ac-
tual act of the spiritual being overtaken by the physical."

I sit back against the booth, trying to absorb what Jamal just said.
All I can think about is my sister and how she reacts to Reverend
Dixon. Like butter. Just like butter.

"Jamal, you can't be serious, man!" Tim's voice breaks my
thought. "You can't possibly be insinuating that women were running around here first, when it's a known fact that men were."

Tim looks at me.

I have a blank look and offer no support for him.

He continues to try to convince us. "We were!" he argues. "Man
was doing fine until the wind blew and his dick got hard."

"Dang, Tim, do you have to be so graphic?" I ask.

"Greg, you grew up in a Christian home and you know that Adam
was the first man on this planet and God took his rib and made
woman."

I shrug my shoulders. "All I know is we here and we gon' be here
and we got to figure this out before the system and AIDS kills us
all," I say emphatically.

Jamal folds his arms on the table and leans, in staring at both of
us. "The oldest living human bones in the upright position that have
been found to date are those of a woman. A black woman."

"He has a point, Tim," I tease.

"But that means that reproduction could never have happened."

"Tim, women have in their bodies only X and X chromosomes.
That means, if you break it down to a simple science, they possess all

natural abilities within themselves to create a female nation, brother," Jamal says. "There was probably a time they could reproduce without the aid of a penis. They had the egg and one sex determiner."

"But not the fertilizer," I interject, making my point.

"That's bullshit. Crazy! Any man knows that women can't *run* nothing but their mouths and niggas to their graves. And those two brothers in the Garden of Eden with Eve should have run a train on her and set her straight for listening to that snake and being disobedient." Tim is practically hollering.

"You and Phil are hopeless," Jamal says as he takes a sip from his ginger beer. "The only two men in the world who think they know all there is to know about women in less than five sentences."

"Hey, don't compare me to Phil," Tim responds. "I got a degree from a decent school, I'm a businessman, and I personally think that I'm a good man. I don't do drugs, I'm not gay, and I work every day at a legal job where I make good money. There is no way in the world I'm going to let some woman come in and melt me down to some sniggling boyfriend chump who will do anything for her. My woman will have to carry her fifty percent, while she watches me carry mine."

"What about being there for her?" I ask. "A woman needs a man's support. Doesn't all that go hand in hand?"

"All these strong sisters want nowadays is a virile brother with stamina and bedroom skills, and I got that covered, you know what I'm talking about?" Tim flashes his white smile. "I'll support her, that's for sure."

Jamal lets out a small laugh. "Tim, you've made your point."

The waitress comes back with our food, and this time, Tim never looks her way. He remains quiet as he digs into his Family Reunion Platter, which consists of short ribs, potato salad, red beans, yams, and a side order of peach cobbler. I have a Black Power Special, which is meat loaf, black-eyed peas, cabbage, corn on the cob, and a large square piece of cornbread. Jamal is eating from a Be Light Plate, which is vegetarian meat loaf, elbow pasta, and a whole-wheat roll. We eat in silence for a little while, but it's cool because the band is now playing "Caravan," and I'm digging it.

"So Greg, you and Adrian planning on getting a house before the wedding?" Tim asks. He acts as if the previous conversation never happened.

"We've talked about it. I would like to."

"What about your honeymoon?" Jamal asks. "Where you going?"

"Cozumel."

"Mexico. That sounds cool."

Jamal wipes his mouth. "So"—he smiles—"Adrian is really the one huh?"

"Yeah, this is it for me. My girl is truly a good catch."

"What do you like about her?"

"It's a lot of things. She's hangs with her girls just as much as I hang with you guys, and that's liberating for me because I don't like a woman who clings."

"Like Cheryl," Tim says.

I thought about Cheryl Coleman. Crazy Cheryl Coleman. She was an old college classmate I hooked up with before I met Adrian. We dated for three months and in that short period of time, she had my phone tapped and had me followed by one of her stupid girlfriends. She would even ask me to keep the bathroom door open whenever I took a piss. "Yeah, Cheryl, man." I laugh a little. "Cheryl wouldn't let a nigga breathe for shit."

"Straight." Jamal drinks the last of his ginger beer. "I remember her. She wasn't secure in herself."

"Yeah, but Adrian is really into this woman thing. She digs being a woman and she knows how to treat people from that aspect. It's like she is a supreme version of a strong, feminine woman and I like that," I say between bites of corn on the cob. "And she doesn't keep tabs on me, even though she doesn't have to."

"Ain't many out there like her," Tim adds. "I could marry a woman like Adrian. She's all right with me. Watch out, Greg, I may take her," he jokes.

"Tim, I can't see you getting married. Why do you say that about Adrian? What makes her different?" Jamal asks.

"Adrian has good sense. She just has an air about her that most of these other women don't have. I don't know, but it's attractive, and my man Greg is damn lucky. I'd kill to be in his shoes." Tim shrugs and dips into his plate again.

"She's well traveled too. Been damn near everywhere," I add.

"Like where?" Tim signals the waitress to bring over a second round of drinks for everybody.

"New York, Atlanta, D.C., and she even spent some time in Europe."

"That's cool," Tim responds. "Adrian doesn't have that well-*traveled* look."

"How is a well-traveled sister supposed to look, Tim?" I ask, slightly offended at his remark about Adrian.

He shrugs. "Like Halle Berry. Halle Berry looks like she's been out of the country a lot. She's well traveled, I can tell. Or like Jasmine Guy. She has definitely been to the moon and back."

"Tim, your senses are warped," Jamal says.

"J, just because you sit in your house all day reading books about the origins of man and I don't, doesn't mean I don't know nothing. I know how to treat women. I buy flowers, expensive dinners, and even a nice blouse or panty set every now and again. I also know how to read women, and most of these sisters don't even have writing on their pages. They have dollar signs. Women, *especially black women,* are shallow, immature beggars and they expect a brother to bend over backwards just to get a kiss. I ain't that kind of nigga. I like the best of what Dallas has to offer. I don't mess with just any old female. The classy, upscale ladies make you work harder, but the rewards are always sweeter. You don't see me running around here like Phil, calling them bitches, do you?"

I turn to look at the band. Tim is going off and I think there's more liquor talking than he is.

Jamal stays tuned in to Tim's loose rhetoric on the woman species and they go into another long conversation.

"Tim, listen at you, man. This shit you're talking is the very reason why we have so many relationship problems between our men and women. What are you tripping on, brother?" Jamal asks. "You don't think the upscale women want to settle? Tim, every woman out there wants security and a man they can depend on at *all* times."

"Jamal, you know as well as I do that black women in America don't want to do nothing but be taken care of, like I said a few minutes ago. They are lazy and shiftless."

"So successful sisters like Oprah Winfrey, Angela Bassett, Tina Turner, and Whoopi Goldberg need you to help them stand on their feet? They're lazy and shiftless? Is that what you are saying? That *these* sisters are lazy?"

Tim pauses and then kicks me under the table. "You hear that, Greg?"

I turn my attention back to the conversation. "What'd he say?"

"He goes off and names some of the most powerful single sisters in the industry to make his point. That's lame, J. That's real lame what you just did. A low blow. You know I'm talking about these sisters who look like a good package and when you get to know them, they turn out to be walking basket cases with baggage for days. Case in point, Cheryl Coleman who Greg just talked about."

"Hey man, don't pull me into this," I interject.

Jamal laughs. "Tim, you are trippin'. All I'm trying to do is understand why you so down on the sisters, when in actuality, they never asked to be put in the situations they are in."

"I take care of women as long as they take care of me. Plain and simple, I am not looking to settle."

"Tim, you even perpetuate their behavior." Jamal looks over at me. "Greg, has Adrian ever asked you for anything?"

"Not materialistic-wise. She be beggin' for my award-winning back rubs, though," I joke.

Tim points at me. "And I would put a hundred dollars on the table and bet that yo' ass be doing it too, like a punk slave."

"You damn right." I laugh. "Because I know what I get for a back rub. Adrian comes correct. Our relationship is give and take."

"You give, she takes!" Tim laughs loud this time. A few folks from the nearby tables look over at us.

"Does Adrian ever keep tabs on you when you go out?" Jamal asks.

"No. Half the time, I just take it upon myself to tell her. If I say I'm going out, she says okay and that's it."

Tim quickly talks back. "That shit is going to change, you watch. As soon as you jump the old witch stick, she's gon' be on you like white on rice. She'll want to know what time you're coming in, who you're going with, how long will you be gone, and then she'll have the audacity to tell you to keep your pager on in case she needs to call, but we all know that's just another way to block your fun. She'll be telling you how to do things you've been doing for years. She'll be picking out your clothes, telling you what you need to be eating, moving your stuff where you can't find it in the name of redecorating. It'll be a miracle if you can even fart out loud in your own home once she gets through with you."

"Tim, I don't foresee any of that happening. And if Adrian for whatever reasons starts keeping tabs, then that's cool, because once we're married, there will be no place I would go that I couldn't tell her. Adrian'll take care of me. I know she will."

"Greg man, you have sold your soul to the estrogen brigade," Tim teases. "See, that's why I never stroke a woman on her legs, because once you stroke a woman on her legs, she thinks you are emotionally involved. Never stroke the legs."

"Is that right, brother. Well, I for one love to be a woman's protection," Jamal says. "If stroking her legs is what will make her know I'm serious about her, then I will stroke them."

"Tim, I would do it for any woman that's my woman, like Jamal said. Take her out if she wants to, bubble baths, body massages. All she has to do is say the word and I am at her command. Women do more than enough for brothers, and we take them for granted."

"That's the spirit, my man." Jamal gives me dap.

"Aw, you two niggas is crazy. These women are going to run your asses slap over." He points at me. "Got you getting married, and J, look at you man."

"Tim, what are you talking about?" Jamal asks.

"I ain't seen you with some pussy since Nixon lied. What is up with that?"

I laugh at that comment. Tim has made a very valid point. The last time Jamal had a girlfriend, his dreds were knots.

"Tim, I'm working on me before I bring any well-deserving queen into my reality. I want to be able to give her whatever she needs, whether it be physical, spiritual, mental, *or financial.*"

"Amen." I give J some dap. My boy is going off on some serious stuff.

"Aw, you two old Michael Jackson and Prince sensitive muh-fuckas." Tim gets up from the table. "I gotta piss."

He struts off, leaving me and Jamal at the table. Tim is always tripping on black women this and black women that, but Tim can be a woman's worst nightmare sometimes.

I remember one Christmas, Eric, Phil, Tim, and I went to a First Friday social at the City Place buildings. The party space was huge, two massive floors wide. There were five large rooms, each hosting different music preferences. There was a live jazz room and an old-school room that housed a DJ that was playing some straight funk masters like George Clinton and the P-Funk All-Stars, the Ohio Players, Chaka Khan, and Con Funk Shun. That room was packed with people. The other three rooms were reggae, urban contemporary, and rap/hip-hop. The sisters were looking fine as hell. If there were any hootchie mamas in the house that night, they were definitely undercover.

Tim was in rare dog form. He was walking and winking at sisters. Before we even got in the party good, he grabbed the hand of this one sister and wouldn't let her go until she promised to dance with him. After that little scene, we all headed to the bar and ordered some drinks. I felt like getting my groove on, so me and Eric went to the old-school room.

I don't know if I mentioned this, but Eric dates nonwhite women on an exclusive basis. Never has dated a white woman in all of his twenty-six years of living. That's not why I like him, though.

Eric is cool. Not like the white-boy-trying-to-be-black cool, but he's real laid-back and nothing seems to bother him. Eric was raised in Jamaica, Germany, Egypt, and Alaska. He was an army brat, but it didn't make him a cocky know-it-all like most men. Eric really can see and respect the beauty and the differences in people outside of his race. I've never asked him does that make him ashamed to be white, but I sure would like to know, because Eric never is seen with other white people. Anyway, Eric and I went to the old-school room and it was packed. The DJ was playing a heavy mix of "More Bounce to the Ounce" by Zapp featuring Roger Troutman. Folks were dancin' and the mood of the room was hyped. This thin sister the color of a Hershey's Kiss came over and grabbed Eric's hand. He sat his drink down and followed her to the dance floor. Eric has rhythm and he was right at home with the music. I looked out the door across the hall into the Jamaican room and saw Tim. He had this sister hemmed up against the wall and he was standing so close to her, I could have sworn their noses were touching. I saw her shake her head no several times, before pushing past him. Right as she walked away from him, Tim reached down and pinched the woman's behind. My stomach dropped and I knew one of two things was about to happen. One, the woman would look at him real nasty and walk away, or two, she would retaliate. She chose the latter. The next thing I saw was Tim's drink fly out of his hand and crash to the floor causing glass to shatter everywhere. The sister knocked him across his head the way a mother would do a son who accidentally cussed in front of her.

Everything would have been cool, but the sister started getting loud, like angry women with no home training tend to do. She was ranting and raving like a lunatic as she threw blows at Tim. He was dodging her punches like Holyfield and I had to hand it to him, he was doing a good job all the while, laughing and saying to the woman, "Damn baby, why you got to be so mean to a brother?"

Her girls came and pulled her away, leaving Tim there. Several brothers walked up and gave him dap, too! It was like something straight out of a caveman movie. I just shook my head and resumed watching the old-school crowd. Eric was holding his own with the Hershey's-Kiss-colored sister and he ended up riding home with her that night, leaving us three deep.

Tim and Phil talked about the ass-grabbing incident the rest of the night. They sounded like Cub Scouts who had seen their first naked woman. The way they talked about the sisters made me wanna holler like Marvin Gaye. For real! So me and the guys tend to take

Tim's comments all in stride and not to heart, because he is a brother with some very masculine values.

I look over at Jamal, who is listening to the band. The bass player is doing better. I can sense a little pocket in his swing as he vibes with the drummer.

"J, what's really going on with you, man? Tim does have a point. We haven't seen you with a woman in a while. I know your ass ain't waiting on Erykah Badu." I laugh.

"Greg, I'm just being careful. I am getting my inner person together. I've actually been meeting sisters everywhere. As a matter of fact, I met this beautiful sister at Reciprocity the other night."

"The little hip-hop poetry joint you hang out at?"

"Yeah, this sister was reading a poem that blew my mind. The name of the piece was 'Deep Inside Revolutionary Threads.' Her name was Freedom Heru." He pauses. "Well, that's what she calls herself. Her given name is April Jordan."

"So what's up with her, why you ain't brought her out?"

"Not yet. Not ready. I want to make sure that she and I have an understanding about our paths as kindred spirits. We are going through emotional cleansing right now, but I dig this sister a lot."

"She just got out of a situation?"

"It's, more or less, we both are just trying to make sure we are not hooking up from lack of comfort. We want to make sure our attraction is not just physical and emotional. We want our motives to be unhindered by societal standards of male-female relationships. But I think she's ready to submit to me."

"Those are dangerous words to a woman on the brink of the millennium."

"Not a God-fearing woman. A woman who knows truth, brother, is a woman who will submit to her king."

"Is that really necessary?"

"Yeah, man. Think about it this way, it's about intentions. I don't care what a woman looks like. She can have nappy hair or hair permed down to her butt, but if her intentions are wicked and she can't accept the truth then I can't fool with her, and I would hope that a sister wouldn't fool with me if I was that way."

I sit back. "But we all know you would never date a sister with permed hair."

"That's not true. As long as she understands that she is in an unnatural condition as a black woman and that we could never have children under those terms, then we're okay. I can't take a woman like that seriously, though, because I'm not wearing a relaxer."

"Is April au naturel?" I ask playfully.

"She's tight as all get-out, Greg my man. She wears her hair braided. I'm diggin' this sister and maybe some interaction and heavy vibes will bring sweet fruit as we get to know each other better. But for right now, I need to be careful 'cause it's just the beginning."

"I was worried about Adrian for a little while in the beginning, too."

"Oh yeah?"

"Yeah, the first time we had decided to sleep together, she told me she never liked being on the bottom. She said being on her back made her feel helpless."

"That shows that Adrian is a strong woman. She must be an Aries."

"Yup."

"Yeah, brother, you got yourself a stubborn no-nonsense woman."

"I guess," I say quietly. "The shit threw me for a loop at first, though."

Tim comes back to the table with a piece of paper in his hand. There's a name and phone number scribbled on it.

"The waitress gets off at ten, so I'm going to swing back through."

"What about your date with Neecy?" I ask.

"I'll cancel. She'll understand. All women do."

"One day somebody is going to cancel on you." Jamal laughs.

He picks up the ticket and we all leave a nice tip on the table. As we walk out the door, the jazz band begins to play "Strange Fruit." The music gives me a strange feeling as I think about how perfect Adrian seemed as I talked about her tonight. I hope I didn't make her seem too perfect, but she is. She is perfect.

**W**HEN TIM DROPS me off, I get in my ride and head over to the salon. Adrian wants me to pick up some movies and return them in exchange for some that we can watch tonight.

AJ's Getaway is located in Oakcliff, on Hampton Street. It's in the same neighborhood that Pops lives in. It's a large salon with seven stations and they are all taken on a full-time basis throughout the year.

Adrian has a good plan working for her. When she first graduated, she taught at Miss Helen's Beauty College for a short time, and once she established herself with the owner and established a clientele, she contracted herself out as a hair and cosmetics consultant. This clientele consists of women who pay top dollar to sport the latest styles as well as styles that enhance their features. From the mayor's wife to the girlfriend of the top drug dealer, Adrian has them on her roster. From there, she was able to open her own salon and establish a central location for up-and-coming hairstylists. She recruits a young, gifted hairdresser, pays half of her tuition, and also pays for the final exam to be licensed. In return, the hopeful works at AJ's for two years. Adrian only takes the top graduates and from the word on the street, girls are scrambling trying to get her to notice their work.

When I drive up, her champagne-colored Lexus is parked up front in the designated spot with her name painted on the curb. The parking lot is packed with cars and I can see a load of women on the inside. There are several women sitting reading books and others watch television as they wait their turn. All the station operators are busy washing, relaxing, curling, styling, or gossiping. I assume the massage room is full, too. When I open the door to go in, the smells of perm, shampoo, and conditioner fill the air and burn my nostrils like they always do. The television hanging in the waiting area is showing some type of male model search on MTV, and the women are watching it seriously and gawking over the men as they appear on the screen.

"Hi Gregory!" It's Kim, one of the hair technicians. She's hot-curling the hair of an old woman who seems to be meditating as her hair gets cooked. Kim has on a pair of yellow stretch pants with a Charlotte Hornets jersey, house shoes, and a towel on her head. One thing I can say about AJ's is that as long as you aren't doing hair butt naked, anything goes. Every now and then the ladies are required to dress with some class, but Adrian usually lets them come as they wish as long as the customer leaves satisfied, rested, and ready to conquer the world with her new hairdo.

"Hey Kim, what's up? How's everybody doing?" I wave. Most of the women speak. I look to the back for Adrian. I can see her in the glass room rinsing someone's hair.

"Greg, you excited about the wedding?" Kim asks. She grins at me, exposing her beautiful smile decorated with one gold-covered front tooth. Kim is originally from Chicago and was recruited a year ago. When I first met her, I didn't know what to think, but she's cool. She actually gets most of the ghetto-fabulous clientele, who are either the mistresses of Dallas's wealthy men or the girlfriends of drug dealers and major hustlers.

"Yeah, you could say that."

"That ring you gave A.J. is the bomb. Looks like something I seen one of my friends wearing. She was messing around with one of the Chicago Bulls and he hooked her up."

"Really? Adrian picked it out. I never really thought of it as a big deal."

"Why not? Boy, you know you hooked Adrian up. I mean, the ring is dope! Is the wedding still going to be in the afternoon?"

"Yeah, are you going to be there?"

"Of course, I wouldn't miss it for the world. I've already started shopping for my dress 'cause I gots to be jiggy with it! Adrian can't stop talking about it, either. You'd think she was getting married to-morrow."

"For real, she was just showing us a sample picture of the cake this morning." Arnelle, the nail tech, joins the conversation. She's sitting at her station munching on some kind of sandwich. "I like those cakes with the buttermilk-flavored icing. How many groomsmen do you have?"

"Five, including the best man."

Arnelle's eyes light up. "How many of them are single?"

"Oooh Arnelle, you need to quit girl!" Kim laughs.

I can't take too much more, because Kim has this annoying deep Southern drawl when she talks. Sounds like Gomer Pyle. It's slow and lazy and I'm trying to grin and bear it.

Kim stops working on her customer's hair to make her point. "Greg, don't tell her nuthin' else, she needs to be tryin' to get Romeo to marry her."

"Girl, you know Rome ain't talking about nothing." Arnelle sucks her teeth as she refers to her live-in boyfriend. "He doesn't even want to go to the fair next month. He's scared he's going to get out there, get into a fight, and violate his parole, so I told him to just for-get it."

I'm trying to figure out when will it be safe for me to walk away from this conversation without being rude. Not that I mind being *in* the conversation, but they've totally pushed me out.

Right as I decide to move, Kim starts talking again. "Greg, are you taking Adrian to the fair?"

"Yeah, we're going the night of the Grambling versus Prairie View A&M game. Adrian likes the halftime band competition."

"See Kim, that's what I'm talking about right there." Arnelle looks at me. "Greg, you's a good black man. Rome will probably sneak his ass over to the PV-Grambling game without me. And if he do, his ass is mine. I ain't taking that shit, 'cause I like the halftime show too."

"Thanks." *Hell, if being a good man is about taking your girl to the fair, then I'm a damn good man,* I think to myself. *Top of the line.*

"Well, you bettuh go see Adrian, she's been looking for you." Kim nods her head towards the back.

I head to the back where the sinks and the hair dryers are. Adrian is putting one of her clients under the dryer. The woman looks at me and smiles. I smile back. Adrian turns around to see who the woman is looking at.

"Hey, stranger," she says as she grabs me and kisses my lips. "I saw you when you walked in."

"Hey."

"It's good to see you today. I've missed you." Adrian walks back around to her station. She places a few combs back in their respective places, picks up a towel, and dusts off her chair.

Several females in the waiting area look at her eagerly, hoping that their name will be called next.

"Loretta, come on," Adrian says as she nods at one of the women.

A woman with blue jeans and a Janet Jackson T-shirt on comes over and sits down. Adrian makes small talk with her and tells her to sit tight until she returns.

We walk outside hand in hand. She unlocks her car door and gets the sack with the movies in it.

"What do you want to watch tonight?" I ask.

"Something with some drama. One of the customers was telling me about this movie called *The Usual Suspects.*"

"Yeah, Jamal told me to check that out too."

"And I also want to see *love jones.* I just love Nia Long."

"Me too." I smile devilishly.

"Greg, don't play. You know that Nia Long is a very well-respected sister in the industry? She looks good, eats well, and I dig her cute figure, not to mention her hair. I met her stylist last year—she is really laid-back, and we exchanged a lot of ideas. But I would kill for Nia's body."

"Why you trying to kill for a body like that? Granted, she is fine, but I like your body, Adrian. These roasty thighs of yours and your booty, neither of which Nia Long can hold a candle to." I grab Adrian by her hips and pull her into me.

Adrian punches my arm playfully. "No woman is ever totally satisfied with her body, Greg. I just think that I could lose a little bit here and there, that's all."

"Well, Nia Long ain't got nothing on you and if you're trying to get rid of your hips then let me help you." I lean in and kiss Adrian. She kisses me back and smiles.

"I love you so much, boobunny." Adrian touches my stomach line and moves her fingers down to my private area. She touches it through my pants ever so lightly, causing me to move closer to her.

"Girl, you're going to lose your job," I joke.

"Then make me," she teases back. "I'll see you tonight and we'll work on these hips of mine, okay?"

"I like that idea, muffin." I grab her and rub my hands over her back. She feels good and I wish I could put her in my car and take her away to some faraway place and just love her. Her almond-colored eyes are looking into mine and I feel closer to her than ever.

"You know I love you, don't you?" she asks.

"Yeah. I know you love me." I'm smiling like Okie-Doke the Slow Poke.

"And I would never leave you, right?"

"That's why I love you, Adrian Jenkins," I say, and kiss her on her neck. "That's one of the reasons you are going to be my wife."

"I can't wait to start our family. You're going to be such a good father." She leans in and kisses me again, this time letting her tongue gracefully slide into my mouth. I don't give a damn who's watching us, because I'm into my woman. When we stop kissing, we hold each other and cherish the moment. Adrian remembers she has a customer waiting and pecks me one last time before going back into the salon. I get the movies and head out.

Any other time, with any other woman, I would be playing my macho role, but Adrian makes a brother lose all his cool. I never think about how stupid I probably sound with her until I get somewhere alone and think about our conversations and how I am when we're together, especially the pet names we use with each other. From muffin to boobunny to lovesnack, sometimes we get carried away, but that's our thang and I love it to death. As I drive along the street, I think about this whole marriage idea. Even though my mother has been away for nineteen years, my parents are still married. I don't think they ever divorced, unless they did it by mail, without me and Shreese knowing. I never got a full explanation on what really happened, and it's hard to get Pops to talk about it. Maybe it's time for a man-to-man. . . .

I DECIDED TO stop by my dad's house before going to the movie store. It took three rings of the doorbell before Pops answered.

"I thought I heard the doorbell." Pops opened the door and let me in.

"What are you up to?"

"Shit, I was reading the paper and I guess I drifted off to sleep."

I followed Pops to the living room. There were newspaper pages strewn over the couch, and a blanket hung lazily to the floor.

"So what brings you over this way on a Saturday?"

"I was in the neighborhood running some errands for Adrian."

Pops smiled. "She got you running errands, huh? Next thing you know, she'll have you buying her female goods at the grocery store." Pops laughs a tired laugh, but his sleepy eyes still twinkle.

"I already do that for her," I huff.

"Good. That's how you make it work."

I wish Pops believed what he just said. Otherwise, I believe my mother would still be here. I used to think that if he begged or put his foot down, then Louise would still be here. Now he sits around giving out the very advice that he should have followed. But I have a wedding and a future wife to worry about—I'm not gonna try correcting his situation. We've been without Louise for so long, she is hardly a subject anymore.

"Pops, I want you to play a song for me at my wedding."

"Oh, son, I don't think I can do that. I haven't touched those keys since your mama left."

I sit quiet. My father is right, and I feel awkward for asking him such a question. He hasn't played the piano since she left, and when he mentions that I feel guilty for asking him to. My mother had always been an awkward subject in my family. I was just hoping Pops would see my wedding day as an event worth getting his fingers back in shape to tickle the ivories, but I guess not. Now, I don't want to talk about it anymore. A slight heat is making itself known in the pit of my stomach. Pops looks over at me.

"Why you want me to play, Greg?"

"Adrian likes this song by Roy Hargrove called 'Things We Did Last Summer,' and I wanted you to play it for her on the piano."

"Roy Hargrove. He's about your age, ain't he?"

"Yeah, Pops. We went to Holmes Middle School together. I took you to see him last year at the Meyerson Symphony Center."

"Now that's a bad-ass old-school trumpet-playin' young cat right there! He's a little loud and was hard on my one good ear, but he's been trained well." Pops's eyes light up again as he recalls who Roy is. "Technique is tight like a mosquito's booty!"

I smile as Pops starts laughing. I can see the life in him struggling to be revived, but Pops's heart is broken, and has been for the past nineteen years. It's hard for him to mask that.

"Well, why don't you call Roy up and have him come? I'll pay for it."

"Pops, you know Roy and I weren't even on the same page back in the day. He was a clown, you know that. Got me in trouble and you told me to quit hanging with him. He and I were never tight after that and I've been out of touch with him. Besides, you can do just as good a job on the piano."

"Yeah, son, but . . . I just don't know." Pops rubs over his plump

belly and looks blankly at the television. "It's been so long, I probably won't know my right hand from my left."

I laugh a little as my pops quotes these lyrics from "Misty," an old
jazz favorite. It reminds me of a game he used to play with me and
Shreese when we were growing up. He would say a line from a song
and we would guess the song title. Now he looks over at me and
starts laughing, too. He's off the wall sometimes, but I love my old
man. He stuck in there with us after Louise left, and I'm grateful to
him for staying. Thank goodness they shared responsibilities when
they were together—otherwise Shreese and I probably would have
looked like throwaway kids. But Pops did Shreese's hair, ironed our
clothes, cooked, and also helped us with our homework every night.
He already knew how to do other things that most men from his
generation didn't do without a woman.

The worst thing Pops had to get through was talking to Shreese
about getting her period. It was horrible, because he made me sit in
the room with him as he stumbled though his reading of the entire
chapter of the *Time-Life Health Encyclopedia* on the female anatomy
and menstruation.

"Did you ask your mother to perform?"

"I'm not inviting her," I said. "I haven't even called her and told
her about the engagement."

"Gregory Louis Alston, I didn't raise you to hate your mother."

"Pops, I don't hate her. I just don't want her at my wedding."

"Why, Gregory?" Pops's voice is almost pleading. "Give me one
good reason why she doesn't deserve to be included."

"I just don't want her there. She hasn't been at any of my other
major events and I don't want her at this one."

"Now, you know she calls whenever something big happens in
your life and I make sure she knows. You never invited her to any of
your graduations and to those fraternity parent events you had in
college, like you did with me, but she always remembers you on your
birthday and Christmas."

"And do you think that's been enough for me and Shreese all these
years?"

"Has it?" Pops has a sad look on his face. "You've never reached out to her, so what are you expecting in return?"

"Pops, you know as well as I do that children need both parents. People just don't walk out on their children like Louise did."

"Son, you'd be surprised. I've seen a lot happen in my life, and what your mother did was follow her dreams. She loves singing and she pursued it."

"So singing is more important than the children you bring into the world? She couldn't take us with her? She couldn't put her dreams off until we were grown?"

Pops leaned up in his chair and exhaled a deep breath. "What is it that you're missing, Gregory, that I haven't been able to give you? What is it that your mother's absence has not afforded you?"

"Nothing." I held my head down in defeat. I mean, how can a person know what he's missing if he's never had it? I just know there is something missing from my life because my mother wasn't there. *I know it is.* Pops is right. He gave me and Shreese everything: love, support, discipline, and much attention. He came to the school when we had programs, he attended every band concert, play, and awards ceremony we ever had, not to mention chaperoning some of our field trips and dances. He cooked dinner for us every night and made sure our ears were clean when we got out of the tub. He did everything.

"Well, then. Don't go blaming her for your anger, because your idea of a family is what you saw on television. Louise did what she thought was right and proper and keeping her from that might have done more damage to our family than good. We just happen to be on the shit-receiving end of the stick. Hell, I miss her just as much, but your mama loves you and she shows that by sending you cards and gifts when she knows you don't even open them."

I sit embarrassed. Pops always defends her, no matter what, and I can never find it in myself to really get to the heart of the issue with him and yell at the top of my lungs how fucked up it was growing up without her.

My mother and father were both extremely involved jazz musicians back in the day. They met at a music festival in Monaco. Pops finished high school and did one year at Juilliard. My mother dropped out of high school after winning a talent show when she was sixteen. Her parents moved her from Houston to New York to do amateur night at the Apollo and although she won two shows back to back, no immediate music career came out of it. She worked part-time as a housekeeper and made the other half of her money as a singer.

My mother, Louise Angelina Alston, became a very popular vocalist who performed with Charlie Parker, Dizzy Gillespie, Charles Mingus, and even Benny Goodman before she was twenty years old. These connections came about when she was in Monaco attending a music festival with some of her singer friends, hoping to pick up a record deal. Pops had a gig playing keys for a small group that Miles Davis and drummer Roy Haynes had put together. Pops had met Miles at a rehearsal one night, and from there he played keys with the group for two and a half years. At the end of the second year they went to Monaco, Pops was looking to start his own band. He formed the Alston Jazz Quartet, and my mother auditioned and was the chosen vocalist. Back then, Sarah Vaughan, Betty Carter, Ella Fitzgerald, and other female singers were on the rise and my mother never seemed to be able to penetrate the market in the United States as a recognized jazz singer. She had a sound that floated between the operatic soul-filled Sarah and the high-spirited Ella. Unfortunately, America was already full of Sarahs and Ellas. Plus, my mother was young and nobody wanted to deal with a teenage jazz singer. Respect in the jazz scene came with age and experience, neither of which my mother had. I suppose that's why she never could get her big break here.

I vaguely remember hearing Mom sing in rehearsals. I was three or four then. She had a voice that could make a man break down to his knees and beg for more. Her singing voice was slow, full of raw soul, and very mellow, but crystal clear. I mean glass-breaking clear. And when she hit those soprano highs like Sarah, everyone in the room would go to shouting and hollering like they were in church. She and Pops used to take me to some of their gigs at the clubs and I sometimes still dream about the smoky rooms full of dark, sweat-lined faces. It's funny, because when she talked, her voice was raspy and low like she was hoarse. Real jazz musicians couldn't get enough of her, and sometimes she did a gig every night for weeks on end. She recorded a few songs, but they were never released in the States and were never enough to get her name in the mainstream.

When Louise became pregnant with me, she was twenty-five and Pops was twenty-nine, but they kept traveling and performing until it was time for me to enter school.

Before then, Mom would take me everywhere with her. Even though I was Pops's "Little Man," Louise hardly let me out of her sight. She would talk to me all the time about anything and everything I asked her about. We would sit at this one particular park in Brooklyn and she would push me on the swings while I asked her a million questions at a time and she answered them one by one. Once Shreese was born and it was about time for me to start school, Pops wanted to move to a city where jazz wasn't prominent, and that was located far enough from the cities that were, like Kansas City, New Orleans, Chicago, and New York. After consideration and debating, we all moved to Dallas. This gave our parents the opportunity to concentrate on raising me and my sister. However, Mom still managed to name me and Shreese after two of her favorite performers. My middle name, Louis, is for Louis Armstrong, and Shreese's first name is actually Nina, for Nina Simone. Only Louise called her Nina, but me and Pops always called her Shreese.

We were happy in Dallas back then. We were a family. Dad began substitute teaching at a nearby grade school and Mom was a cashier at Joske's. In the evenings, when they came home, Mom would sit me down at my drum set and Shreese would play the keys with Pops, and we would play jazz tunes together. Mom seemed happy with us. Seemed. That's why I can't comprehend why she left.

When it started, no one saw it coming. At first, she started taking trips to and from France. She had gigs there, and Pops was understanding. Because of her traveling out of the United States so much, he began teaching full-time. I remember, three nights before my eighth birthday, Pops had put me and Shreese to bed. It was a Friday night and I was still up, lying in my bed like a convict sentenced. I hated going to bed and would sometimes lie awake hours before drifting off to sleep. The phone rang and Pops picked up the line in the hallway. A few minutes later, I could hear him shouting into the phone. I'd never heard him sound so angry. The last thing I remember him saying was, "I hope you and that drum-playing, backbiting Lester have a good life!" He slammed the phone down and I jumped under my bedcovers. It scared me to hear Pops yell like that. It was the one night in my life that I remembered wetting the bed. The next day, Pops got up and went through the usual routine with us. He put our clothes on us, fixed breakfast, and took us to school. I knew something was wrong. Pops's eyes were red and sleepy as if he had been up all night. He had that look on his caramel-colored face that made you understand that no questions were to be asked.

When my birthday rolled around, my mom called. I was excited and glad to hear from her. Her voice sounded like the first warm, sunny day after a long winter. I wanted to tell her I heard Pops shout at somebody the other night and ask her who it was and why was he shouting, but I didn't want to ask over the phone. I asked her when she was coming back, and there was a long silence. When she began talking again, her voice was quivering. I became nervous and scared. The emotions that my parents had been displaying made me uncomfortable. She told me that she would see me at Christmas, and that was it. We saw her at Christmas for the next five years. The last time I saw her, I was thirteen and Shreese was ten. Pops never dated again, nor did he bring any other woman into our house. He stopped playing his piano, I quit playing the drums, and Shreese started going to church every chance she got, praying to God to send our mother back.

I don't know . . . sometimes I think that because I got my degree and I ain't slangin' drugs or laid up with children all over the city calling me Daddy, all the hurt and damage I felt as boy just aren't there. But every time I come across a situation where a mother is not in her child's everyday life or am faced with my own personal dilemma with my mother, I just want to start running. Running so fast, until the wind can no longer get to my lungs quick enough to keep me standing. I want to punch somebody and then go to sleep and never wake up, because sometimes it hurts that much.

I'm angry at my mother and I would love to have her at my wedding, singing to me and Adrian. I want her to meet Adrian and love her the same way I do. I want my mother to be living in the same house with Pops, because that's where she belongs. I want her to call me and hassle me about not coming to see her or call her, even though only a week has passed by. The exact way Tim's mother does him sometimes. That's what mothers are supposed to do. I'm not asking for too much, and I think what my mother did was unfair, selfish, and fucked-up. Real fucked-up.

## 7

B ABY, TAKE THE popcorn out of the microwave and hurry up, the movie is about to start."

Adrian is laughing at me because I'm trying to carry this hot-ass bag of popcorn and two Cokes.

She's lying on the couch like a princess, wearing a Victoria's Secret shorts-and-tank set. The burgundy colors against her skin excite me when I look at her. *The Usual Suspects* is in the VCR and it has already started playing. I climb onto the couch and almost drop the bag of popcorn.

"Ouch!" I drop the bag on the coffee table.

"Greg, you should have poured it in a bowl." She giggles.

"I should have let you get it, that's what I should've done," I say as I shake my burning fingers in the air.

Adrian grabs a pillow and rests it comfortably between my legs before laying her head on it. We watch the movie and when it's over, we climb into bed exhausted.

Even though Adrian has a silk head rag on her freshly permed do, she still looks good. I stroke her arms and hips as we lie together. She smells good and I'm glad we are able to share moments like these.

That's where most women tend to go wrong, if you ask me. Some women can't just lie in bed with a man and enjoy the moment. They start twisting and turning like something's wrong with them; then, when you ask them are they okay, they lie and say yes, knowing good and well that something is on their mind. Then they wait until sleep has a brother by his neck and they start talking and asking all kinds of what-if questions. That really gets on my nerves. My last serious commitment was with this aerobics instructor named Jamie. She was fine, beautiful, and we had a lot of common interests. The only problem was that she asked so many questions, I thought I was auditioning for her love! We would lie in bed and she would question me to sleep. I would wake up answering her shit. Finally, one day, I asked her why'd she ask me so many questions, and her response was "To see where your head is at." Now, don't get me wrong, but if you want to see where my head is at, asking me a thousand questions a day isn't going to get it. Half the time I was lying to her, anyway.

See, I'm a man of quiet action. Adrian seemed to pick up on that immediately. She doesn't hardly ask me anything and when she does, they are questions I don't feel threatened by answering. She's a woman who knows her man. Sometimes, I get thrown off because she doesn't ask a lot of questions, but it's cool because I've had my share of nosey sisters.

"Greg, don't forget we're having dinner at my parents' house tomorrow," Adrian whispers, interrupting my thoughts.

"Okay." I pull her closer to me and kiss her neck. I forgot all about tomorrow's trip to the Jenkinses' home. Now, this is what I am not looking forward to. I love Adrian's parents and they seem to like me, but her family strikes me as kind of odd.

The best way I can put it is, they seem somewhat sheltered. Compared to my family, anyway. Her parents don't say much, but when they do, the comments are off the wall. If I wasn't Adrian's fiancé, the perfect word for her folks would be "slow."

## 8

RUFORD AND JOYCE Jenkins greeted us at the door, both smiling like we were holding winning Lotto tickets. Ruford immediately stuck out his right hand. "Gregory, son! It's good to see you again! Come on in!"

"Same here, same here," I say, smiling.

"Oh, Gregory, how are you?" Mrs. Jenkins grabs me and kisses me on both cheeks. "I'm cooking something good for you today."

"Fine, Mrs. Jenkins," I respond. "Thanks for taking the time out to cook, you really shouldn't have."

"Oh, it's nothing for the man who's going to be our son-in-law!"

"Well, y'all come on inside, out of the heat." Mr. Jenkins steps back inside the house and we follow. The house smells good. Whatever Adrian's mother has prepared, I'm ready to eat it.

We sit in the living room letting the cool of the house surround us. As soon as I see the big-screen television settled quietly in the corner, I think about the Dallas Cowboys and Denver Broncos football game I'm missing.

"So, are the wedding plans going okay?" Joyce asks. She walks into the kitchen, which is open to the living room. She's a tall woman with big hips. Her hair is pulled back in a single braid decorated with a handmade barrette. She has a cigarette lit in an ashtray near the stove.

"Mom, they're going fine," Adrian snaps. "We've got everything covered."

I look at her and she isn't smiling. Adrian never enjoys coming over to her parents' home. She thinks they have always been a bit overbearing, but I think they're cool. Joyce doesn't seem to notice Adrian's cranky behavior. She looks at me with a porcelain grin on her face as she stirs whatever she has brewing in the pot.

"Your sister told me you two were having problems finding a photographer," Joyce says. "Adrian, I told you Mr. Henderson two blocks over can do just a good a job for half the money you're talking about spending."

"Mr. Henderson fell asleep at Arlette's wedding and missed the kiss! How can you expect me to want to use that man?" Adrian barks. She shakes her head unbelievingly and huffs.

"We're still looking, though," I cover as I rub my woman's shoulders. She's uptight every time we come over here. "Thanks for the reference."

"Adrian, have you found a dress yet?" Mr. Jenkins asks.

"So far, I've found one, but I'm still looking to make sure it's what I want to wear."

"Well, make sure it's angel white with a long train," Joyce says. "I'll die if you walk down that aisle without a long train. The ladies at the lodge are looking forward to being there."

Adrian lets out a long sigh as she gets up and walks to the back of the house. I want to go and check on her, but something keeps my ass glued to the sofa.

"We are so proud of Adrian. She's come a long way," her father responds. He has a toothpick in his mouth that moves up and down when he talks. Mr. Jenkins is tall and I can't imagine why Adrian isn't taller than five seven. Both of her parents look like basketball players. I know her mother played in a league some years ago, but her father never played any sports from what she's told me.

"The good Lord knows we have always wanted what's best for her," Joyce adds. She comes into the living room and sits on the side of the recliner next to her husband. "Sometimes, I just didn't know about that girl."

"If you're trying to sell her to me, then you've got a buyer," I joke. "Sold."

The Jenkinses laugh with me, but I feel like they're laughing at me. They always seem to be laughing at me. I sit back on the couch to help steady my nerves.

"She's special. The only one of my children who always went against the grain and didn't let anyone tell her what to do," Mr. Jenkins says. "Grit iron."

"Headstrong. Always has been," Joyce adds. "But you should know this by now, Gregory. After all, three years is the longest we've ever seen Adrian commit to something other than hairstyling." She gets up and goes back to the kitchen. I'm hoping Mr. Jenkins will turn the television on so we can watch the game, but no such luck. He's sitting with his head against the La-Z-Boy as if there's no television.

"How's that job going?" he asks.

"Good. I'm on the verge of getting a new account. If I do, then Adrian and I will start looking to buy a house a lot sooner."

"Yeah, that computer industry is where it's at." Mr. Jenkins laughs a little.

I lean in on my lap. "So, how do you think the Cowboys are going to do this year?"

"About as bad as they did last year. Cowboys all drug-free now, too. They can't play if they ain't high. Emmitt Smith can't carry that team alone and Deion can't catch a football, hit a baseball, and carry the Bible with two hands. He's going to have to choose one or the other."

*Good,* I think. *He's talking about football. Maybe he'll click on the television.* I laugh at his statement about Deion. "Yeah," I respond. "He's a jack-of-all-trades."

"And you know Michael Irvin isn't going to be worth a rat's tail."

"You think?"

"Shoot yeah, I think!" Mr. Jenkins leans over the recliner and grabs the remote. I lean back onto the couch, ready for some football. He's still talking, but I can tell he's going to click on the game. "I think Michael Irvin is on that stuff. You can't make me believe otherwise. O. J. Simpson, Rodney King, and Bobby Brown too! They all on something that got 'em acting like heathens."

Mr. Jenkins presses the remote button and I can immediately hear the sportscasters talking. The screen is clearing in, and I can see the camera panning across the field as the teams break their huddle and get ready to play. It's the third quarter and Denver is up by fourteen points. Just as the players line up for the hike of the ball, Joyce walks into the den.

"Ruford, turn that television off, it's time to eat."

Mr. Jenkins hits the power button on the remote and the big screen goes silent. I slump on the couch. He looked over at me and smiles. "That's why I didn't turn it on in the first place."

I return the smile, hip to his words.

"She can't stand for me to watch football when she's here. Normally on Sundays she's at a meeting, church, or some sorority function."

"Thank God Adrian likes the sport," I say. "Maybe we should cook next time and invite you and the missus over."

"Now you talking. Adrian used to watch football with me when she was little. She's always been a tomboy. Nothing like her sisters Angel and Alanya."

We both get up and head to the dining room. Adrian comes from the back and helps her mother set the table. The table is laid out with four place settings. A small bowl of salad sits next to each plate. A steaming bowl of vermicelli noodles is placed in the middle of the table with a covered pot next to it. Adrian brings in some homemade meatballs. They look good enough to be finger food. My stomach growls and I'm thankful the food is ready. Mr. Jenkins blesses the table and we all sit and begin dinner. I notice Adrian isn't saying much, but she doesn't appear disturbed by her own solemn mood.

"Adrian told me you two decided on not getting married in a church," Mrs. Jenkins says. She is spreading her homemade sauce from the covered pot onto her noodles. I look over at Adrian. She's not looking my way.

"Yes ma'am. We want to be married outside."

"Adrian never was much of a church girl," Joyce responds. "But she knows I want her to have a church wedding and that's why she's being difficult."

Adrian looks at her mother and cuts her eyes. Mrs. Jenkins never glances Adrian's way.

"Angel and Alanya would go all the time, but not Adrian. She would kick and scream, so I would leave her here with Ruford. She was a daddy's girl straight from the womb."

"Joyce, stop meddling. Gregory don't want to hear all that. You liable to run the boy off. You make Adrian sound like the child in *The Exorcist* and you tell the same story every time the boy is over here."

"It's okay." I smile. "I think every family has certain issues that make it unique."

Adrian is eating quietly. I look over at her and wink. She winks back with a shy smile. She is the exact image of her father: thick, dark hair, soft eyes, and the same skin tone. But when she smiles she reminds me of her mother. She's smiling now, but Joyce is not. She has the look on her face that mothers give when they choose to be quiet for the sake of peace, but really don't want to. Sometimes I envy my fiancée for having a mother who is concerned about her. But I know I don't need my mother and there is nothing Louise can tell me to make me change my mind. I think I'll call her tonight and tell her about the wedding just to prove to her that I was able to find me a woman who is going to stay with me and not walk out on me, like she did to Pops. Yeah, that's what I'll do.

After dinner, Adrian and I stay long enough to catch the end of the game. The Cowboys lose by a touchdown. Mr. Jenkins is probably right. Emmitt isn't playing with the same spunk he had in '91 and '92, when they won back-to-back Super Bowls. When we get ready to leave, Adrian takes my hand and squeezes it gently. Her parents bid us farewell and we head to Adrian's.

"Are you staying the night?" she asks.

"No, I have to make a phone call and get some things straightened out about the wedding."

"Like what?" Adrian is looking at me. I am happy that she is concerned, but I really don't want to talk to her about my mother.

"I just need to call some family members and make sure their addresses are correct."

She leans over and touches my face. She plants a kiss on my lips. "Call me if you need me," she whispers.

"I will."

She gets out of the car. Adrian is understanding, warm, sweet, and caring. Everything I want in a woman. I watch her walk to her apartment and disappear inside. I drive off and head home, ready to face one of the biggest monsters of my life: talking to my mother.

IT'S ONLY SIX P.M. when I get home. That means it's around midnight in France. I figure my mother is probably just getting in or getting ready to go out. I grab my phone book from my briefcase and look up the number. Someone picks up on the first ring.

"Bonjour?" The voice is that of a man. I can tell he isn't French by the way he fucks up the word. It sounds more like "bunshure." There are several voices in the background, people laughing and music playing.

"Yes, is Louise Alston available?"

"Sure, un moment." The watered-down Frenchman puts the phone aside and I can hear the voices more clearly. I can hear a song in the background. They're playing Sarah Vaughan. The song is unfamiliar. I've never heard it before, which is strange because I have all of her recordings, everything she ever recorded all the way up until her last song on the Quincy Jones *Back on the Block* CD. My stomach has butterflies and I swallow hard to get rid of them. I realize the voice singing in the background is not Sarah's but my mother's. The phone falls silent and I can hear another line being picked up in a quieter area.

"Yes?" the raspy voice asks. It's her. A voice I haven't heard in years. I can't say anything. Her voice is familiar, as if it were yesterday that she told me she loved me.

"Hello? Is anybody there?"

"Hi . . . It's me . . . Greg."

She chuckles a little. "Gregory Louis Alston! How are you doing, son? Baby, it's so good to hear from you!"

*She's faking it,* I'm thinking.

"How are you, and how is everything going back in Texas?"

"It's fine and I'm fine." All of a sudden I feel urgent for some water. My throat is dry and it's hard for me to swallow.

"Is everything okay? Is Nina okay?"

"Yes, Shreese is fine. We're all doing fine." *Without you!*

"I was entertaining some guests, that's what all the noise is, but it's so good to hear your voice, Gregory. It is warming my heart."

I can hear her sniffling. I can feel myself struggling trying to stay mad at her, but I can't. I haven't talked to her in so long, it feels good to just hear her voice. Her beautiful raspy voice.

"Where's your father? Did he make you call me?"

I smirk at the thought that she's right and doesn't even know it. "He's home and yes, he talked to me about giving you a call."

"So, what's going on with you? I have all night to talk to my only son."

She still has a way of making me feel special but I'm keeping my guard up.

"I'm getting married in March."

"MARRIED??!! Who are you marrying, and when is all this supposed to happen?"

"Her name is Adrian Jenkins and we're getting married next spring."

Louise sits quietly on the phone. I don't know if she has put it down or not. I clear my throat to break the silence. After a few seconds she speaks to me. "When, Gregory Louis? What month did you say again?"

"March."

"Then I will be in Dallas at the end of the month and stay until the wedding."

"I'm not asking you to come here."

"Gregory, I know that, but I am still your mother. I don't know this girl, and I don't want to be a stranger to her, regardless of what you may have told her about our relationship."

"I've never told Adrian anything about you not being around."

"Exactly. You haven't spoken to me since you were eight, so I'm willing to bet you haven't told her anything at all. You think just because I move to France and don't see you for several years, I am no longer a part of your life? I know you don't want me there, that's no big secret, and I've always tried to respect what you wanted."

I sit in silence for a moment. I don't know what to say to this question. I do feel that way, and I don't need her here. "I'm just calling to let you know I'm getting married. Don't think this is a sign of me going out of my way to have you come here."

"I'm not asking you to go out of your way. I'm coming to Dallas because I want to see my family as well as attend your wedding. I want to be there to share it with you and make sure all hell doesn't break loose." She laughs at her comment. But I'm not laughing with her.

"Just understand that I'm not asking you to come," I repeat. I feel like I'm eight again.

"That's understood, but I'm still looking forward to it. Besides, I haven't seen your father or Nina, aside from the few photos I have, which are old, and this will give us all a chance to be together."

*If she's thinking we're going to be one big happy family again, she is dead wrong,* I'm thinking. *So much has changed since she left, and I can't even tell her. How can she be so calm and sure about her visit here? Why would she want to come home to a man who's dead on the inside, a daughter who has gotten lost in the cracks of religion, and a son who just doesn't want her here? What can she possibly bring to a table that has nothing on it she can complement?*

"Don't forget to make your hotel arrangements." I say. My voice is dry and I can feel it about to crack.

"Hotel arrangements? Child no, I'm staying at my house. Your father could use the company and I have some things to do there anyway."

"I don't think that would be a good idea."

"Why? Is he seeing someone?"

"No, but . . ."

"Well then . . . it's settled." She laughs again. "Tell Nina that I will be home and she should get ready, because we're going to have a good time together, just mother and daughter. I'll see you then, Gregory."

I want to tell her she can't just come here like she won the lottery and make all of our lives better. I want to tell her that our levels of sanity can't tolerate her staying at the same house she left, and that we can't take any more of the hurt she's caused. Especially with my father. He's been hurt enough by her absence! I fall back onto my bed. "Bye." That's all I can form my lips to say. I can't even tell her off the way she should be told. The way she deserves to be told off after all this time.

She hangs up.

I hold on to the receiver, wondering if calling her was a good idea after all. I'm hoping she doesn't come down here and make my life more complicated. I head for the shower and prepare for my next day at work, but all I can think about is my mother's upcoming visit. I don't know how I'm going to keep myself busy until then. I guess work and the wedding are the best answer.

THE ATMOSPHERE AT the office is festive. We got the Dillinger account this morning! They sent a rep over to sign the contract. I decided to have lunch catered in Data Tech's main meeting office, which seats up to twenty-five people comfortably. Someone brought a CD player and put on some new music by a brother named Rahsaan Patterson. I dig his music and I feel like getting my groove on. The Dillinger account will allow me to sit pretty the rest of the year and then some. I actually don't have to work hard on any more accounts until January. That's good, because the wedding is going to take up a lot of time as the new year comes.

LaShawn and the other Group Three members are all packed together in a small group in the meeting room. They're talking and celebrating by tapping together paper cups full of Pepsi.

LaShawn is at the center of the circle. She has on an olive-green two-piece pants suit that looks good against her shiny black skin. LaShawn wears her hair natural, close to her head, and her petite face sets it off just right. She reminds me of those young sisters you would see in *Essence, Seventeen,* or *Braids & Beauty.* Tim is standing near her. Scary, but they look damn good standing together. I wonder if Tim is interested in being a stepfather? I can see them happily living together in a small home with LaShawn's daughter, Aija. And they would have African and African American art all over the place. LaShawn's little girl would even have an all-black doll collection. My thoughts of Tim and LaShawn are interrupted by a tap on my back.

"No luck, man, Tim has already tried to hit that."

Phillip is looking at me smiling. "What are you talking about?" I ask, surprised that he's read my mind.

"LaShawn. She's not interested in him." Phil leans on the wall next to me. He's holding a cup of punch in his hand. "I saw you looking at them and figured you had something up your sleeve."

"Oh, so he already approached her?"

"Yeah, he took her out and she told him she wasn't interested in dating him." Phil drinks from the cup and tosses the rest in a nearby trash can.

"Seriously?"

"LaShawn is a serious sister, but I bet I could get into her panties." Phil sucks his teeth. "All she needs is an all-night-long brother such as myself. Ain't no shame in my game."

"Phil, leave her alone, man. Stick with the hootchie mamas and 'hood rats. You should be ashamed of yourself." I laugh.

"Aw man, you don't think I can get a corporate woman like LaShawn?"

"Phil, she has a child and she doesn't need to be played with," I argue. "She is respected by every man in this office. You shouldn't even be thinking about getting with a woman like that. She's climbing the corporate ladder and doing a damn good job."

"Cool, but I know what she needs to climb up on." Phil is looking at LaShawn like a hungry wolf looks at unsuspecting sheep.

"Phil, when was the last time you dated an educated sister?"

Phil shakes his head. "I don't know. Man, a woman is a woman. It don't matter if she's educated or not. They all got a little freak in 'em." Phil straightens his tie and double-checks his jacket buttons.

"I'm just here to remind them where they come from. Give 'em a li'l somethin' to keep from going to the other side."

I lean in and whisper to Phil, "With you around here, sisters should be scrambling to the other side. You are a scary brother."

Phil looks over at me and smiles. "And don't you forget it." He daps me five and sucks his teeth in an arrogant manner.

Phil and I walk over to the group and join in the conversation. LaShawn looks at me, but she has this crazy please-don't-ask-me-any-questions look on her face. At first I start to ask her is there a problem, but I decide against it.

"Hey Greg! Congratulations on getting the account." Tim shakes my hand. I want to laugh at the fake corporate voice he uses in the office when others are around.

"Thanks, but you really need to say that to Group Three. They did the hard work." I turn toward the group members. "Good presentation, ladies and gentlemen."

"Mr. Alston, does this mean a raise for everybody?" jokes Arthur, one of the group members.

"Sure, and a Mercedes to go with it," I respond. Everyone laughs.

"Mr. Alston, this will give you time to plan for your wedding now that the biggest account has been closed, won't it?" It's LaShawn. She's staring at me hard.

I feel uncomfortable and look away as I answer her question. "As a matter of fact, Ms. Denton, it will. It will give me and Adrian plenty of time to get our pictures done, taste-test the food, and find a house to live in."

"You and Adrian are getting a house?" she asks.

"Yes, we decided to get that done before the wedding. Now it's a reality, with us getting the account."

"Wow, she really is into this whole marriage thing, then?"

"Why wouldn't she be?" I'm thinking LaShawn really does know something I don't.

She laughs it off as if she doesn't want to give any more clues to what it is that I don't know. "It's just that back in the day, Adrian was not into marriage. She was always real tough on her views about it." I ease up when LaShawn says the word "tough." "Well, her dad did say she was a tomboy when she was growing, so maybe it took her a while to adjust her views. I can guarantee you, she's very much for this union."

"That's cool," LaShawn says with a dreamy look on her face. "That's real cool."

"Shoot, Ms. Denton, you make it sound like Greg's fiancée is a football player or something." It's Phil and he's instigating.

"No, it's not that, Mr. Putnam," LaShawn replies. She cleared her throat. "Adrian was just hard-core a few years back. She didn't have the gentleness in her that you-all are familiar with." She smiles her girlish smile and walks off, leaving me and Phil standing together.

I'm glad she walked off, because I don't like the vibes I'm getting from her.

After the mini reception everyone heads back to work. I'm full and sleepy, so I get to my office and shut the door. The phone rings before I can even sit down. I press the intercom button. "This is Greg."

"And this is Adrian. Hey you."

Her voice makes my good day better. "Baby, I was just thinking about you." I pick up the receiver, taking the phone off intercom.

"And I was thinking about you, too. What are you doing?" Her voice is warm and it makes me hold the phone closer to my ear.

"Nothing. Just got back from a big lunch celebration. The company paid for lunch today to celebrate the Dillinger account I told you about."

"Wow, sounds like it was nice."

"It was. Now I have more time to concentrate on me, you, and the wedding. Speaking of which, one of your past customers is interning here."

"Who?"

"LaShawn Denton. She said she knows you from—"

"Lancaster. Yeah, I remember her. How is she?"

"Promising. She said you had a big impact on her life. What was that about?"

"Girl stuff. Having babies and keeping them versus giving them away." Adrian laughs and then changes the subject. "So, what else is going on?"

"You tell me," I tease.

"Why don't you leave early from work, and I'll show you what else is going on." She's teasing me and I can feel my pants tighten in the crotch.

"When do you want me knocking at your door?"

"How does two o'clock sound?"

"Sweet."

"Okay, then, I'll be waiting. I love you."

"I love you too."

We hang up and my penis is as hard as Chinese algebra. I try to think of something else, but Adrian got me all worked up. I look at my watch and it's only twelve-fifteen. I get up, flip my computer off, and head out of the office anyway. Shit, opportunities like this don't happen often, so I'm going to enjoy them while I can. See ya!

I STOPPED BY my place to freshen up before going to Adrian's. By the time I get to her place, it's nearly two o'clock. There is a note on the door that reads: USE YOUR KEY. I take my keys and find the one to her lock and open the door. Immediately, the remix of Maxwell's "Whenever Wherever Whatever" starts playing from upstairs. I look up, but can't see anything. There is a lit candle in front of me with a note attached. I pull it off and read it:

> *Take off everything but your tie and underpants, come upstairs, and be introduced to romance.*

Thank God I have on my Calvin Klein underwear. I strip to my draws and tie and head upstairs. When I walk into Adrian's bedroom, she is lying on the bed. The only things she has on are a purple g-string and her toe ring. My penis is rock hard against my briefs. My girl is looking good! She wiggles her finger for me to come over. I get in the bed with her and she starts kissing me all over. I grab her petite waist and pull her on top of me. She smiles and continues to kiss my chest and navel. I wouldn't mind at all if she went on down, but the last time she did, I came too soon and she got mad at me. I couldn't help it, Adrian's got skills. That was also the same night we got into it because I wouldn't go down on her.

Don't get me wrong, I have been known to linger in the valley, but this one particular night, Adrian wanted it bad. I mean, that's *all* she wanted, and I couldn't do oral on her and get up with a hard dick. We had just started dating and I wasn't used to one-sided pleasures. I couldn't see myself going out like that. That was before. But as our relationship has progressed and my love for Adrian has grown, she gets served quite often without having to do too much in return. She likes oral a lot.

One time, she put my ass in a headlock. My neck was sore for two days. We have a lot of fun in bed and it's always something new. Even after three years.

Another time we did it in Pops's bathroom. He'd invited us over for July Fourth for barbecue. He was cooking and had run to the store to pick up an onion. I was just about to come when I heard him walking down the hallway. He knocked on the bathroom door. I covered Adrian's mouth. She was giggling hysterically as she stood leaning over the sink with me behind her. Pops turned the knob, but we had locked the door. He started whistling and went back down the hall. We finished and came back into the kitchen where Pops was. After an uneasy silence between us three, all Pops said was "Make sure you wash your hands before you eat."

When I think of all the crazy things I've done with Adrian, it amazes me how some brothers like Phil and Timothy get off trying to play the macho role all the time. I've found out that if you let yourself be a sensitive brother, then your girl will pretty much be down for whatever. And I do mean *whatever,* like what Maxwell is singing about. I'm sweating now and Adrian is doing her thing. Her eyes are closed and she looks like she's enjoying herself. I like that. I like to see her having a good time with me. I'm giving my love to her the way she likes it. Adrian can go years before she comes. Seriously, she can do me about four good orgasms before she gets her first. I'm game, because we like different positions. It takes me a long time to come, so our intercourse usually lasts about fifteen minutes or more.

Most brothers are too busy trying to look like they're killing the kitty-cat, or they close their eyes and imagine the sister they're with is someone totally different. Not me. I check on my girl to make sure the position is right, she's feeling good, and she wants some more later. I would never let her walk away unsatisfied. That's how you lose a good woman. Give her some whack lovin' and bam! She is AWOL on yo' ass!

WHEN ADRIAN AND I finally wake up, it's damn near nine o'clock. I have to go home and get ready for the next workday, and she has to get ready too. She watches me get dressed. "Your sister invited me to go to church with her this Sunday," she says.

I continue to put on my clothes. "Are you going?"

"I think so. It's been so long since I've gone to church."

"Well, don't let Shreese turn you into a holy roller."

"I won't. Your sister is really nice, and I don't understand why she's so involved in church the way she is at such a young age."

I think about my mother. "It's a long story."

"Do you think she really wants to be that way?"

"I think it's safe for my sister. Shreese needs to be dependent on something. In this case, that something is church. She eats, drinks, and sleeps church." I grab my tie and put it in my pocket.

"It has to do with your mother leaving a long time ago, doesn't it?"

"Among other things."

"You want to talk about it?"

"Not now. Just be careful with Shreese. She wants to save the world, you included. She's a little overbearing."

"Well, I promise I won't become a holy roller and I won't ask too many questions." Adrian rolls over, grabs her house robe, and slides into it. She follows me downstairs and stands at the door as I prepare to leave.

"I will talk to you tomorrow."

"Okay," she whispers.

She closes the door behind me as I head for my car. This is the first cool September night we've had. The breeze rushes through my clothes and the smell of me and Adrian fills the air around me. I go through the day's events in my mind and decide the one thing I need to do is call my sister. I haven't talked to Shreese in several days and I'm overdue for a sister-to-brother talk. I'll call her tomorrow. Mondays are set aside for her usher board meetings. She usually doesn't get home until after eleven. I don't know how she keeps her job at that advertising firm with all the churchgoing she does.

Anyway, I'll call her Tuesday because I have to tell her that Louise is coming. But right now, all I want to do is go home, hit the shower, and catch the end of *Monday Night Football*.

## 10

LASHAWN DIDN'T COME to work today. She left a voice mail that she had to go to school and get her financial aid papers signed. I forgot it was time for her and the other interns to return to school. I was meaning to question her about the remarks she made concerning Adrian when we were all at the reception yesterday. I wanted to also make sure that LaShawn is doing okay. Lately she's been alienating herself from me and I've been wondering why.

The office is quiet except for the chatter of the receptionist, who is on the phone gabbing about some book she was reading. I decide to go and visit Eric and Tim. They both work upstairs in the finance department as accountants.

When I get up there, the first person I see is Simone. I begin to think about Tim and his supposed threesome with her and one of her friends. She sees me heading her way and smiles. Her cat eyes catch my attention, but I keep my pace and distance.

"Hey Greg, how are you?"

"Ms. Lacy, it's good to see you. I'm doing good, and yourself?"

"Fine. Are you gearing up for the big day?"

"Yeah, and I put you on the invitation list."

Simone smiles coyly at me. "Thanks," she says. "I'll be looking forward to this one. From what I hear, the wedding is going to be simply gorgeous."

I walk past her, feeling awkward and unsure of what to say. It's hard talking to someone when you know their secrets. Knowing that Tim had wild, unadulterated sex with Simone and trying to pretend I don't is difficult.

Eric and Tim are both at their desks when I turn the corner where they sit. Tim is on the phone, so I walk to Eric's desk instead. He's leafing through a magazine with Tyra Banks on the cover in a bikini. The magazine is wrinkled and has food stains on it as if Eric has never given it a rest.

"What's up, E?" I ask.

Eric swivels around in his chair. He has a new haircut that gives more exposure to his green eyes and blond eyebrows. "Nothing, Greg man, just sitting here checking out Tyra."

"Yeah, I've noticed you've worn that magazine out."

"She's beautiful, man," Eric says. "The perfect black woman. I'd be her slave anytime, no pun intended." He laughs. "So, what's up?"

"I was just coming up to see what you guys were doing. It's quiet downstairs. All of my groups are working on projects and I just finished setting up presentations with two more prospect companies."

"That Dillinger account put us all over. I went looking at some Land Cruisers yesterday. I was checking out the FJ80 fully loaded with dual battery kits, side steps, and a Pioneer sound system."

"You thinking about buying one?"

"I don't know. I'm not ready to pay that kind of car note, but my sister and her husband have one and it's nice as shit." Eric looks around, making sure none of the other accountants heard him cuss. "They even have New Zealand sheepskin seat covers."

"I feel you. I may get a utility vehicle after Adrian and I get married."

"Yeah, because when you start having crumb snatchers you'll need the extra space. Your Accord may not take the punishment a child gives a car."

"You ain't lying, man. Adrian would probably shit in her britches if one of our kids wasted a Happy Meal in her leather car seats."

I look over and Tim is hanging up the phone. He sees me and smiles. I walk over to his desk.

"Tim, what's happening?"

"You the man, you tell me."

"I was just coming up to hang around for a bit."

"How are the wedding preps coming along?"

"Cool. As a matter of fact, by the time March rolls around, we won't have to do nothing but show up dressed and ready to get married."

"What about your wedding night? You ready for that?"

"What do you mean?"

Eric leans back in his chair. He's smiling. "Greg, don't tell me you haven't thought about the wedding night." He runs his hand over his cut, causing some of the blond hairs to move out of place.

"Yeah man, you got to set it out right for your girl," Tim adds.

"What are y'all talking about?" I feel incomplete as two of my best friends toy with me.

"You know—rose petals in the bed, giving her a foot massage, making her beg," Eric says.

"Adrian gets all that now. As a matter of fact, Adrian gets enough lovin' from me," I brag.

"Oh—well then, you're going to have to set the real shit out for her," Tim whispers. He has a crazy expression on his face. "Man, you just might have to visit the dark land."

I revert to stupid again, not knowing what they're talking about. Eric starts laughing so hard his face turns crimson. "I've only been there three times. Remember that chick Peaches I dated?"

Tim shakes his head. "That dark land is some serious shit, Eric. I can't believe you've gone there that many times."

"Well, you know I like adventure, and Peaches spelled adventure from the time I met her."

"Eric, I can't believe you dated a sister named Peaches." I laugh. "Even the hardest of brothers know to stay away from black women named Peaches."

"For real!" Tim scoffs. "That's like asking for chitlins, ham hocks, and collard greens on the same plate at a Juneteenth family reunion!" He snickers at his own joke.

"Well, her real name was Dana, but her girlfriends called her Peaches. Anyway, I went to the dark land on her and she called me for months after that. I couldn't get rid of her."

I become curious again about this sacred talk of the so-called dark land. "Were you two serious?" I ask, still ignorant about the unknown place.

"Yeah, but she had some hangups about me being white. Most of them do. They want to be with me, but are too afraid to take me home to meet the relatives."

"Well, Eric, what do you expect after four hundred years of slavery?" Tim asks.

"Tim, don't start that shit with me, man. I ain't never cracked a whip on nobody's back and I have never acted any different toward you guys."

"Listen at that. 'You guys.' " Tim laughs, imitating Eric's deep voice.

I interrupt to keep Tim and Eric from getting into a heated debate about race and get them back on the subject at hand. "Anyway, what does slavery have to do with the dark land?"

"Man, the dark land is the freak move you pull on a woman you really dig," Eric says. "It's where you explore the most intimate part of a woman's body to achieve maximum pleasure for that special woman."

"Yeah, like she's the only woman in the world deserving of the critical steps a man takes in the bedroom," Tim adds. "It's the freak move of all freak moves."

"Between the sheets," Eric adds. "If you do this, Adrian will have Greg on the brain and she will be at your beck and call."

"She might get your name tattooed on her cookie." Tim laughs hard under his breath.

"Well, what the hell is it? You two sound like you've discovered the Dead Sea Scrolls or the lost island of Atlantis."

"Greg, visiting the dark land is basically licking the crack of a woman's ass in the heat of the moment," Tim whispers. He begins to giggle like a Boy Scout looking through his first issue of *Playboy*. "Right before she reaches her climax, you take your tongue and lick her ass. Make it wet."

My stomach flutters at the thought and I groan out loud. "You muhfuckas is crazy!"

Eric and Tim are staring at me like I've lost my mind. "I ain't licking the crack of no woman's ass." I try to keep my voice low. "That is foul. Straight foul!" I continue to laugh, knowing that these two have actually done it.

"Greg, you got to be down on your wedding night with Adrian," Eric says. "You love her, don't you?"

"Look, I don't give a damn if you pay me a million dollars, I ain't licking the crack of her ass." I point at them accusingly. "You two are out of control. Next time you come to my house, bring your own glasses, 'cause you can't drink out of mine anymore."

Eric leans back in his chair and continues looking at Tyra Banks. "Suit yourself, man."

"I can't believe you would even consider putting your tongue there."

Tim shakes his head. "Hey, sometimes a man's gotta do what a man's gotta do." He pats his chest.

"Well, Greg, if you ever decide to go to the dark land, let us know. We're here for you," Eric says.

I laugh nervously. "With friends like y'all, I don't need crack cocaine." I head back to my office. Tim and Eric's words of advice are lingering in my head. I picture myself going down on Adrian, but not to her butt. I shake my head again in denial of the thought, but can't help smiling at Tim and Eric.

I finish the rest of my workday, trying to figure out what man in his right mind started that freak move and why did he have to tell the next man? I would do anything to please Adrian, but sometimes you have to set limits. I don't know, maybe I'm just being a square. A continuous L7. I'll think about it some more. I mean, if Tim has done it, then it can't be that bad. I hate to say it, but I'd expect some old crazy shit like that coming from Eric Giles's mouth. He's my friend and all, but we all know that white folks are the masters of freaky-deaky.

WHEN I GET home, all I want to do is lie down and take a nap. Before I do anything, I need to call my sister to tell her Louise will be in town soon. This time when I call, a male voice answers. "To God be the glory."

"Is this 555-7567?" I ask.

"Yes it is," the thick male voice answers. "Can I be of some service to you?"

"No," I said with direct irritation in my tone. "Is Nina Alston available?"

"Oh yes. Sister Alston is here. Please hold on, brother."

*What in the world is going on?* I think. *And who in the hell is he call-ing "brother"?*

"Hello?" Shreese's voice takes some of the edge off my anger.

"Shreese, who was that answering your phone?"

"Oh, Gregory, this is you. I didn't know who this was demanding information without saying hi or how are you or nothing. That was Pastor Dixon that answered my phone."

"What is he doing over there?"

"We're studying some scriptures together. We're in the glorious book of Proverbs. The practice-what-you-preach book of the great Basic Instructions Before Leaving Earth. You need to be over here."

I ignore the last remark. "Are you alone together?"

"Yes."

"Shreese, get that man out of your apartment. Have you lost your mind?"

Shreese sits quiet for a moment. "Gregory, I will talk to you later. Now is not the time for this kind of discussion." She's angry and I can tell she's trying to conceal it.

I lower my voice quickly to try to calm myself and make her feel at ease. "Shreese, I was calling to tell you that Louise is coming to Dallas at the end of the month." I don't like to upset my sister, so I hope mentioning our mother will change her mood.

"How do you know?" she asks with challenge in her voice. She has every right to not believe me. It's no secret that I call Louise on a less-than-regular basis.

"I called her and told her I was getting married, so she's coming up to stay until the wedding."

"The Lord is good all the time!" she yells.

In the background I can hear Reverend Dixon respond, "And all the time the Lord is good! Yes He is!"

"Shreese, do me a favor," I say with a serious tone in my voice.

"What, Greg?"

"Get that man out of your apartment for me."

"Gregory, I am a grown woman, a God-fearing woman, and I don't think who I have in my apartment is any of your business. All I'm trying to do is be faithful to the works of the Lord and Savior. Why are you so against that?"

"Shreese, I'm not against you trying to be a better Christian, I just think—"

"Well, Gregory, I don't care what you think."

*Click!*

I can't believe my sister hung up on me! Shreese has never in a million years hung up in my face. Fuck it, I ain't calling her back. If she wants to hang out with that pimp preacher then so be it! She just better hope God can keep her safe from him, because I'm not going to. I have too many other things to worry about. Most important, my mother's upcoming visit. She's not even here yet, and already shit is starting to fall apart.

## 11

**B**EFORE I KNOW it, the end of September has arrived. Dad and I are at the airport waiting for flight 1702 from France to come in.

I feel distant from what's about to happen. I feel like a friend of the family just present to support my father, who is obviously glad to be here. He's dressed up in some khaki slacks, a green shirt with brown suspenders, and some chestnut-brown casual shoes. At his request, we went to the mall and searched hours for his outfit. Pops went and got a fresh haircut and shave, too. He actually looks ten years younger. He talked all the way to the airport about anything and everything just to show he wasn't nervous, but I could tell he was. I'm a little nervous too, but I refuse to let it get me excited. I know he's still in love with her, so he has good reason to be nervous. Hopefully, he has thought about this visit and won't get his hopes up. I don't think I can stand to see him vegetate any more than he already has from her leaving the first time.

The terminal is packed for a Thursday and I'm surprised at how many people I see. It's funny because when I was little, airports used to scare me. The planes seemed like steel bird-monsters as they came and went. Then, to be walking among all those strange people from strange places really freaked me out. Now, they just appear as faces without names. No threat at all. One of the airline workers comes and unlocks the terminal door.

The 747 pulls up to the gate and turns facing the window we're looking out of. Pops stands up and walks around to the entrance. I sit waiting for the passengers to begin coming from the walkway between the terminal and the plane. After several minutes, the airline worker finally opens the door and passengers begin flooding out to greet their loved ones.

I join Pops at the entrance. He's smiling, and I can tell that his hopes are up by the way he stands near the gate peeping down the corridor looking for her. When he sees her, he quickly steps back, runs his hand over his new shirt, and waits.

I immediately notice Louise when she steps off the walkway and into the terminal. Her smile reveals the glow she passed to Shreese. Same petite face. Same pecan skin tone. She's wearing a peach silk pants suit with a white silk shirt underneath. She's beautiful. Her skin is smooth and her eyes are beaming. She looks untouched by time except that she no longer sports long hair. It's short to her head, but it's perfect on her face. She has picked up some weight but she still looks like she could go an extra mile or two. Her face lights up more when she sees me and Pops standing at the doorway.

"Adolphus and Gregory! Oh, it's so good to see my family!" She walks up and hugs us both. Pops hugs her back, but I just stand there like a bump on a log, unwilling to place my arms around her. I don't feel connected to this woman who is holding on to us as if this one hug will make us know each other again. She smells like gardenias. It's a smell that I've been familiar with all my life because it's the perfume she wears. I can't believe she still wears the same scent. Her soft skin against my face reminds me of nights when I was small and I sat in her lap as we sang songs together, so I pull away lightly to keep from insulting her and to maintain my hard feelings about her return. The smell still lingers against my skin, and my mind flows to the nights when we would sing and the smell of gardenias cascaded across the room comforting me as a child. She taught me the words to "Embraceable You," and it became our song. We would sing it every night before I went to bed. Every single night until she left. When Nina came along, our duet became a trio. I miss the smell of gardenias, but as I stand back and look at Louise, I hate the fact that she is the one who makes me miss that smell. Pops grabs her bags and she walks between us, holding his arm and my hand.

"So, how much has Dallas changed since my last visit?" she asks. "It already feels different and I bet it has changed a lot." She looks around us, but I can tell she's not really interested in the surroundings. For just a second, I can see that she's nervous too, but I can also see she's sincerely happy to be with us. The spring in her steps forces me and Pops to keep up with her.

"Yeah it has," Pops responds. "I'll take you around later and let you see what's new and what's been closed down."

"Gregory, you're looking more and more like your daddy every day. Handsome as ever!" she says to me and squeezes my hand.

"Thanks." I feel like a void, a hole in the wall. I don't know how to respond to her. I reach up and rub my chin, realizing that my shave isn't as close as I thought it was. "How was your flight?"

"Long, honey. I'll tell you this, that's one thing I regret about being so far away. Sometimes it seems like the plane isn't ever going to land."

"Kind of like people." I retort. Once I've said it, I feel bad.

Louise looks at me, still smiling. "Yes, son, just like people." She pulls Pops closer to her and resumes her happy-go-lucky mood with no regard to going head-to-head with me about my remark. "Where's Nina? She didn't come?"

"She had a meeting at church," Pops answers. "She'll meet us at the house."

"Since when did church become more important than meeting your mother at the airport? I just talked to Nina about a month ago and all she kept asking was when was I coming back to see the family. Well, here I am, and where is she?"

"Lou, her church life is important to her, and I think some young pastor up there has caught her fancy."

"Really!?!? Looks like I may be down here for two weddings, then." She laughed.

I don't find it funny at all, but keep that to myself.

"It's about time Nina started getting ready to settle down too. I wish she'd've told me she met someone."

"Lou, this relationship is new for Shreese. Give her a little room, she'll come around."

"Gregory, have you met this man?"

"On a few occasions."

"Well, what do you think of him?"

I shrug. "He's really not my idea of the kind of man who will make Shreese happy, but if that's what she likes, then who am I to spoil it?"

"Baby, you are her big brother. If you think she could do better, then I think you should tell her."

Okay, now she's trying to regulate how I should be towards my own sister. I wonder, has it ever dawned on her that maybe telling Shreese what kind of men she should or should not date is really her job and not mine? I hold my breath and count to three in my head, then release it quietly. Now is not the time to let Louise know how I feel.

There is a thoughtful silence held between the three of us. I'm sure we're all thinking about the many changes that have taken place since our family was handicapped by my mother's leaving. Now it seems we're stuck with the task of bringing her up-to-date on all the important things that she missed in phone conversations.

"So, Gregory, tell me about your fiancée, Adrian."

"There's not a lot to tell. She's a self-employed beautician."

"Does she have any children?"

"No."

"Does she like jazz music?"

Pops laughs at this question.

"She likes jazz, but she's more into the younger generation. She listens to Eric Reed, Terence Blanchard, Harry Connick, Jr., and Mark Whitfield."

"Mmm. Sounds like a winner to me," she says. "I've done work with Terence and he is something valuable to the music industry. Sounds like this Adrian has good taste, son."

"And she's a beautiful girl, too," Pops adds. "Looks like fresh-made butterscotch pudding."

I feel my face heat up as Louise and Pops laugh together. They laugh as if they'd just laughed together yesterday. It almost sounds like music. And I don't care if she's worked with Terence Blanchard. What does that have to do with me and Shreese not having a mother around?

When we get to the baggage claim, all five of her bags roll out onto the conveyor belt just as we walk up. I grab some of her luggage and Pops grabs the rest. I linger behind my parents as they hold on to each other talking and smiling. By the time we get through customs, I've had enough of their giggling and hand-holding, but they don't pick up on the bothered and obviously embarrassed look on my face. I'm relieved when we finally get her bags loaded into the car and head to Pops's house.

They talk all the way. I find out from listening that Lester, the drummer Louise ran off with, died seven years ago. I sit in the back wondering why she never returned home to us after the contract was up, because even then, she would have been welcomed back.

"So, how is the music career going?" Pops asks.

"Oh, Adolphus, it's great. You know, since that tour a couple of years ago I've been working on the CD. Well, when it finally came out, we partied! Ooooh we partied! The people in France have a totally different appreciation for jazz music than over here. But of course you know that. I get love everywhere I go."

She turns around in her seat and looks at me. "Greg, you would love it. I know you would." Her hands begin to move with her every word. "I'm a regular at a restaurant named La Coupole. It's where Louis Armstrong used to compose some of his music. The folks love me there. 'Dolphus, you remember, that's where you took me when we did that gig where you and Sticks ran out without tipping the waiter and the police came looking for you."

Pops laughs a laugh I've never heard before. It's wild and liberated. "Oh, yeah. I forgot about that. Man, Sticks outran those cops." He laughs that laugh again. I sit in the backseat wondering who Sticks is. Louise tells the story all over and I act interested for a while. Then I look out the window at the passing scenery.

She picks up on the nonchalant attitude and although she continues smiling, she turns back around in her seat. "That's enough talk about the old days—this visit is for my children. My son is getting married and I will do all that I can to help make this a happy occasion for him," she responds cheerfully.

When we get to the house, I help take the bags out of the car. Louise and Pops go in ahead of me. Louise looks around as she removes her jacket. She is still smiling. "Mmm, Lord, Lord. This house ain't changed a bit. Adolphus, why you didn't take all these old pictures off the wall?" She's standing in the hallway looking at the pictures like she's in a museum. "Lord have mercy, looka here." She points at a picture of her and Pops onstage at a club.

"Take them down for what?" Pops asks. "Those pictures ain't bothering nobody but you, Lou."

"They're just so old. They look as untouched as they were the last time I was here." Louise laughs out loud. "Lord have mercy, I forgot you had this picture of me, you, and the guys at the Three Deuces in Chicago. Look at my hair. Thank God those bouffant hairdos went out of style." She's still casing the wall. I don't understand how she can stare at all this history she left behind and not show or mention one iota of guilt.

I get up to leave and just as I do, the doorbell rings. "I'll get it," I say, rushing to answer the door.

Shreese and Adrian are standing there together.

"Where is she?" Shreese asks. "Is she here yet?"

I let them in. Shreese walks past me without giving me the usual hug.

Adrian walks in and plants a much-needed kiss on my lips. "Hey baby, you look stressed. Is everything all right?"

"Now it is," I say as I smile and take her hand.

When we walk into the living room, Shreese and Louise are hugging and crying in each other's arms. Shreese is holding Louise tight and I am angered that she can be so forgiving to the woman who moved out on us nineteen years ago.

Louise pulls back, still holding my sister's shoulders. "Girl, look at you! Just as pretty as the last time I saw you! Oh Nina! My baby girl is all grown up. And I do mean *all* grown up!"

Shreese looks like she's witnessed a miracle. "Mom, it's so good to have you home. I've been praying for this day so long," she cries. "God is a good God!"

"Well, stop all that crying and cheer up, because I will be here long enough for us to catch up and you can tell me everything you've been doing." Louise looks over at Adrian. "And you must be Adrian Jenkins, the fiancée and my future daughter-in-law." She reaches out her hand. "I'm Louise Alston, Gregory's mother. It's a pleasure to finally meet you."

Adrian takes Louise's hand. "Same here," she responds cordially. "Greg hasn't told me much about you." Adrian looks as if she doesn't know what to say.

"That's because Greg wanted us to get to know each other on our own terms. He hasn't told me much about you, either, but I can tell you're a gem."

Louise continues to hold Adrian's hand and she waves us all over towards the couch. "Come on, come on. Let's sit down and talk, I know there's a lot to be done between now and March." We all sit down in the living room. Pops is in the kitchen fiddling with dishes. I guess he had plans to make dinner.

"So, have you two set a date yet?" Louise asks.

"March twenty-second," Adrian answers.

"Are you having a traditional ceremony?"

"No, they're not," Shreese interrupts. "They're not getting married in a church, Mom. What do you think about that?"

Louise looks at Shreese strangely, but ignores the remark. "I always thought traditional weddings were so boring, anyway," she says. "What do you have in mind for colors, minister, and music, Adrian?"

She looks down and notices the silver ring that adorns Adrian's toe. Louise sends a quick look my way. I catch it, but she looks away quickly when our eyes meet. It was the exact same look she gave me when I was seven and I tried to lie to her and tell her that I didn't stick my fingers in her freshly made cake, although the small holes in the icing and the chocolate on my shirt gave me away. The first thing she said to me was "Gregory Louis Alston, don't you take me for no fool." I'll never forget that day, because she whipped me for attempting to lie to her. Adrian doesn't notice and begins to answer the question.

"We're going to be outside. I love nature, and I think marrying in the spring, outside, shows that we respect and love the beauty that God creates during that time of the year. The colors are red and black, the minister is a spiritual priestess, and we're using live music."

Louise and Shreese look at me. I get up and go help Pops in the kitchen. I think listening from in there would be to my advantage.

"A priestess?" Louise asks. "What belief are you?"

"I don't claim any religion, Mrs. Alston. God is not a religion for me, but rather an expression of who I am and a reminder of how I should live my life. God is a lifestyle for me. I think that marriages should revolve around the union of two souls who have decided to combine their goals, wishes, and desires. Marriage is a union, not a religion," Adrian answers.

"God put marriage together, so why would you let Greg convince you to marry outside of the church?" Shreese interrupts.

"Nina!" Louise sounds surprised. "Girl, God made everything. If we could only get in touch with God based on church affiliation, then this world would sho 'nuff be something else," she huffs.

I can tell Shreese gets quiet. Louise continues to talk to Adrian. "Adrian, have you and Greg thought about the style of the ceremony and the importance of what you are about to do?"

"Mrs. Alston, Greg and I have dated, argued, loved each other, and been best friends to one another for three years. I love him and I think we understand what we're about to do."

I'm in the kitchen cheering my baby on. Neither Louise nor Shreese has any right to try to find fault in why I want to spend the rest of my life with Adrian. Louise's mellow voice echoes through the room.

"I just want you to know that Greg is the only son I have. I love him with every breath I breathe, and him getting married is important to me because he's committing to something that I know he's had to come into his own understanding and interpretation of. The person he is marrying is important to me because when he hurts, I hurt, Adrian, and I don't want you two to hurt each other because of a difference in interpretation. I want you to be as happy as you possibly can, but I want you to understand that Gregory is like his daddy. He plants his feet in something and the roots grow deep." When Louise finishes talking the room is quiet. The only sound we hear is Pops opening a can of corn with the electric can opener. I don't think he's paying attention to any of the conversation going on in the next room. I walk back into the living room and they all look up at me. Louise looks at me and her face is beaming again. "Gregory, she's wonderful. She knows where she's going, and I wish you two the best."

"Thanks." I hope Louise doesn't think I need her approval to marry Adrian. Surely, she isn't giving me her approval as if it matters.

Once the food is prepared, Pops yells for everyone to come eat. After a long and overdone prayer from Shreese, we all dig into our plates.

As I look around the table at my family, I can see what should be. Except, I know and understand the hurt and confusion that makes this scene at the table unrealistic. My mother destroyed a perfect family setting. I feel like I'm part of a visual figment. A piece of unfinished art.

It's not so bad having Louise home, I guess. She has been the only one to really talk seriously to Adrian about our engagement and in a small way, I can appreciate the talk she had with my fiancée. However, this is just the beginning, and now that Louise is home, I know some shit is going to happen. It's unavoidable. Too much pressure has built up and our family can't walk around here forever acting like her leaving never affected us. My dad may have his roots planted deep, but my mother never had the strength to keep hers planted—and in the process of uprooting, she exposed all the other roots around hers.

All I can say is, I'll do my best to hold my peace with her until she leaves in March.

## 12

I'S MID-OCTOBER and the weather is starting to change. The mornings are becoming cooler and today is the first rainy day we've had in three weeks. Pops used to tell me that rain was a sign of bad things about to happen so new things could take place. Sitting in my apartment looking out the window, I think about what those bad things may be. The window doesn't offer much of a view, just part of the parking lot and the open baseball field across the street, but it's perfect for days like this.

Today Louise and Shreese are going shopping with Adrian to look for furniture and carpet for the house. Adrian fell in love with a re-modeled home towards the west side of town, in the Winnetka Heights Historic District. She loved it so much, I put down the deposit on it immediately. It's a four-bedroom two-and-a-half-bath with a study. All the floors are hardwood and all the windows, with the exception of the ones in the bathrooms, are huge, landscape style. The room designated as a study faces east and the sunrise from the window is breathtaking. It sure is going to beat the stank view I have from this flat. We're not scheduled to move in until the beginning of the year, because of some unfinished renovations, but it's okay. I've started to value spending time like this alone.

Adrian and Shreese have really gotten close in the short time that Louise has been home and my sister has started hanging around more. They've been going shopping together and spending more time on the phone, and Shreese is really open to Adrian's liberal pro–black woman views. So much so, that the last time I saw Shreese, she had her hair cut to her shoulders and curled. A hairstyle she once swore women would burn in hell for, since it involved cutting. She looked good, too.

Lately, my sister has been flaunting behavior totally opposite to what I've been used to. Before, she always had this serious look on her face. The kind of look a librarian might give you if she catches you putting a hardback in the magazine section. Shreese is even wearing colored lip gloss now. Maybe it's a little bit of Adrian and Louise that's bringing forth this change in my baby sister. She still hasn't apologized from when she hung up in my face, and I haven't forgotten, either. The ugly side to all this is that she's still hanging around pimp-man, Reverend Dixon. They've been spending more time together, as well.

I found out his first name is Ulan. What kind of name is that for a man of the cloth? Seriously, he looks like a Derrick or a Kevin. Either of those names would fit him perfectly. Those are the kinds of names for brothers who run around getting all the booty they can at one time and then wonder why women try to slash their tires or burn their houses down. Skirt chaser. That's the kind of vibe I get from this Ulan Dixon man. He's suave, too. I'm talking about the gold nugget ring, the German-made car he drives, the expensive shades he wears, even the way he walks. It all screams ladies' man. Shreese can't get enough of this pimp preacher, and I would like to think that my baby sister knows better, but in my heart I know she doesn't. I'm determined to protect her and send his no-preachin' ass on its merry way. Especially before he sweet-talks Shreese out of her panties. I don't even know if my sister is a virgin or not. God forbid he takes that from her and leaves her high and dry. I'd have to kill him then. I can imagine. I'd be on the front of the local newspaper in handcuffs. Police would have me surrounded and the headline would read something like MAN MURDERS MINISTER FOR TAKING SISTER'S CHERRY. It's a shame that after all that, they wouldn't put my name in the headline. I don't know, maybe his monkey ass wouldn't be worth the trouble. I'll probably just call him and threaten him. No, I would definitely hurt the man.

I need to get up and get dressed. I have an appointment with a marriage counselor in an hour. Adrian doesn't know I'm going. Louise set it up and asked me to consider going to see this guy. I figure it's the least I could do considering she's been very supportive so far. He's the grandson of an old acquaintance of hers. At first I protested, but then after thinking about being counseled by the priestess, I reconsidered. I'm not saying this woman can't counsel me and Adrian effectively. It's just that, some of these freethinking people don't have a valid grip on reality and I can't afford sitting in an office talking about healing the world when my future is at stake.

This guy Louise asked me to go see is actually a clinical practitioner and counselor. He's supposed to be one of the best in Dallas. This is the part of getting married I don't like. I mean, why should I be counseled on marrying the woman I love? Even if this doctor makes me realize that there may be some things about Adrian I don't like, that won't stop me from marrying her. I'd marry her if she had one leg, no hair, a glass eye, and a mole on both her cheeks.

The other thing I need to do today is go visit Uncle Bennie and his family. He's been on my case about not coming to visit. The rain is letting up, so I better get dressed if I plan to make my appointment on time.

DR. LEN BRINGHAM meets me at the door of his small home. He's converted part of it to an office. He leads me to the back room, where he holds his sessions. There are all kinds of Roman art on the walls, and a red Persian rug lines the floor. He's spent a lot of cash on this place.

When we get to the office, I'm even more impressed. There are books lining the walls and some sit neatly on the floor beside his desk. I'm checking it out and I like the feel of the place. Dr. Len is half white, half Japanese looking. I try to figure out which of Louise's friends he looks like, but I can't place him. Knowing my mother, Dr. Bringham's grandfather could be some horn player she met in Belgium or Spain. Someone I never met as a child. I sit in a brown leather chair facing the desk and wait for him to start the session.

"Gregory, I'm Dr. Bringham. It's a pleasure to meet you." He extends his small pale hand. I shake it and resume sitting. He removes a tape recorder from his desk and places it on the stool next to him.

"Do you prefer to be called Gregory or Greg?" he asks.

"Greg is fine."

"So, I understand you're getting married in a few months?"

I take a deep breath and let it out. "Yeah, March the twenty-second to be exact."

"Most of the people I counsel who marry in the spring tend to stay together longer." Dr. Bringham is fiddling through his desk drawer as he talks to me. I'm annoyed at his rudeness.

"Really?" I ask. "What's the difference?"

"There is less stress in planning a wedding than there is in the summer and fall months. Most couples who marry in the spring don't hassle with relatives traveling from long distances and if there are any children involved, school keeps them busy so they aren't interfering with the preparation process as much." He pulls out an ink pen and I am relieved that his fiddling through the drawer has stopped. "And for the most part, the weather is exceptional."

"That makes sense," I add. The doctor is saying some interesting stuff. "I can tell that everyone is excited about the wedding being in March."

"Also, spring couples tend to be happier their first year together."

"Really? You know, you may be right, because Adrian and I met in the spring three years ago."

"Where did you meet her?"

"At a club." I clear my throat, thinking that I probably sound silly, saying that I met Adrian at a club. I feel like I should have said a museum or a grocery store.

"Was she alone?"

"No, she had two of her girlfriends with her."

Doctor Bringham hasn't turned on the tape recorder. That's good. That way he won't be able to play over how stupid I sound now. I need to loosen up. Don't want to give him any reason to think me and Adrian won't make it.

"She sounds like a fun and adventurous woman."

"She is. She's independent, smart, charismatic, and stable. I like that in a woman."

"What do you like in a woman? Stability?"

"Yeah, I mean who would want a person who is unstable?" I say smartly.

"Well, sometimes stability brings balance to instability."

"What do you mean?"

"There are people in this world who are too stable. Finicky and neat. Straight, to-the-point kind of people. Being with someone who is equally *un*stable can make both lives balance."

The doctor is starting to play mind tricks, but I'm ready for him. Nothing I say is going to make me look bad or unprepared for marriage.

"Well, I've had all the instability I need in my life." *Damn! I've opened up the floodgates!* The doctor leans back in his chair and rotates from side to side. I can tell he's about to hit me with the big question.

He leans down and places his hand on the tape recorder. "Do you mind if I begin recording?" he asks.

Now I'm nervous. I don't want my private life recorded, but I'm not too ashamed to have him do it because I don't have anything to hide. I mean, it's just some simple questions with simple answers; how stressful could it be? "Sure," I hear myself say.

He presses the record button, leans back, and continues the session. "What kind of instability are you referring to?"

"Well . . . I mean when I was young, my mother went to France to pursue a singing career and that made things hard on me, my sister, and father."

"So your sister was the only woman in your life for several years?"

I clear my throat. "Yes."

"Tell me about your sister."

"Shreese is kind of a fanatic. An extremist of sorts. She finds something she's interested in and jumps in headfirst."

"Is she married?"

"No." I laugh. "Heavens no."

"Tell me about your fiancée. What is she like?"

I lean back on the chair and think about Adrian. Her face becomes a fresh picture in my mind. "Adrian is the kind of woman who doesn't remind you of anybody. She doesn't nag like a mother would do. And she's not nosy like a kid sister would be. Being with her is like being with your best friend. She is really good at what she does and she gets along with everybody."

"She sounds like your mother. Louise is good at what she does, she gets along with everybody, and she lets you do what you want to do, right?"

I feel my foot twitch. "Ah . . . yeah, you can say that. Except, Louise left. My mother wasn't committed."

"Is Adrian committed?"

"Yes. She's staying here. She likes Dallas. She loves me, no doubt."

"Your mother loves you, too."

"I'm not trying to marry my mother," I snap.

"Do you and Adrian spend a lot of time together?"

"It's average. We both have busy lives. She loves to hang out with her friends and I definitely don't neglect my homies, but we find time to be together."

"Do you think Adrian's upbringing is a reflection of the woman you have fallen in love with?"

"Yeah. She comes from a two-parent home and her parents get along fine. She has her own business, just like her grandfather did, and she's always done community-oriented services. Her upbringing is a validation of the woman I love." I reposition in the chair. I feel like I'm having to prove myself to this man, and I don't like it.

"She tells you that she loves you often?"

I look up at the doctor. He's not even looking at me. I feel insulted that he would even question me knowing whether or not Adrian loves me.

"Yes. She tells me all the time," I reply.

"Do you tell her you love her all the time?"

"Yes," I say with aggravation in my tone. "Open expression is healthy for both of us," I snap.

The room is quiet and Dr. Bringham looks at me with a casual smile on his face. I feel like whipping his nosy ass. This is the main reason I didn't want to come here. I'd rather be somewhere with the guys watching a game or two.

"Are you okay?" he asks.

I avert my eyes and clear my throat. "Yeah, I'm cool."

He leans up in his chair, causing a loud squeaking noise. "Do you and Adrian have a good sexual relationship?"

"Yeah, we do."

"What kind of things do you disagree about in the bedroom?"

"Turn the tape off."

"Excuse me?"

I point to the stool next to his desk. "If you stop the tape, I'll tell you."

Dr. Bringham leans down and turns the tape recorder off. When he smiles at me, his slanted light-brown eyes look damn near closed. "Okay. Now do you care to tell me?"

"We disagree about oral sex. Sometimes she likes only oral performed on her and I ain't down with that." I feel a little better making him turn off the tape recorder. I feel like I'm back in control of the situation.

"Why aren't you willing to perform oral sex on her and let that be the end of it?"

"Because I like a full round of sex with Adrian. I mean, I like being with her from A to Z, not just A to P. But to be honest with you, that was an issue a while ago. We've gotten over it since then."

"Did it affect your performance?"

"Sure it did. I mean wouldn't you be a little reluctant to initiate sex if you ran the risk of your woman telling you she only wanted oral sex, leaving you with a rock-hard, aching penis?"

He smiles slightly and shakes his head, as if he hears me but isn't agreeing with me. "Has Adrian's performance been affected?"

"No. As a matter of fact, her desire for oral heightened and she pretty much lets me know when she wants it because she becomes more relaxed. More uninhibited about it. We were able to level it off and eventually things were back to normal."

"So she never asked you to perform oral sex on her after that?"

"No. She doesn't have to. I know when she wants it."

"You know because she becomes uninhibited, as you said."

"Yes. And because she knows I don't like to do that without being able to enjoy the full acts of our sex life, she doesn't hint to me that much anymore. Adrian and I got through it and left it at that. Our relationship is very open and we talk about everything."

"Greg, can I turn my recorder back on now?"

"Sure," I say with a flip of my hand. I'm satisfied that I've shut him up. I'm also glad I'm not a headshrinker, because this shit is way overrated.

The doctor stands up and pours himself a cup of water from his purified water fountain nestled near the door. I stretch my legs, letting them pop like old wood.

"Water?" he asks.

"No thanks," I say. I wonder what he's going to conclude from all this. Hopefully, he won't say some bullshit to me about putting my wedding plans on hold.

He comes back over and sits at the desk. I play our conversation over in my mind and come up with nothing negative to discredit me and Adrian's engagement.

"So, how's your mother doing? My granddad tells me she's a big hit over in France."

"Huh . . . oh yeah. She's doing fine."

"I have two of her original recordings she did when she first moved there."

I get curious about the relationship between the two. "How does your granddad know my mother?" I ask.

"My grandfather paid for your mother's living expenses when she first moved to France. He basically sponsored her and Lester Woodbine."

"The drummer?"

"Yes. My grandfather owned a recording studio overseas, but it was bought out by a Sony subsidiary about six years ago."

I sit stunned. I can't figure this whole thing out with my mother. First, I find out that she leaves town with another man to go live in France. Now, I've come to find out that she and the other man were living together while another man paid their bills. I've got to get out of here, because now all kinds of perverted thoughts about Louise are running through my mind.

"Your mother is some singer, you know."

Dr. Bringham's voice snaps me back to reality. "What's that?"

"I was talking about your mother. She's a great singer and a good friend of the family."

"Yeah," I say blankly. I rise from my chair and look at my watch. "Well, is this all there is?"

"Sure, and it's on the house. Good luck on your wedding."

We shake hands. I feel better knowing I didn't have to pay for the session.

"So, you don't have any words of advice for me?" I ask.

"Well, you will know the success or failure of your decisions when the time comes. You seem to have it all in perspective and you are ready for marriage. You are ready. Don't forget that Adrian is a woman who is very independent in nature. It's in her blood to go after what she wants and to create her own. She's strong and it appears that you love her very much, and that's good. That will make it easier for you to strain out later, when things between you two get really tough." Dr. Bringham smiles as he walks me to the door. I start to question what he's talking about, but I'm sick of him already and I need to get over to Uncle Bennie's.

"Thanks," I say and head to my car.

ON THE RIDE over to Uncle Bennie's, I think about what the doctor told me about my mother. Even though I hate to admit it, I'm fascinated by her. Every time I find out something new, it's like finding a dollar when all you have is a penny in your pockets. With her in town lately, it's been like having a jigsaw puzzle in front of me and not having a clue as to where to start to get it put together to see the finished result.

Last week, Adrian and I took her out to eat at a spaghetti place downtown. The entire time we were there, Louise asked Adrian a million questions. Adrian seemed to have the nosy bug too, because she asked just as many questions of Louise. I was glad Adrian was asking questions, because it kept me from having to.

My mother just released her first CD in France after all this time. The title of the CD is *Rivermoon Blues.* I almost choked on my Sprite when I heard the title. Rivermoon is the name of the street we lived on. Shreese and I grew up on Rivermoon Drive, where Pops still lives. I guess she was sad that she left us behind so she felt compelled to relay some kind of message on her CD. Well, that's too bad, because it's her own fault and I ain't trying to have a pity party for her. Louise still seems a lot less friendly towards Adrian. I picked up on it the first time they met, but I figured it was because Louise had been away so long. But now it's bothering me. I mean, Louise is not rude or blatantly unfriendly towards my girl, but the way she treats her is odd. Like she doesn't want Adrian to get to know her. Maybe it's just my imagination. I haven't been around Louise enough to know how she reacts to new people, but the wedding is right around the corner and I'm sure her true colors will have come out by then. And when they do, I want to be right there. Uncle Bennie always said my mother had some funny ways. I guess leaving her family was only one of them.

## 13

NCLE BENNIE'S HOUSE has five cars in front of it when I pull up. His house always looks like it's full of company. When I was growing up, I loved to come and play with my cousins, Bennie Junior and Aretha.

Uncle Bennie never married after Aunt Linda passed, but he did date several women. From my memory, every woman he dated had kids. It was as if having children was a prerequisite for any woman who dated him. It would always be me, B.J., 'Retha, and Reese along with two or more other children running around the house playing hide-and-seek, cops and robbers, and other group games. And I got in trouble every time we went over. It never failed.

One time I broke one of Uncle Bennie's prize-winning fishing poles. Uncle Bennie had gone out with one of his lady friends and she left her three bad kids with us. Their names were Keith, Keilon, and Katrina. These kids were mean and they cussed like baby sailors. I went to the garage and got one of Uncle Bennie's fishing poles to play with. I had played with them before and didn't think anything of it. Keilon followed me outside and asked me what I was doing. I told him I was playing with the fishing pole. He told me I didn't know how to do no damn fishing and snatched the pole out of my hands. I told him to give it back. When I reached for the pole, he whacked me across the head with it. Lucky for me, Pops had taught me a few boxing moves, so I lunged at Keilon and knocked him on the ground. I grabbed the fishing pole and held it between my hands as I stood over him. I put on this real crazy face and told him, "This is what I'll do to you if you don't get outa here!" I raised one leg up and placed the bottom of my foot on the pole and pushed with all my might. At first, the bamboo bent with my foot, then all of a sudden, it snapped. A piece of the wood popped Keilon square in the forehead and he ran in the house crying to his brother. Needless to say, all the other kids came into the garage where I was. Shreese started teasing me when she saw the broken pole. "Ooooh! I'm 'on tell on you, Gregory! You broke Uncle Bennie's pole!" Keith came over and punched me hard. My face burned where he had hit me. I started crying, and that's when B.J. and Keith started fighting. All of a sudden this big masculine voice shouted, "Hey! What in the world is going on here!?" It was Uncle Bennie and he was pissed. Uncle Bennie and his lady friend had driven up and come in the house without any of us knowing it. They both started grabbing us and spanking our asses. Then when I got home, Pops lit into me again for breaking the pole.

Now, as I look at it, the garage I used to play in is full of car parts, old air conditioners, and rusted furniture. I walk around to the front of the house, ashamed that I haven't been to visit my father's brother sooner. When I knock on the door, I hear a child on the other side trying to open the door. I assume it's one of Aretha's kids. The door opens and a girl no higher than my knees looks at me. All of a sudden she runs down the hall yelling, "Gregory's at the door! Gregory's at the door!"

I pull on the screen and it's locked. Then I hear Aretha's voice. "Cicely, did you unlock the door?" I hear the small feet of the child come back down the hall and she unlocks the screen door. I follow her into the main room, where everyone is sitting. The television is on and they're watching an old movie with Eddie Murphy playing

some cornball Detroit police detective that's out of his district in
California.

Uncle Bennie looks up. "Hey Gregory Bean! Boy, I didn't think
you was ever gon' make it over this way!" He stands up and gives me
a hug.

"Boy, you looking better than ever," Aretha adds. She remains
seated on the couch, rocking a boy infant on her lap. I lean down and
give my cousin a kiss on the cheek.

Cicely runs up and grabs my leg. I bend and give her a hug. When
I stand back up, she runs down the hallway to the back.

"Have a seat, have a seat," Uncle Bennie tells me. I plop on the
couch next to Aretha and the baby.

"How's everybody doing?" I ask.

"Oh, we're holding our own," Unc says. "B.J. will be back in a
moment, he ran to the store to get the baby some milk."

"Has Stephanie had the baby yet?"

"Any day now. B.J. can't wait," Uncle Bennie says.

"Gregory, you ready to walk down the aisle?" Aretha asks.

She looks tired but hopeful as she rocks the baby on her lap.
Aretha used to be fine back in the day. So fine that I used to wish we
weren't cousins. She was thick in all the right places and it showed
when she wore jeans. Guys used to follow my cousin home and offer
her rides in their cars and she would tease them by flashing that well-
known Alston smile their way and keep on walking. Me and B.J.
would have to fight niggas just to get them to leave her alone. Now,
at thirty-one, her hips are large and rounded from the two children
she's carried, not to mention the one on the way. Her face doesn't
glow like it used to. You can tell she's been through some heavy
emotional situations. No doubt, dealing with two different men,
neither of which is really worth her time. The only thing that holds
a hint of what Aretha used to be is her eyes. They still look like the
eyes of a fourteen-year-old know-nothing teenager. I still think she's
the prettiest. Her skin is smooth except for the two marks. One near
her left eye where she fell off her bike when she was nine and another
that extends from the back of her ear to part of her neck. A stab
wound from fighting a chick over her first baby's daddy.

"Yeah, I'm ready," I answer.

"I can't wait for your wedding. I bet it's going to be nice." She smiles.

Uncle Bennie looks at me. "How's Adolphus doing? He told me Louise was in town."

"Pops is holding his own. He's been on cloud nine since she stepped off the plane."

Uncle Bennie lets out a weak laugh. "I remember when you couldn't split them two apart. Louise was all yo' daddy talked about. One time she was late coming home from a gig, and Adolphus called the cops and told them to look for her." Uncle Bennie is laughing. I'm wishing we could talk about something else.

The front door opens and seconds later, B.J. and Stephanie walk in. Stephanie looks like she's carrying twins in her oversized belly. A modest smile crosses her face.

I stand just as my other cousin, Bennie Junior, steps into the room. He halts when he sees me. "Look what the wind blew in! Greg! What's up, man!" B.J. places the sacks he was carrying by the couch. We grip and hug.

"Hi Greg, it's good to see you," Stephanie says.

"Steph, it's good to be seen," I reply.

B.J. picks the sacks up and takes them to the kitchen. Stephanie takes the baby from Aretha's lap and heads to the back. The Bennie Alston house still feels the same. Everywhere you look or go, there is some human activity going on. B.J. comes back into the living room. He's smiling big. We go way back and I feel bad that I don't spend as much time with him as I did when we were kids.

"Where's Adrian?" he asks. He comes and sits next to me on the couch.

"She's out with Shreese and Mom, looking for carpet."

"Man, how is Shreese? She still going to that church, Mount Cannon?"

"Yeah, she's still there."

B.J. lets out a sly laugh. "Man, I remember when she wouldn't play with us. Remember? Your sister used to preach full sermons on the back porch to Corduroy and them dolls."

I nod my head in agreement. "Not too much has changed," I say.

"She would sit in this living room and preach sermons to Aretha's dolls, too."

We all laugh at the memory.

"Is she dating anyone, Greg?" Aretha asks.

"I don't know. Last time I called her, the pastor from Mount Cannon answered the phone."

"You mean the pastor was at her house?" Aretha's mouth falls open. "I went to high school with Ulan Dixon and I still can't believe he's preaching. Who would have thought?"

"She's going to end up being a preacher's wife, you just watch," B.J. proclaims.

"Naw, Nina ain't gon' be no preacher's wife no time soon," Uncle Bennie interjects. "Nina was always different after Louise left. Now that her mama is back, things will change."

"I don't think Louise is here to stay," I say to my uncle.

"Don't matter if she does stay or don't," he responds. "Nina Shreese Alston got her prayers answered. That's all that ever mattered to your sister, ever since she was a little bitty thang."

We all sit quiet in the living room after that. Eddie Murphy is doing that crazy laugh of his, keeping our silence company.

Before too long the sound of a baby crying fills the house with noise once again. Stephanie comes from the back with the infant in her arms. Aretha gets up and joins her in the kitchen. I get up to leave. Uncle Bennie looks up at me.

"You gone?"

I stretch and straighten my pants. "Yeah, I'm supposed to meet Adrian shortly."

B.J. and Uncle Bennie get up to walk me to the door. Aretha looks out the kitchen at me.

"See you later, Greg. Don't be a stranger."

"Okay, 'Retha," I yell back as I head out.

Uncle Bennie places his hand on my shoulder. "That's right, Gregory Bean. You know where we are, and it's always somebody here." He smiles. "Don't let it be March before we see you again."

"Yeah, and tell Shreese 'nem we said hello," B.J. says.

Uncle Bennie walked me to the door, but B.J. steps out of the house with me and walks me to my car. "So, when's the big day again?" he asks.

"March twenty-second."

"We'll be there."

I lean against the car. "You still going to adopt Stephanie's baby?"

"Man, I don't know." B.J. has this look on his face that proves he's confused and needs some solid answers.

"What's up, cousin? Talk to me."

He leans on the car next to me and crosses his arms over his chest. "I met this girl."

"Aw hell." I chuckle. "We all know what that means."

He holds his hands out and uses them to express his words. "Nah, cuz, it's not like all them other times. This girl is the one for me. Her name is Tawanna. She's fine, makes good money, no children, and she wants me to move in with her. It's the perfect opportunity for me to get out from under my dad's roof and show him that I can do something with my life."

"Do you like this girl?"

"Yeah, I dig her. I dig her on the for real."

"What about Stephanie?"

"She's useless right now. Nobody wants to hire a woman that's nine months pregnant. Even when she wasn't pregnant, she couldn't hold a job. They fired her from Wal-Mart three months ago for being late all the damn time." My cousin looks up at the golden-orange-colored sky. "Greg man, I don't know. I love Stephanie, because she's seen me through some seriously hard times, but living with Dad, 'Retha, and her kids has closed in on me. There's never any peace and quiet, I'm always running errands to get diapers and milk, and I can't tell you the last time I was able to sit and watch a game without being interrupted because some cartoon or women's show was on. I'm playing the role of father and husband to women that I shouldn't have to do that for. I mean, Aretha is my sister, so I don't mind, but Stephanie has become a burden of sorts. But I owe it to her to stay around."

"Has Unc said anything to you about moving out of the house?"

"Aw man, you know my dad. He ain't going to say much because he don't mind me being there, but I can see it in his eyes when he looks at me. I feel like I'm not a real man because I'm still living under his roof."

"So, what do you plan to do?"

"I was thinking, and this is what I came up with. After Stephanie has the baby, I will adopt it so the kid will have a father figure. I'll break up with her and pay child support. It's the least I could do. I just don't want to see another kid grow up fatherless."

"Bennie, that's stupid," I say as I fiddle with my car keys. "Tawanna may not tolerate something like that. You paying on a kid that's not even yours? Think about it."

"I know, but I don't want to just throw Steph out. She needs a roof over her head for her and the kid."

"Look, she found you when she was pregnant by another man, so what makes you think she can't find some other brother to take care of her? I'm not saying that there isn't anything you can do for her, but tying yourself down to another man's responsibility isn't the answer. Especially when you have a perfectly good woman, who will work and help you get on your feet. You and Tawanna can start your own family. Don't let Stephanie put all of her burden on you when she's not even willing to get up and make it to work on time. It would be different if she pulled her own weight, but from what you're telling me the only thing she's pulling is you. I climb into my car and start the engine. "Just think about what you're saying, but ultimately, you are going to have to follow what sounds best to you."

B.J. looks unsatisfied with my advice. He's never been too good with decision making or with women. He's probably making this situation harder on himself than it has to be. He usually does.

"Well, I'll think about it." He stands back away from the car and grips me one more time. "Hey, thanks cuz. I'll be hollerin' atcha." B.J. retreats into the house. I pull out of the driveway and head over to Adrian's.

My cousin, Bennie Junior, has always had women problems, ever since I can remember. He's never had a steady, decent girlfriend, someone he could depend on. The women he's dated in the past have always caused him problems, and he always leaves a totally together woman for a woman who lies, cheats, and has kids she doesn't take care of. When he first graduated and got a nice-paying job at a roofing company, he moved out and got his own place. Everything in his apartment was new. Brand, spanking new! Then, he started shacking with this sister he met at a car wash. I only met her once, but the vibes she gave off were trouble. I don't know all the details behind what exactly happened, but I do know she ran all five of B.J.'s credit cards up, wrecked his car twice, and came to his job one time too many trying to fight him. The fifth time she came was the charm that got him fired. Ever since then, B.J. has been living with Unc.

Pops says it's because Bennie Junior meets his women on the streets. I don't know about that. I would have to beg to differ, because I've met some tight women on occasion when hanging out with B.J., but they were too old to bring home.

I think Bennie Junior just has bad luck. When he met Stephanie she was thin as a toothpick. She was cut, though. Fine as all get-out. Bennie fell in love with her immediately. Even after she played on him and got pregnant by some nigga she couldn't get out of her system. I still think she's secretly seeing the father of her baby. I think this because not too long ago, B.J. came home and Stephanie was taking a shower in the middle of the day. She claimed she was hot and sweaty, but B.J. said the air was on inside the house and she didn't have any reason to be outside. I didn't say anything about my suspicions then, because Bennie never listens to me half the time and I didn't want to waste my breath. Now that he's found a working woman who can care for him the way Adrian cares for me, I think he needs to move to higher ground from Stephanie.

It's high time my cousin got back on his feet and reclaimed his responsibility to himself and stop attracting all these brain-dead women. Hell, ain't nothing to it but to do it, right?

## 14

**A**DRIAN IS LATE meeting me. I decide to wait for her outside since the day is cool and clear. When she finally drives up, she's all smiles. I get out of my car and we hug and kiss each other in the parking lot. The Caress soap she uses religiously is still fresh on her skin from this morning. She has several bags piled in her backseat and I help her take them into the apartment.

She immediately runs upstairs to her room and changes clothes. She comes down in a pair of off-white linen shorts and a tan smock shirt.

"How was your day?" she asks me.

"Tiresome. What about you?"

She sits on the floor and begins to remove the polish from her toenails. "Productive. Hanging out with your mom and Shreese was different, to say the least." She laughs.

"What did y'all do?"

"Well, after we left the carpet place, your mom took us to this Afro-Caribbean art boutique in Addison."

"Addison? Why in the hell did she take you all the way out to Addison?" I ask. Addison's the far north section of Dallas, where the black faces are few and far between.

"She knew the owner and they had some nice pieces of work. She got us four statues from Kenya for the house."

"Figures," I say under my breath.

Adrian ignores my comment. "Then, we went to Lord and Taylor's and bought Shreese some outfits."

"Couldn't you have gone to Wal-Mart or Target, where Shreese usually shops? I guess Louise is trying to buy your love the same way she tried to buy mine."

"Your mother wanted to go someplace nice, so we went there instead. Louise isn't trying to buy nothing from me. If anything, she's going out of her way to make sure that we have a nice wedding."

I shrugged. "What did Shreese have to say?"

"Nothing. As a matter of fact, Miss Thang got a pants suit and made an appointment with me for Tuesday. She's going to get her hair cut shorter and styled." Adrian looked up at me. I'm frowning big-time.

"So, Gregory, what is up with you and your mother? She can't do nothing right where you are concerned. Ever since she's come home you have been nothing but fickle with her. Why are you being so wishy-washy about your mother? One day you're Son of the Year and the next it's like you don't know her."

"I just have a small problem with her coming here and spending her money as if it's going to make up for lost time. She's trying to buy her way back into my life, and that can't change what she did."

Adrian stops painting her toenails. She stares at me with a look I've never seen on her face before, her lips pursed and her eyes plainly serious. "Don't flatter yourself, Greg. Besides, what is wrong with being different or changing for the better? At least she's trying to accept the fact that your life is your life." Adrian is practically yelling at me. "Your mother has lived a different life, but does that make it wrong? I mean, sure, she left, but it's not like she abandoned you. You still had a good life and you still are the son she always knew you could be and not some disappointment! She wanted to sing, so she did. She left. So what?!!"

"Why are you so worried about it?"

"Because! All my life I've been different and I know what it's like to want to follow a dream but not be able to because family try to make it seem like it's a crime. I've always been the one nobody could adjust to. The tomboy. My parents! My sisters! Nobody could adjust! Your mother hasn't done anything but come here and try to be supportive of this engagement and all you can think about is yourself and your fucking personal pity party!" Adrian jumps to her feet and stands over me. Tears are rushing over down her cheeks and onto my shirt. "Gregory, I suggest you get off this motherfucking high horse and quit tripping!!! I WOULD GIVE MY ONLY SOUL TO HAVE A MOTHER LIKE YOURS!!!!" Adrian runs upstairs and slams the door.

A small porcelain figurine falls from a shelf and onto the plush cream carpet. I sit on the couch stunned for a moment. I don't know what has gotten into Adrian to make her go off like this. I run upstairs behind her and knock on the door. From the other side I can hear her crying.

"Adrian baby, I'm sorry." I knock lightly one more time. "Look, I didn't think you would be offended by all this. Open the door and talk to me." She's still crying on the other side. I turn the knob; the door won't open. "Adrian baby, open up. I just want to hold you and talk about this."

Moments later I hear her unlock the door. I open it and she's standing nearby. Her eyes are tearful and her lips quiver. I grab her and hold on to her. She lets her emotions loose in my arms and cries some more. I lead her over to the bed and lay her down. "I'm going to make you some hot tea." I flip the lamp off in her room.

As I walk towards the door, I step over the clothes Adrian wore out today. A small piece of paper is dangling from her pants pocket. I think about her being late, and curiosity sets in. I want to know what's on the ripped piece of paper. It has that call-me-sometime-when-yo'-nigga-ain't-home look to it. It looks like it was torn off a receipt or something. I kneel down and pick the clothes up from the floor. The paper falls from the pocket and lands quietly on the carpet. I pick it up and look at it quickly before setting it on Adrian's dresser. Shreese's number is scribbled on the top and below that is the name Carla Perrone, with flight information listed. Looks like she's coming to town soon.

I've heard Adrian talk about this person on a few occasions. They're best friends who fell out some years ago. As a matter of fact, when I first met her, she talked about Carla a lot and even whipped out pictures, but it's been a while since her name has come up, and I really haven't cared to ask. Women fall out with each other all the time, friends one day, enemies the next lifetime. So I gather that they're friends again. I do know Carla did some hair shows for Adrian and that she was a big help in getting clients when Adrian first started doing hair. My mind is set at ease as I put the paper in Adrian's purse. Adrian has been doing way too much and she needs a break. I put the clothes on the chair in her room and go downstairs to make the tea.

By the time I bring it to her, Adrian is sleeping. She looks like an angel as I sit next to her. I leave her undisturbed and go back to the living room.

When Adrian wakes up and comes downstairs. I'm lying on the couch watching a college football game. She comes over and lies on top of me.

"Greg, I'm sorry," she says as she nestles into my chest.

I place my hand on her back to comfort her. "Baby, it's okay. I should be the one apologizing for tripping about Louise."

"My mother could take some serious lessons from yours, that's for sure." She sniffs. "It's just always been so much pressure on me to be Little Miss Prissy like my sisters. Your mother is just so . . . *free* that I couldn't help but get angry when you copped an attitude about her. You have it good and you're not realizing it."

"Hey, let's concentrate on us," I say as I kiss the top of her head. "Our parents have lived their lives and nothing they've done or said should keep us from living ours."

Adrian strokes me, relaxing me all over. "You're right," she whispers. "You're absolutely right."

LOUISE HAS CALLED me every day since she's come to town. Sometimes she just calls to say hello; other times she's updating me on something new she's done for the wedding. She and Adrian have spent a lot of time together, but I still sense that Louise is apprehensive when around her. Considering Adrian is not her daughter, I can see why, but I pick up on a different vibe. It's as if Louise doesn't want to get to really know her. I try not to dwell on it because I promised Adrian I wouldn't bring up our parents anymore. I'm still worried about her. She's taken more time to herself lately. I'm cool with it because if there are some things she needs to get straightened out with herself, then I will give her all the room she needs. I love her and I believe giving her the space will only benefit our relationship in the long run.

TODAY IS THE last day for our interns to be around before they return to school full-time again. They actually left in September, but we invited them back for an appreciation reception. It's a Data Tech tradition. The reception is at a local restaurant out on Walnut Hill, on the north side of town.

When I get there, all the interns are seated at a table with Phil, Eric, Simone, and other Data Tech employees. It feels good not wearing the normal suit and tie around my coworkers. I was quick to throw on some Levi's and one of my ETSU alumni sweatshirts. I invited Jamal and Adrian out, but Jamal is the only one who has shown up so far. Adrian said she would be here, but there's no sign of her yet. Tim comes in minutes after I do and sits next to me.

"What's up, my man?" he says.

"Nothing but the rent, bro. What's up with you?"

"Same stuff. Women on me like white on rice."

"So who's the lucky lady this week, Tim?" Jamal asks.

Tim looks at us and smirks. "Yolanda Mulligan, owner and CEO of Landa's Delectables."

"What kind of shop does she have?" Eric asks from across the table.

"What kind of word is 'delectables'?" Phil laughs. "She must be uppity."

"Gourmet desserts, pies, and sweet treats," Tim brags. "She is a first-class lady all the way, and finer than Tina Turner could ever hope to be."

"Mr. Johnson, I'm going to be like you when I grow up," Franklin, one of the interns, comments with a smile. Tim raises his hand in the "Stop" position. "No, my son, the world can only take one Mack Daddy at a time. And right now I am in the prime of my career."

We all laugh. I look down the table and LaShawn is talking to Simone. I figure the conversation must be deep because neither of them has heard a word the fellas have said. "Hey LaShawn," I call to her. "How's school so far?"

She looks over at me. Her eyes seem to be admiring me. "It's good." She smiles.

I look over at Simone and she cuts her eyes at me. "Gregory, you interrupted our conversation. Do you mind?"

"Aw Simone, the man was just being cordial." It was Phil and he was nursing his third hurricane.

"No Phil, it's cool," I say.

"Phil, don't get loud with me. I will call you out you keep on," Simone blurted.

"See, that's what's wrong with bitches!" Phil yelled. "Always using bullshit to come down on a brotha!"

Everyone stops smiling. A few of the interns look outright scared.

"Yo Phil, chill out," Eric says.

"No, FUCK THIS! Simone, pull my card, you trifling trash bitch!" Phil gets up from the table and looks at Simone and LaShawn. Spit is spewing from his lips wet with liquor. "You two dyke bitches been gettin' on my nerves since day one! Pull my card, I DARE YOU!"

The entire table gets quiet. Some of the interns look like they are about to break. LaShawn's mouth is open and instantly her eyes are full of tears. Tears appearing too frightened to fall.

Simone's catlike eyes squinch so tight, you can barely see the white in them. She gets up and stands facing Phil. He looks like Fred Sanford would look against an Amazon version of Aunt Esther.

Simone pulls no punches. "I may be a dyke bitch, but you ate this dyke bitch's pussy! Fuck you, Phil Putnam! You ain't nothing but a little-dick-having fart! FUCK YOU!" Simone snatches her purse from the floor and looks at LaShawn, who is crying up a storm. "I'm sorry, LaShawn," Simone says as she leaves the table.

I look up and Adrian is standing not far from Phil. She'd witnessed the entire outburst. She stands like stone, with a disturbed look on her face. I can see the anger in her eyes. She goes over to LaShawn, who is now sobbing heavily. Adrian and two other females take her to the bathroom.

Tim is laughing like a wild man. "Phil, I can't believe you, man! I can't believe you called Simone out like that."

Phil looks at everyone remaining at the table. "Man, Simone Lacy pissed me off! I ought to beat her stupid ass for saying that." He sits back down and orders another drink. "Fuck her, man."

"Phil, don't you think that's enough?" I ask, referring to the drink order.

He ignores me. Tim is still laughing. "Phil, you fucked Simone for real?" he asks.

"Man, I was drunk when I was with her. That bitch was all on me like white on rice."

Jamal gets up from the table. "I'm going to play some games, anyone care to join me?"

Franklin and the remaining interns join Jamal and head to the arcade area of the restaurant. Tim is still egging Philip on. "Tim, how did you find out she was a lesbian?"

"I saw Simone at this house party the night after we got the Dillinger account. It was out in Arlington. Me and some of my boys had been invited. It was a huge house. I'm talking about seven or eight bedrooms, swimming pool, Jacuzzi, all that shit. Well, anyway, we get up in there and I had to pee. We'd drunk a case of beer before heading out there. When I asked, half the fools in there were high and couldn't tell me shit, so I ventured off to go look for the toilet myself. I stumbled upon this room. The only light in it was this blue light from a closet that was wide open. I walked in and it wasn't nothing but bitches in there butt naked all over each other."

"Oooh damn!" Tim said excitedly. "I would have been in heaven!"

"Tim, chill out, man," I say, still interested in the story.

"Well, I thought I was too," Phil continued. "Shit, I came in the room and started taking off my clothes. Then, this white lesbo looks up at me and says, 'The bisexual room is down the hallway.' At first I started to cuss her ass out because I ain't no homo, but just as I was about to, I looked up and there Simone Lacy was big as day. She was lodged between two women that were freaking her down."

"Damn, that's a shame. I thought Simone was fine too," Eric says.

"She's still fine," Tim argues. "She's just not fine for us." He chuckles.

"No, this definitely takes away from her fineness, if you ask me," Eric answers.

"Anyway," Phil continues, "that Monday at work, I tell Simone that I want to hook up with her and if she doesn't agree, then I would tell about seeing her. She agreed, but after we fucked, she tried to get sassy with me and there was tension between us ever since."

I'm stunned, still thinking about the nature of this conversation. "Phil, what did that have to do with LaShawn?"

Phil brushes the thought away. "Aw man, I was just pulling her card. I didn't know she was a lesbian. I didn't mean to put her in this."

"Well, now you know," Eric interjects. "Now we all know."

A brief moment of silence passes between us. The waitress brings Phil's drink over and sets it on the table in front of him. He takes a swallow and sits quietly.

"Well, since the truth is setting us all free, I got with Simone too." Tim admits. "The girl is good in bed, and I would do it all over again if she asked me."

"Tim, you are a pathetic brotha." Eric laughs.

"On the real tip," I add.

Adrian and the other women come out of the bathroom. LaShawn is between them, their arms around her shoulders. Her eyes are puffed from where she has been crying. Her sorority sweatshirt collar is soaked with the tears that have cascaded down her face.

Phil gets up and goes over to her. "LaShawn, I apologize for what I said. I was talking about Simone. I wasn't trying to accuse you of being gay, too."

"It's okay," she sniffs. "It just caught me off guard that you would say something like that about me, because I'm not gay." LaShawn looks at us. Her eyes lock on me before she walks back to her chair and sits down. I feel like a kid being punished. Her eyes hold the hurt she's feeling.

Adrian is clearly upset. She walks by Phil and sits in the empty seat next to me. I hold her hand, but she doesn't smile at me. The waitresses start bringing out everybody's food. Eric goes to get Jamal and the others.

I lean over to Adrian and whisper in her ear, "Baby, I'm sorry you had to walk in on something like this."

"It's okay. It's not your fault," she responds coldly.

A few of the guys speak to Adrian. The mood at the table is solemn. The joy has been taken out of the whole evening.

WHEN WE GET to my apartment, Adrian's mood still has not changed. I can tell she's thinking about what happened.

"Are you okay?"

"Yeah, I'm just bothered by what Phil did, that's all."

"That was messed up. I think it was those drinks he had."

"Maybe, but I wouldn't blame it all on the liquor."

"I felt worse for LaShawn. I think if she hadn't started crying, then it wouldn't have been so bad."

Adrian looks at me. "Greg, what about Simone? Phil put her business in the street and you're thinking it would have been okay if LaShawn hadn't cried."

"Adrian, I'm talking about the mood at the restaurant. I realize that Simone's feelings are still at stake."

She sits on the bed and takes off her pants. "Phil has some serious issues. You don't just up and do people like that. He needs his ass beat one good time. He's pompous, arrogant, a loudmouth, and an obvious woman-hater."

"I think he was more upset with her being gay."

"Even more of a reason for Phil to be kicked in the nuts, because he still slept with her after the fact. He's got problems."

"I know, baby."

"Why does stuff like this still happen?"

I grab her and pull her in next to me. "I don't know, baby. Maybe one day it won't."

"Greg, what if that had been our daughter?"

I take a deep breath. The thought actually makes me shudder. "Hopefully it won't happen to any of the children we have in the future."

Adrian gets up and finishes getting undressed. When she climbs into the bed, she snuggles in next to me. I hold her tight as I feel the world around me and my fiancée being cracked by my friends and my family.

## 15

EXT MORNING THE phone rings early. I hear it but can't force myself to move to get it. Adrian reaches across me and picks it up. From the sound of her voice, I can tell it's someone from my family. Adrian hands me the phone and I croak a greeting.

"Hello?"

"Gregory, this is your mother. Could you please come over right away?" Her voice alarms me. I can tell she's trying not to throw me into a panic, but it isn't working. Her voice shakes as she asks me to come over, and the first thing I think about was Pops. Something has happened to my father.

"What's the matter?"

"It's your father, he's—"

"POPS!?!? Is he okay?"

"Baby, I hope so. He found Corduroy dead this morning. Right after he bagged the dog up, he came in the house and locked himself in the bathroom. I've been knocking on the door for the past hour and he won't answer, but I can hear him moving things around in there. I was hoping that maybe you can get him to come out. I'm so worried about him."

"I'm on my way. Just continue to talk to him and see if he will come out." I reach over Adrian and hang up the phone.

"What is it, baby?" she asks groggily. "Is it an emergency?"

"No. I just need to make a trip over to Pops's and take care of something."

"I'll come with you." She moves to get out of the bed, but I pull her back. She falls comfortably against the pillow.

"No, it's okay, baby, I won't be gone too long."

Adrian almost immediately falls back into her sleep. I pull on a pair of sweats and a T-shirt, grab my keys and wallet, and rush out the door.

When I get to the house, Louise is standing at the bathroom door knocking softly, calling Pops's name. When she sees me, she stands back to give me room. Her face looks worried. It's a look I never imagined she could even be familiar with.

"He's still in there," she says to me.

I knock on the door. "Pops?" There's no answer. I knock and call his name again, but there still is no answer. Then I hear the sound of things being moved around as if Pops is in there cleaning under the cabinets. The doorbell rings, and Louise hurries down the hall to answer it. "That's Nina. I called her right after I called you."

When Shreese steps into the house, Pastor Dixon steps inside behind her. Mind you, it's seven-thirty in the fuckin' morning! I look at her like she has lost her ability to think. She returns an even colder stare, graced by a thin-lipped smile. She greets Louise with a kiss and introduces her to Dixon but says nothing to me. Not a damn word. I go back to trying to get Pops to answer me by knocking on the door. "Pops, come on out." Still no answer.

Shreese walks up next to me and knocks. "Daddy, it's me, Shreese. I just want you to know that Jesus loves you, Daddy, and nothing is too much for you to bear, okay?"

At that moment, I can't do anything but walk out the front door. I'll try to climb through the small bathroom window like I used to do when I locked myself out of the house back in the day. My mind is swimming even more because not only has Shreese brought Dixon into a private family matter, but I notice her car is nowhere in sight. All I see is my car, Pops's car, and Dixon's Mercedes. I shake my head, disappointed that Shreese would do what I think she's doing.

I walk around to the front right of the house and climb on a water bucket to reach the bathroom window. I snap the screen off and raise the window, surprised to find it still unlocked. We never locked it when I was small. I pull my leg up as high as I can to grip the windowsill and hoist the rest of my body up, but my muscles scream out and I have to let go and regroup. The second time isn't so bad, and I pull myself up just enough to have one leg inside and the other outside while I straddle the windowsill, bent at a ninety-degree angle. Smoke hits my nose as I take a moment to catch my breath. I immediately know what it is. The window is set on the wall where the tub is and I will have to fall down into the tub and look out the shower curtain to see if Pops is okay. I lean in, prepared to fall, and rip my shirt on a nail as I fall through the window into the bathtub. A sharp pain rips through my legs as they land in the tub. The noise is enough to make me realize I shouldn't do this ever again. I get on my knees and pull back the shower curtains. Pops is sitting on the bathroom floor, Indian-style. There is a towel underneath the door covering the crack and Pops has the butt of a joint, as round as a cigar, dangling from his lips.

"Greg. Son, what the hell is you doing? You gon' break your neck climbing through that window."

"Pops, what are you doing man? Louise called this morning worried sick because you had locked yourself in here and wouldn't come out. That's not cool."

The smell of the joint is strong. Pops has his eyes closed like he's meditating and he's obviously high. He opens them and looks at me again. The whites of his eyes are the color of cranberry juice.

"Son, this is long overdue. I know the joint may surprise you 'cause I never smoked around you and Shreese, but I had to send Corduroy to dog heaven in style." His words drag but his eyes still have the sparkle in them that makes my dad seem younger than what he really is. I can't believe he's smoking weed, though. I experimented in college but never liked the way it made my mouth feel, like I'd sucked on cotton, and now here I sit with my old man. A seemingly seasoned weed-smoking professional. I sit on the side of the tub and watch him smoke away his blues. He has one of those after-sex grins on his face.

A heavy knock on the door startles me. "Gregory, is Dad okay?" It's Shreese, and I have a right mind not to answer her at all.

"Well, ain't you gon' answer her?" Pops is whispering like a four-year-old. When I look at him, he starts giggling again, then takes another puff from the blunt.

"Yeah, he's fine," I snap. Pops drags on the joint once more, then gets up, wets the roach, and flushes it down the toilet.

"Greg, you know your pops is getting old. When I walked outside this morning and saw Corduroy laid out like lightning had struck him, it scared me. Corduroy saw you and Shreese grow up. Remember I brought him to your graduation?"

"I know, Pops."

"That dog was the best goddamn dog a man could ask for," he preaches. It's hard for me not to laugh, because Pops is high as a kite and he looks out of place sitting in front of me with his draws and T-shirt on. The only thing I can think is, this is how I will look a few years down the road.

"I got to thinking about me and your mama." Pops chuckles. "How good we used to be together and how good it is to have her back home. She's brought a lot of life back into this house. She sings every night in the shower and I feel like a teenager in love again."

I pat him on the back to show my support. "But Pops, you scared everybody locking yourself in the bathroom. All of us will miss Corduroy, but you can't go around locking yourself in the bathroom like this."

He grabs a can of air freshener and sprays the room around us. "Well, Gregory. Sometimes a man needs time to think about life and the decisions he's made." He looks at me seriously. "Sometimes a man has to stop and think about the things he's let pass him by and why things happen the way they do. Corduroy never hurt nobody, but he's gone now, which means I'm alone. I tried to do right by my kids and my wife, and look at me. I'm old, I'm separated, and I don't have nothing. And now, I don't even have no one to share my nothing with. I don't want to die this way. Like an old dog in an empty backyard."

"Pops, you've done a good job raising me and Shreese, and you've all but given us the world. The grandchildren will come. Corduroy was old, Pops. Sure he was faithful and around a long time, but he still was a dog, Pops, just a dog."

"Hell, so am I," he says. "Look at me, son. I gave up the world instead of giving it to you. I let all that go so that you kids could have some stability in your lives, and I've been waiting for those rewards, but they don't look like they're coming, 'cause I'm too old. Old just like Corduroy, and tired like Corduroy."

I laugh. "Not in dog years. Cord was old for a dog. Pops, you still have time to get on your feet and make things happen. You just have to get out, meet you a nice woman, and show her what you got."

We laughed together.

"Greg, I'm talking about love between two people. Love that never faded and a love that may have a second chance. Son, there's no reason for people to live like I have. I made a mistake by letting your mother walk out of this house and now I know I can't let her leave again. I still love your mother."

I cringe a little. "Pops, why didn't you ever find another woman? You chose to be alone, man."

"That's because your mother was and is the only woman I have ever loved. She can't be replaced. There's a lot you don't know about your mother and me."

"I know all right, but it doesn't change the fact that she left."

"So you can honestly sit on that tub and tell me that you don't miss your mother or that you no longer remember the things about her that make you proud to be her son?"

Pops has a point. Even in my anger, there are things about Louise I cherish. Things that only Louise and I shared. I brush the last comment away and avoid answering. "Look, Pops, I love you and I want what's best for you. If that's what you want, then who am I to say you're wrong for wanting it?"

"Do you still love your mother, Gregory?"

"Yeah . . . I love her."

"Do you think you still need her?"

"No. I'm grown now."

"Are you sure, son?"

"Pops, come on now." I laugh nervously. "Louise lost her chance when she walked out. I'm twenty-seven now and fully capable of handling my own dilemmas. Hey, I thought this was about you and not about me."

"It is about you, son. You just don't know . . . but it is."

There is a long silence between us. Pops gets up from the floor and looks at himself in the mirror. I raise up from the edge of the tub and grab his robe off the door hook to slide it on him.

"Well, don't you think we've been in this bathroom long enough?"

"I guess so. Your old man ain't getting any younger."

"But you still got what the women want." I laugh.

"Shit, then tell me where I put it, because ain't no women been 'round here looking for it."

I unlock the door and we walk out. Luckily, no one is waiting at the door. The smell of the weed is still strong, regardless of the air freshener. I'm going to have to buy Pops some incense if he's going to continue this habit. I can hear Shreese singing a hymn, and Louise is in the kitchen preparing breakfast. The aromas of her homemade biscuits and bacon and eggs fill the house.

Pops goes to his room to put on more clothes and get himself together. When I come into the living room, Shreese and Pastor Dixon are seated next to each other singing some song about Jesus being on the main line. He's holding her hand, stroking her palm as he leans in trying to stay on key with her.

She jumps up and meets me. "Is Daddy okay?"

"Yeah, he was just depressed about Corduroy." I move in front of Shreese. She is facing the living room, but Dixon's view of her is blocked by me standing in front of her. I look behind me where Shreese is trying to look and see Dixon sitting on the couch staring around the room. Shreese realizes what my intentions are and continues with our conversation, eager to get back to the couch next to Dixon.

"Yeah, when Mama told me Cord was dead I was hurt, too. It's a shame that the Lord giveth and taketh away in such ways unbeknownst to mankind."

I stare at my sister. "Shreese, are you sleeping with Pastor Dixon?"

She looked at me with a smart-aleck look on her face. "Greg, that is none of your business. How could you ask me something like that?"

"It's my business if you come up pregnant or if you have sex with him and he has no intention of marrying you."

Shreese leans on one leg and puts her hand on her hip. "I think you're jealous, Greg. Dixon is a man of God and I am a lamb looking for salvation. Can't you see he's helping me with that? Can't you see how supportive he's been to me and to our family? Job, chapter five, verse two reads, 'Surely vexation kills the fool and slays the simple.' Gregory, your jealousy is making you simple in the eyes of God."

"Jealous? Girl, that hustling preacher got you hemmed up running around for him like a chicken with its head cut off, and you say I'm jealous?"

"That's right. I found someone who has their stuff together and who loves the Lord. Pastor Dixon isn't a hustler, either. He is supportive, warm, and a seeker of truth."

"Seeker of truth my ass, Shreese. He hangs out at clubs and car washes for Christ's sake!"

"Don't you curse at me and don't use the Lord's name in vain!" Shreese yells. "Pastor Dixon only goes to clubs to preach the word of God. He wants this sinful world to know the goodness of Jesus and to give them a chance at repentance. Why can't you see that, Gregory?"

I want to grab my sister and shake the everlasting shit out of her! She really believes what she's saying, and she believes Dixon is the way the truth and the light. "Shreese, all I want to know is, are you sleeping with that man in there?"

Shreese looks around the room. When she looks back at me, there are tears in her eyes. "No I am not! There, are you happy!?!"

My sister has never lied to me and I can tell, even through her tears and frustration, that she's not lying to me now.

"But I want to sleep with him," she admits. "He talks about marriage, so I know this is the man God has sent to me."

*Now we're talking,* I'm thinking. *There's still time for me to nip this whole relationship in the bud, like a big brother is supposed to do.*

"Shreese, why do you want to sleep with a man like that?"

"Greg, he loves me, and with God on our side we can start a great ministry. He wants to have children and a family, everything that will make my life complete."

"Has he asked you to marry him?"

"No, he just said he would like to someday soon. Once the new sanctuary is built and he buys more land for a community center. Will you please get off my back about this?"

"Do you love him?"

"Yes."

I can feel my stomach turn into knots. "Shreese, I just think that he is all wrong for you. No pastor has any business in a club."

"Gregory, I told you that he's—"

I grab her shoulders. "I know what you told me. But I know you deserve better. You do deserve love and a family, but you also deserve a man who respects you enough to stay out of your home at all hours of the night and who has enough decency to stay out of clubs. I don't care if he can pray up a storm. There is someone better out there for you."

"He's a preacher. There *is* nothing better," she whines. Her tears have disappeared and Shreese is becoming aggravated.

*Should I slap her now or later?* I think. My sister has the straw that's about to break this camel's back. "Well, promise me that you won't have sex with him until after I get married in March. Can you do that?"

"Gregory, this is silly, Pastor Dixon would never ask me to have premarital sex with him."

*Like hell he wouldn't!* I think. "Look," I beg. "Just promise me you won't. And quit letting him spend the night and leave the sinning up to me."

"Dang, boy, I promise," she snaps. "Now move out of my way so I can go eat breakfast." She pushes past me.

I still feel uncomfortable about my sister seeing Ulan Dixon, but there's only so much I can do or say at the moment. Shreese's heart belongs to Mount Cannon Baptist Church and it's going to take some time for me to convince her that Pastor Dixon is a cat nigga.

Louise sets the table as Pops comes and joins everybody for breakfast. This time Ulan does the prayer. I bow my head with everyone, but as soon as he starts praying, I pull my head up because I don't want no part of his prayer. To my surprise, Shreese is looking right at me. She's mad at me, and I feel awkward with my head up. She rolls her eyes away from me and resumes with the prayer.

When Ulan finishes, he immediately starts complimenting Louise on how good the food looks and smells. I try to observe everyone's reaction to this man without being obvious. Louise is being cordial and saying thank you every time he says something nice to her, but there is a hint that she has picked up on his sneaky vibe. Shreese is quiet, but not unusually quiet, and Pops is eating up some stuff. He hasn't looked up from his plate since the prayer was over. I guess I'm the only one who isn't happy to see my baby sister with this man.

Every now and then I look over at Ulan. He has this big cheese-eating grin on his face. His skin is a dark brown tone, the color of a Brazil-nut shell. He only wears two rings, one on each hand. I can tell one is a college football ring; the other is a solid gold nugget ring with a diamond in the middle. Reminds me of a pimp ring. Uncle Bennie used to have a similar one back in the day. Pastor Dixon doesn't have on the usual gold chains I've seen him wear at church. I guess it's because it's so early in the morning and he didn't have time to put them on. His hair is dry, too. Didn't have enough time to put on the S-Curl activator, huh? He looks at me and smiles. "Greg,

Shreese told me you're getting married," he says between bites of sausage and toast.

"Mm-mm," I say through a mouth full of biscuit. "I am getting married."

"Church wedding?"

Louise jumps in. She sounds defensive. "No, Gregory is getting married outside." She cuts a sharp look at Shreese, who doesn't catch it.

"Sounds nice. Church weddings can become monotonous," he says with that stupid, cheese-eating grin still on his face. "But good Christians abide by the law of the Good Book. Church is holy ground, you know."

"Tell him about the priestess, Greg," Shreese says. There's enough sarcasm in her voice to feed the hungry. I can't believe she's being messy like this, but I should have known. Uncle Bennie has told me about church women and how messy they can be. He should know because Aunt Linda spent a lot of time in church and a lot of time crying in front of the congregation testifying for forgiveness from God because she had gotten caught up in some he-said, she-said. Even though I miss her, Aunt Linda was the reason Uncle Bennie stopped going to church. One Sunday, she got up in front of the congregation and told them about him suffering a small mental breakdown, and he never forgave her for that. She embarrassed him by begging the church to pray for him and the family. With Aunt Linda it was always something. She even had a fight in the church once, but I never got the full story on that. All I know right now is I have to be careful dealing with Shreese and Ulan because they are looking for something to get holy about.

"A priestess?" Ulan says. "Is that the new unconventional route to getting hitched?"

"I wouldn't say that. We're being married by a woman who is just as qualified to marry people as any church minister is. She's actually an ordained spiritualist."

"Where was she ordained?" Ulan asks.

"Ghana. But her homeland is Burkina Faso."

"Is that in Africa?"

I feel like he's challenging me, but I'm on my shit. "Yeah, it's in Africa. West Africa, to be exact."

"What religion?"

"There is no denomination, if that's what you're asking," I reply. "The ceremony will be held in accordance with African traditional religious beliefs, on the whole."

"So you're jumping the broom like the slaves used to do?" He laughs.

*Where did this corny motherfucker come from? I guess the next question he's going to ask me is how are Adrian and I going to get the bones through our noses.*

"No. That's actually a tradition that was popularized through slavery, so no, we're not jumping the broom at the wedding, but we will use the broom as a symbol of shared responsibilities," I say arrogantly. "This priestess will take us through a ritual that brings us closer to nature and our true selves."

"The birds and the bees, huh?" He's still got the grin on his face. "So you'll have the different spirit gods to see you through. That's good if you worship more than one god," he says and places a forkful of eggs in his mouth. He's trying to be funny.

"No, actually only one God will see us through," I snap.

"What God?"

Now I know he's challenging me. "Well"—I lean back in my chair—"not the God that separates my people and has them running around here thinking Baptists are better than Methodists, or that only committed church members go to heaven. *Or* that you have to die to get to heaven." I got that from Jamal. I never look up at Ulan until I finish saying what I want to say. "Actually, it's the same God who watches over pastors that claim to preach the word in clubs and hotel rooms in spite of their own shortcomings." When I do eventually look at him, I have a cheese-eating grin on my face and he's no longer smiling. Shreese starts shaking her head as if I've just bought a first-class ticket to hell.

"Well . . . God is a good God," Ulan responds loudly. "And there is a heaven as real as the very chair you sit in. Its streets are paved with gold and the angels sing sweet songs all day." He's speaking in his preacher's voice. Word-singing again, like he does at church. Shreese has her eyes closed and her hand raised at the table. "Thank you Jesus!" She says joyously.

Louise and Pops have stopped eating. Pops still looks blunted as he smiles and looks at the pastor, shaking his head in agreement like he's listening, but Louise looks like she's in a courtroom observing a circus act. She looks totally stunned as she stares at Shreese.

Pastor Dixon is still on a roll. "Heaven! Is a good place!" he yells.

Pops is startled, but he continues to smile. I sit and look at Ulan and my sister like they have lost their minds. Ulan gets up from the table and wipes his mouth. "Mrs. Alston, I enjoyed the meal. Mr. Alston, I appreciate your hospitality, and Greg, man, I hope you have a successful engagement and wedding."

He reaches out to shake my hand, but I refuse it. Shreese jumps up behind him without saying a word. Louise smiles and gets up from the table also. She walks them to the door, being as hospitable as she can. When she returns, I'm finishing up my eggs and bacon.

"Do you want some more breakfast, Greg?" Louise is looking at me as if nothing has happened. I stare back at her, and hesitate to mention what just happened at the table between me and Ulan. I'm mad that Ulan Dixon tried to show me up in front of my family, and I want to talk about it.

"No, I need to get back to my place and clean up." I get up from the table and take my plate to the sink.

"Well, son, keep your head up. That minister didn't mean any harm," Pops says. "He's just doing what he's been led to do as a Christian man."

I don't say anything. I look at Louise and she looks like she could argue that point, but she doesn't say anything either. I wish she would! I pat Pops on the back and tell them both I will see them later.

On the way to my place, I think about the past two days' events. It's enough to make a brother like me want to drive to Mexico and not return. Life should not have to be this complicated for anyone. Especially me.

## 16

CHRISTMAS IS THE worst time of year for a man. We hate to even think about it. We're expected to go buy trees, put up lights, put together bikes, warm up the car, barbecue the meat, bring in the firewood, and on top of all that, purchase an expensive gift for the woman we love. That puts me between two rocks and a hard place with the women in my life. I love Adrian, so she gets a gift right off the bat. I love Louise because she's my mother, but I'm not feeling like buying a big gift yet for her, and Shreese and I are still going head to head about her dating Pastor Dixon, so she ain't getting a damn thing. I know Christmas is supposed to be celebrated in the spirit of giving because Jesus is the reason, but I have to keep it real. Shreese has gone over the deep end and all I think about is how disappointed she has made me.

Now that she's gotten her hair cut and started wearing fancy pants suits, she has gotten besides herself. She and Pastor Dixon have been strutting around town claiming to bring the word of God to the masses. They even have a small thirty-minute segment on the public access channel, called *Praise with the People*. Pops told me she came by last month selling prayer cloths for twenty bucks apiece. I'm glad I wasn't there. I would have taken it and wiped her face while yelling in her ears, "WAKE THE FUCK UP!!!!" She's even gone so far as to leave five- to ten-minute prayers on my answering machine at home and my voice mail at work. It's a bit much when your own sister, who's never dated a man in her life, ends up with a no-good pastor who just so happens to have a shitload of charisma.

But Adrian and I have been getting along fine. She introduced me to the maid of honor, who just so happened to be Carla Perrone, the longtime best friend of my fiancée and the woman whose name I saw on the piece of paper three weeks ago. I never mentioned that to Adrian. I figured she would tell me later. She said Carla just moved here from Washington, D.C., for a job relocation, and just in time for the wedding.

Carla is Greek-Italian. She actually looks like a light-skinned black woman, except her nose and thick eyebrows are clearly Mediterranean. She's a buyer for a small furniture gallery that just opened up a store in Dallas. I like her. She's the coolest woman I've ever met. She wears her hair cut above her shoulders and it's real curly. Like a young Rita Moreno. The only drawbacks I see in Carla are that she smokes Black and Milds and she wears these straight-leg pants suits that make her look hard in the figure area. She doesn't wear makeup, either. A definite plus from me. She's smart like Adrian and they have a lot of the same mannerisms. Carla laughs like Adrian and they both have this left-hand movement they do when they are heavily involved in conversation.

Anyway, I think this woman is cool and a welcome change from the soulful lip-smacking sisters at the hair salon. I think Tim could really dig her, because she seems like his type. Or Eric, since he likes exotic-looking women. Carla is about as exotic as they get in Dallas. Most of the women you meet here are either black, white, or black and white. Since I only date black women, it's no big deal for me, but Tim and Eric are always searching for women who look like they were zapped down to Earth from the planet Beautiful or something.

I remember Eric brought this gorgeous woman over one night. I won't mention what race she was because I don't want to embarrass her or disrespect her culture. Her name was Sameelah. This woman was beautiful! I'm talking about so beautiful and fine that you knew no matter where you went with her, niggas were going to be player-hating. When I first saw her, all I wanted to do was clock Eric upside his head and steal her. You know, pull one of those South Dallas moves on 'im and trick him for his woman. I felt that way until she sat next to me for a while. This woman had an odor on her that would make a horse want to swat her with its tail. She was funky! Not musty-funky, but from-another-country funky. To this day, I can't describe it, but it took me two weeks and thirty incense sticks just to air my apartment out. Eric said he never noticed her odor. Bullshit! You could smell this woman a mile and two houses away. I guess that's the price you pay for a woman like that. A woman from the planet Beautiful or something! She ended up leaving Eric for someone of her own ethnicity, which was good because after a while, Phil started making smart remarks about her body odor. Eric wasn't too upset about her leaving although he did mope around for two days.

So maybe I will try to hook Carla and Eric up. I don't see nothing wrong with it, and who could it hurt?

Louise called me this morning. She's coming over to wrap gifts she bought for Pops and Shreese. She said she wrapped mine last night and put it under the tree. She should be over any minute now. I still haven't washed my dishes from three days ago. I hope she doesn't say anything. Actually, I hope she does because it will show that she cares. Every now and then, she acts like my mother, and it makes me feel important. I like having her around, but I still feel uncomfortable showing it. As I take the wrapping tape out of one of the boxes in my hall closet, the doorbell rings.

When I open the door, Louise is standing there with two large shopping sacks.

"Go to my car and get those boxes for me, Greg." She's out of breath. I slide on my running shoes and go retrieve the boxes. When I come back, she's standing in my kitchen running water over my dishes and placing them in the dishwasher.

"You don't have to do that."

"Well, it looks like you think you don't have to, either. These dishes look three days old."

How'd she know that? See, mothers know everything. Louise has her moments when she is the exact kind of mother I know I missed having all those years.

Once she gets the dishes loaded and turns on the dishwasher, she joins me in the living room.

"Well now"—she looks around—"you have it nice and cozy in here with the fireplace going."

"Yeah, it's supposed to get down to the forties tonight."

She looks at me and smiles. This is our first opportunity to spend time alone since she's been here. "Do you want some tea or coffee?" I ask.

"What kind of tea do you have?" she asks in her raspy voice.

"You have a choice between cinnamon apple spice tea and spearmint tea."

"I'll have some spearmint tea, then."

I get up and go put some hot water on the stove.

"Where's Adrian?"

"Gone with one of her friends to order furniture for the house."

"Why didn't you go? It's your house, too."

I laugh a little. "Because I will be paying for the house, so the least I can do is let her decorate it."

"Boy, you don't mean that. You should hang out with Adrian in all environments. You may learn something new about her."

"We do go to different functions together when we can. Besides, decorating is not my thing."

"You sound like your daddy." She laughs. "He didn't do any decorating or coordinating for the house on Rivermoon. I chose the house, he signed the papers. I found the carpet, he had it installed. I bought curtains and furniture, and he picked the kind of toilet paper we would use." She laughs again. "Adolphus just made sure everything was there and in place when I brought you and Shreese to your new home."

I stand in the kitchen silently listening to her weave stories I never heard before. Louise is having a moment and I don't want to disturb her. "And the first time he had to mow the yard, I thought I was going to die laughing. Child, your father and his brother Bennie had went out and bought this modern gas lawn mower. Back then, a gas mower was a luxury for black folks. Your daddy thought he had moved up in the world buying that thing. I guess they thought they were going to have the whole yard finished in an hour. So, they wait until the heat of the day is at its peak and get out there and start mowing."

She's laughing and this time, I laugh with her.

She continues. "Bennie fell out first. I guess that heat got to him because he hit the ground like I don't know what! Choppy 'nem from across the street came over and helped carry him in. I stayed inside trying to get him to come to, while your father went out to finish. About ten minutes later, Choppy was at the door again with Adolphus across his shoulders!"

"Who is Choppy?" I ask.

"Oh, he was Ms. Thompson's boy from across the street. I can't believe you don't remember big Choppy. He was a big boy for his age. He was twelve or thirteen and stood all of six feet. He was slow in the head and Ms. Thompson kept him at home all day. He died of a brain tumor not long after you started school, but that summer before, you two used to play together."

"I don't remember him at all," I say solemnly as I cut some lemon slices and put them in the mugs. "You know Ms. Thompson died about five years ago."

"Yeah, your daddy sent me one of the programs. She was a good woman. She kept you and Shreese a lot when we would go to late-night gigs."

"I remember some of those overnight trips." I make the tea and sweeten it with honey. I take the mugs of tea into the living room and set them on the coffee table.

"So, what did you buy Pops and Shreese?"

"Oh, nothing. Just some things I think they would enjoy for a long time." She sips her tea. "Gregory Alston! This is the best tea I've had in a long time. Tastes like the tea Bennie used to make for me when I would go sing."

"He taught me what I know." I smile. I'm enjoying being with my mother. It's hard referring to her as my mother, but now it feels appropriate.

"Your Uncle Bennie is something else. I don't think I ever saw him and Adolphus fight or argue or nothing."

"They're still the same."

"Adolphus told me that Aretha is expecting another baby. Did Bennie Junior ever settle down?"

I think about B.J. and the last conversation we had. "He's trying," I say in his defense.

"I sure hope so. Bennie Junior was always a floating child to me. He never stayed anywhere long and was hardheaded. Mm-mn, that boy was hardheaded. You and him couldn't stay away from trouble when you were together.

"I know." I laugh.

"I'll never forget when he made you stand in the toilet. You were about three and he had to have been five. We were visiting for the summer and Linda and I had come in from shopping. There you were, standing in the toilet, crying your heart out. When I asked you what you were doing you said Bennie Junior told you that if you stood in the toilet and counted to three hundred, Santa Claus would come to your house early." She breaks out in her hoarse laughter.

I smile, vaguely remembering the incident.

"The funny thing about it all," Louise continues, "was that you would always get confused when counting high, so you were crying because you didn't know what came after thirteen." We both laugh. I feel embarrassed that she has such a story to tell about me.

*Boy, was I dumb back then,* I think.

I begin wrapping one of the boxes she had taped up. Louise sits sipping her tea and watching me. I'm at a loss for words with her, but I know what needs to be said. "Why did you go to France?" I ask.

She shakes her head dreamily. "I don't know. I was young and I wanted to sing. That was all I ever wanted to do, Gregory. Singing has always been my life."

"So leaving your family behind was the thing to do?"

"No," she responds. "I tried to get your daddy to come with me and bring you two along—we didn't have to pay for anything. But Adolphus had settled in. He was comfortable going to work and coming home to a family. I loved my family and being with my children, but I'd never planned on planting my feet in Dallas. I always looked at our situation as temporary and I was ready for us all to go on the road."

"So what happened?"

"We had been renting the house for a while, and Adolphus wanted to buy. I was doing gigs here and there, off and on, trying to get a record deal. Blue Note Records was on the decline and I was getting desperate. A friend from California called the same week we were supposed to sign the papers to buy the house and told us of an opportunity in France that guaranteed a record deal. There was a guy named Joe Bringham who had a small record label called Swing Time, and they wanted to do a live recording in France. He wanted the Alston Jazz Quartet and me to be the band to record. He offered to pay for all moving expenses, families included. I immediately said yes, and your father immediately said no, which goes to show how much we really knew each other after all those years."

"What happened after that?"

"I left. I just up and left. I was afraid to tell 'Dolphus that I was going so I decided to tell him once I got overseas. When I called him he cussed me so bad, I shook. But nothing compared to the day I called you on your eighth birthday and you hung the phone up while I sang the birthday song to you. That was the first time I regretted leaving. I wanted to come home, but I had signed a contract by then. A five-year contract that threw my life into a ball of confusion and locked me down in Europe."

"What about Lester Woodbine?" I asked. "I remember Pops yelling at you that night about Lester the drummer. I thought you two ran off together."

"Greg, it's not what you think. Your daddy knew nothing was going on between me and Sticks. That's what we called Lester. Sticks left with me, that much is true, but he had a woman over there. Her name was Felicia. She was a young, pathetic-looking white girl, too. You should have seen her." Louise shakes her head and smiles at the thought. "Anyway, we had to form a whole new band because 'Dolphus, Mootchie Rankin, and Dexter Sanders stayed in the States. Sticks was my drummer, that's all."

"He never told us what happened. We never talked about why you left."

"To be honest, son, I think the whole band was against going over there and letting a white man pay our way until we could get on our feet. They were all proud black men who had been through enough with the whites in the music industry here. But Lester and I had decided that money is green, and the folks over in Europe have a totally different appreciation for music, especially black music and jazz. I think your father was mad that Lester crossed over the line."

"But why did you quit coming to visit?"

"The last time I came to visit, you were thirteen and Nina was eleven. You both treated me so bad that I decided to quit wasting your time by coming home. That's when you stopped calling me Mama. Shreese wouldn't give up her church nights to spend any time with me and your father was barely talking to me back then. I was hurt."

"You hurt us. What you did was selfish."

"Greg, I don't expect you to understand, and I apologize for bringing you and Nina into this. What I did *was* selfish, but I have always loved you. Don't think anything different." She takes a long thoughtful pause. "All I've ever wanted to do was sing jazz and be good at it." Louise grabs her mug and sips some more tea. "Europe gives me that chance."

I still feel compelled to talk. "We used to make wishes for you on our birthdays, at Christmas, when we saw falling stars, and any other time we had opportunities to make you appear from nowhere. I remember wishing for you at one of Bennie Junior's birthday parties as he made his wish and blew out his candles." I laugh. "It's funny how as a child I made you feel unwanted when all the time I wanted you home. I knew I loved you, but I hated what you did more." I inhale slightly. "I still hate what you did." I look at her for some form of comfort.

She looks at me and gives a half-smile. "It's okay. Like I told you before, I am your mother and sometimes dealing with angry children is part of my job description. But I hope you don't spend the rest of your life hating what I did, because one day you will have your own children, and they will make decisions based on soul needs and not on the needs of others." She grabs a box out of one of the sacks and begins taping it closed. She looks up at me one more time and smiles.

"I was young and foolish. Very foolish, Gregory." Her lips quiver for a second and she starts wrapping another gift.

I continue to wrap the box I have as I think about what she's said about soul needs.

"You know I don't hate you, right?" I ask without looking up. I want her to feel better and to know that I forgive her.

Even though something inside me is still angry at her, I think it's more my resentment towards myself for coming to conclusions without ever giving her a chance to tell her side. I know she's right, because I can remember the times I wouldn't talk to her on the phone, or wouldn't sign my name to her birthday cards. I wanted her to beg for my forgiveness, but what I wasn't willing to do was forgive. Now, I feel like I can start.

She puts everything down and reaches for my hand. I give it to her.

"Gregory Louis Alston, thank you for being the son I knew you would be. I never wanted anything from you that you weren't willing to give. There's no way I could have expected you or your sister to be happy about my leaving. I hoped you two would grow up with passions of your own. Something you loved so much that you would lay down your life for it if you had to. Only then could either of you understand why I left. I just hope that when you settle with the woman you really love, you can make better decisions about the lives of your children than I did." Her grasp becomes firm and I squeeze back.

We release our hold on each other and continue wrapping gifts.

"What do you mean by 'the woman I really love'?" I question, not letting the statement slide.

"Oh, I just meant when you settle down with the woman you

love." She never looks up, but she has an expression on her face that clearly means she's holding back. It's the same look she had when Ulan and I had words at the breakfast table, and this time I'm not letting it drop. Louise and I just bonded and opened up to each other and there is no reason I should feel uncomfortable trying to figure Lou—my mother's statement out.

"Adrian is going to be my wife, so why is it all of a sudden you can't say her name? I do love her and I think you owe her that much respect when referring to her."

"Oh Gregory, I wasn't thinking anything by what I said. If you want me to say Adrian, then there, I've said it. Adrian."

"You've treated Adrian strangely since you met her. That day you met her, I saw you look at her funny. I noticed that. And the day you called my apartment and she was here, you didn't even greet her. She told me you just asked her to put me on the phone. You don't have to pretend. Why don't you be up front with me concerning your feelings about Adrian?"

"Well, to tell you the truth, son, she's a little too quiet for me. I just always thought you'd marry a woman who was more spirited. I've met millions of women around this world who Adrian reminds me of, and that just isn't what I expected. Quiet people have never been my favorite type of people, based on personal experiences, and that's why I may act standoffish from her, but I don't mean for it to show. I'm sorry if that offends you and I will try to do better."

I accept my mother's apology. Hopefully she's sincere. "Just give her a chance, because you haven't been around her long enough. Your experiences can't define everything, and Adrian really likes you. I think you should at least stop judging her based on others you've met who remind you of her."

"Gregory, let's not get into how I feel about Adrian. What matters is that you have my blessings, and you do, one hundred percent. You're right, I haven't been in your life long enough to know what you like or dislike, and my feelings about Adrian are irrelevant."

"But your approval means a lot to me right now. Don't you understand that?"

"And I do approve, son. I approve of how happy I see you when you're with her. What matters to me is how she makes you feel, not how she makes me feel."

"So, do you like her?"

Louise laughs. "I personally think you could do better by finding you a nice young jazz singer, but she'll do if she can appreciate the music."

We laugh together and continue wrapping the gifts. This moment feels good to me. I never thought a day like this would happen and I could actually start coming to grips with my anger and my resentment of Louise. One thing I can say without a shadow of a doubt is that I'm glad she's here.

By the time we finish wrapping the gifts and getting the scraps of paper from the floor, it's almost seven o'clock. Louise gets up to leave and I walk her out to her car.

"So, are you doing any gigs while you're in the States?" I ask.

"No, I canceled everything for your wedding."

"Oh." I'm disappointed.

"Your father wants me to go down to Sambuca's club and do a set, but I told him to forget it. For once in my life, singing is not the priority. You and Shreese are." She smiles. "Besides, seeing the old gang might kill your mama." She laughs.

"Nah. I think you could handle it."

"I'm cooking New Year's dinner at the house and I want you, Adrian, and your friends to come over. We'll set it out with a great big party with lots of food and drinks."

I smile and look out over the parking lot. "Okay. Sounds good." I shut the door and watch her put her seat belt on, start up, and drive away.

She waves as she leaves, and I return the favor. Although I'm skeptical about Louise's intentions towards Adrian, I think talking with her has made a big difference and now Adrian and I can get our lives back on track. We've been distant from each other lately, and I know Louise's presence has hurt my relationship with my fiancée more than it has helped. Adrian tolerates her because she is my mother, but I'd rather Adrian not deal with Louise at all if she feels uncomfortable around her. Hopefully, my mother is serious about changing her attitude and Adrian will notice it. She loves my mother, I can tell by the way she has talked about her lately, but at the same time, Adrian and I have spent fewer nights together, our sex life is virtually nonexistent, and the last time I went to visit my parents, Adrian declined to go with me. But now, everything can be put back in motion and we can begin to close the crack we've started falling through.

The nip in the air causes a chill to run up my spine as I head back into the warmth of my apartment. I'm smiling big, feeling good that I am no longer one big ball of anger and confusion where my mother is concerned. I've got a roof over my head, food in the fridge, love on my mind, and finally . . . a mother for Christmas!

## 17

I T'S NEW YEAR'S Eve and everyone is at my parents' home except for Shreese and Ulan. They are at church with other members, bringing in the new year. Shreese invited the family to attend the service, but I think only Aretha stopped by, and now she's here with everybody else at my parents'. She even has a date. The brother looks sorry if you ask me, but it's her world and I ain't trying to spoil nobody's night.

Jamal is here with April. I mean, Freedom Heru. She's good-looking just like he said, thin and elegant. Deep brown skin and long thin braids. I really like the tattoo on the back of her left shoulder. It's the shape of the ankh symbol, but if you look at it close, it's a black woman holding a child. The artwork is cool.

Eric brought a woman he met at a Christmas party last week. They both have on the same colors, black pants with red shirts. He introduced her as Darcell McElroy. She's exotic and very ethnic-looking, the way he likes them. He said she was part Thai and part Indian, but she looks like a Native American with slanted eyes. She's not that pretty, though. Her grill is messed up, meaning her teeth are jacked, stacked, and two or three are cracked. But mouth closed, she's the bomb.

Tim came alone. Last year he had three different dates at three different times. I guess this year, he's decided to settle down and bring in the new year stag. Since Adrian's friend Carla is here, I'll introduce them instead. Who knows? I could be the next great Cupid.

Phil is here with some woman who looks like she could use some sleep. She has huge bags under her eyes and she's sitting on the couch like a zombie. When I asked her did she want something to drink, she stared at me for several seconds before answering. I started to get right in her face and yell, but she eventually came around and gave a polite "No, thank you." Phil isn't even paying her any attention. He's skinnin' and grinnin' with Arnell, the nail tech from Adrian's salon.

Pops, Uncle Bennie, and three other older men are outside in the garage playing dominoes. Bennie Junior comes in with a new woman. I assume he got Stephanie out of his life. This woman looks a lot older and doesn't quite fit the description of the one he told me about over a month ago, who was his age. He walks over to me and gives me some dap. "What up cuz!" he says loudly. The alcohol on his breath heats my face.

"Hey B.J.," I reply, pulling myself from his grasp.

He pulls the woman next to him, by his side, and introduces her. "This is my woman, Phyllis. Phyllis, this is my soon-to-be-married cousin, Greg."

She extends her hand to me and smiles. "Hi Greg, it's nice to meet you."

"Same here."

Bennie Junior leans in and whispers in my ear, "Fine, ain't she?"

I look at him and smile. Phyllis looks like she could be here with Unc. She's not bad-looking, just old. Her eyes are big and her glasses are kind of thick, but she's attractive to say the least.

"Would you two like something to drink?"

"Yeah cuz." B.J. laughs. "Let me have some of that Alizé and give my woman a Sprite. She's driving tonight!" He pulls Phyllis up against him tighter and lands a fat kiss right on her neck. She giggles for him to stop, but it only leads B.J. into more kisses.

I head for the kitchen to get their drinks. On my way, I see Tim checking out the CD collection. Across the room in the hallway, Adrian and Carla are looking at the family pictures on the wall. I call Adrian over and she walks to the kitchen with me. I get a Sprite from the pantry and she puts ice in the cups for me. "Why don't you introduce Carla to Tim?" I ask. "I think they might hit it off."

Adrian looks at me and laughs. "I think Carla is doing fine being single. Besides, didn't you say that Tim was a player?"

"You misunderstood me, baby. I said Tim was a player because he hasn't found the right woman," I say, trying to clean up my initial statement.

"Hm-mm, I bet."

"Adrian, you don't think they'd hit it off? It would be good. Me, you, Tim, and Carla."

"No."

"Why?"

"Because Carla told me she's here to enjoy herself and she isn't looking for a relationship right now."

"Oh, and I guess you believed her?" I say defensively. "That's just a shield. You did the same thing with me when I met you, and look at us now, on the verge of being married."

"Yes, I do believe her. I know Carla and she's not like me, Greg. If she says she's not looking, then she's not looking."

"Whatever. *I'll* hook them up by myself, then," I say. "And when they get married and are thanking me for hooking them up, don't you say a word." I grab the drinks and kiss Adrian as I walk out of the kitchen.

She hits me on my butt and follows me out. I take B.J. and Phyllis their drinks.

Tim is still checking out the CDs and Carla is in the hall by herself. Adrian has disappeared in the crowd.

I jump on the opportunity to introduce them. "Hey Tim, come here man, there's somebody I want you to meet."

"She ain't no mud duck, is she?" he jokes. I walk him over to Carla. She smiles as she sees us approach her. "Hey Greg," she says. "I was just admiring all these wonderful pictures your parents have. I didn't know they knew so many famous jazz musicians."

"Yeah. I have to show you the photo albums someday," I say, trying not to seem so rushed to have her meet my homie. "Carla, I want you to meet my best friend, coworker, and best man, Tim Johnson." Tim extends his hand and Carla takes it.

"Tight grip." Tim smiles. "Nice. I take it that you're a business-woman?"

"That I am," Carla says. "A very good businesswoman."

"Carla just came here from D.C., to open and run a gallery here," I say.

"Art?"

"Furniture."

"Did you go to a special school to learn that?" Tim asks. Before Carla can answer, I excuse myself and leave the rest up to fate and destiny. I still don't see Adrian, but I figure she's somewhere being a hostess, because several of her beauty shop friends are here.

Jamal grabs me and gives me dap. "Greg, your parents know how to throw a party."

"Thanks man," I say as we both look at the room full of people.

"When are you going to take me to see the new house?"

I feel bad now. Two weeks ago I told Jamal I'd take him to see the house, and I still haven't gotten around to it. "Soon, man. As a matter of fact, Adrian is having the furniture delivered the second week of January, so how about after then? At least you'll have somewhere to sit and the place will look decent."

"Bet. I'm going to hold you to that." He smiles.

"Hey. I've been meaning to tell you that Freedom is a nice-looking sister. You two complement each other well."

"Thanks, brother. She and I have been kicking it strong. She's a good woman."

"Does that mean I may be hearing wedding bells soon?" I ask.

"Man, I don't know about that." Jamal laughs. "But it seems to be definitely heading in a positive direction."

I look at him questioningly. "Does she brush her teeth with baking soda?"

"Yeah." He grins. "And she uses a natural deodorant, the whole nine yards."

"J man, I'm happy for you."

He nudges me. "I saw you introduce Adrian's homegirl to Tim. You trying to hook them up?"

"Yeah. Her name is Carla Perrone. She just moved here from Chocolate City. I think Tim'll like her."

"It's about time that brother slowed his roll."

"For real."

I see Adrian come out of the bathroom. She waves at me and goes to mingle with some of her friends.

Louise comes out of the kitchen, tapping a small spoon against a glass with wine in it. "Can I have everyone's attention, please?" She repeats herself several times before everyone is finally quiet.

Adrian comes and stands near me. I pull her in front of me so I can hold her. Pops and his friends come in from the garage. Pops's eyes are red. I look at him and shake my head. I know what they've been doing. He giggles with Unc.

"Excuse me, gentlemen," Mom says as she gives Pops and Uncle Bennie a hard stare.

They stop laughing, like two embarrassed kids.

"I would like to take this time to celebrate two people in this room tonight," she says. My heart begins to beat fast. I look down at Adrian and her face turns beet-red.

"The first person is my son, Gregory Louis Alston."

"Go Greg!" Phil yells from the couch. Several guests laugh and clap.

"My son is about to get married to a wonderful young lady, Adrian Jenkins." She pauses as Adrian's girlfriends cheer for her. "I would like to recognize them. They will be wed on the twenty-second of March and I hope to see each and every one of you there." Everyone in the room claps and whistles as my mom raises her glass and sips. She smiles and continues talking.

"Secondly, I would like to ask Adolphus Alston to come forward."

She turns and looks at Pops. He's high and giggling. He straightens up and stands next to Louise. He puts his arm around her waist. I wish Shreese were here to see this. Pops hugs Mom closer to him.

She ignores the gesture and continues smiling. "Someone revealed to me some time ago that Adolphus had started slacking on his piano playing. I don't know why, but I do know that God has given this man a gift that he should not let go down the drain." Mom grabs Pops's hand. "It took a lot of thought and planning. With the help of Adrian, I was able to contact some friends in New York and present Adolphus with his Christmas present."

"Baby, Christmas was a week ago," Pops says. Several guests laugh.

"I know, and you've been pouting ever since I gave you the other gift."

"Shit, I didn't need no luggage set. I don't go nowhere." Pops manages to get a roomful of laughter this time.

My parents look like they're doing a variety-show skit. Sonny and Cher. Captain and Tennille. Marilyn McCoo and Billy Davis, Jr.

"Now, Adolphus, don't you start with me." Mom laughs. It's good to see her and Pops getting along. "Anyway, as I was saying, I wanted to give you your real Christmas gift now. It's a little late, but the timing is still perfect." She reaches into her blazer pocket and pulls out a case with Pops's eyeglasses in it. She hands it to him.

"Woman, these were already mine!"

"But this wasn't," Mom says as she leads Pops to the backyard. We all follow and look out the patio door. Sitting in the middle of our patio is a Boston grand piano. Several guests gasp. I even hear Tim behind me say, "Damn!" Mom opens the patio door and the cool breeze runs into our faces and through our clothes.

Pops walks up to the piano and runs his hands across the polished Macassar ebony. It looks like it has full sostenuto, too. Mom went out. She went all the way out. The air is cool and still, and when Pops sits down and runs his fingers across the ivories, I hold my breath. He puts his glasses on over tear-filled eyes. Mom sits next to him by the piano and lays her head on his shoulder.

Pops lays his fingers on the keys again and this time, he plays. The notes warm my insides. It's been a long time since I heard him play, but once he starts, I feel five years old again.

I don't recognize the tune he's playing, but Mom giggles and Pops leans over and kisses her on the cheek. They're sharing a secret moment and everyone on the patio allows the sacredness to stand unaltered and unbothered. Several of the beauticians are crying, too. I see Jamal holding Freedom and they both have their eyes closed as if they are the only two in the room.

Mom sits up and begins singing. It must be an original piece, because I've never heard it before. Mom sounds like Sarah Vaughan tonight. The tune is bluesy.

As she lets the notes and words flow from her vocal cords, everyone in the room is mesmerized. I feel heat rise in my stomach and then to my throat. My eyes burn as I blink to keep the tears back.

Mom's voice fills the night around us, but Pops's playing is like gold. He doesn't even look like he's concentrating as the chords flow from the Boston grand. I had forgotten what it was like to hear him. Some of the chords he strikes remind me of when I was little; the visions are blurry and unclear, yet I feel excited and nostalgic.

The doorbell rings and I leave Adrian's side to go answer it. When I open the door, two large brothers and a muscular white guy are standing there.

"We're here to move the piano inside," one of the brothers says.

"Come in. It'll be a minute." I let them in and we walk to the living room where everyone is still being serenaded by Mom's singing.

"Don't think I'm crazy for loving you, baby, / But I can't help seeing you're good. / And if I could give you my love on a menu, / I'd let you order what you would. . . ."

Tim pulls Carla out on the patio, and they begin to dance. He holds her close by the waist. They look good together. I smile as I see Carla close her eyes and lay her head on Tim's shoulder. Adrian leaves the patio and goes into the house. Several other couples head out onto the patio and dance. I'm diggin' the scene.

When Mom and Pops finish, everyone applauds and yells.

I go get the movers, who are eating in the kitchen. Afterwards

I go look for Adrian. I find her in the guest bedroom, lying down. The light is on and she's lying on her back with an arm across her forehead.

I sit beside her on the bed. "Baby, are you okay?"

"Yeah." She sniffs. "I just have a slight headache. I think the excitement and the cold air just weren't good combinations, that's all."

I can tell she's been crying. I smile a little, because I know the scene between my parents probably touched her and she's ashamed to admit it. I remove her shoes and begin massaging her feet. She moans, but it still doesn't look like it's enough to soothe her headache.

"You ready to go home?" I ask.

"No, I just need a minute. I'll be back out in a little while. Go ahead and enjoy your parents. They need you here."

I lean over and kiss Adrian on the forehead. I think she's been stressing out lately about the wedding, her family, the house, and the shop.

She rolls over on her side away from me and closes her eyes. I flip off the light and leave the room, allowing her to get some well-deserved rest.

The movers have gotten the piano moved into the living room. The loveseat had to be moved up against a wall. Pops is playing again, and one of his friends is standing next to him playing a saxophone. Mom is doing riffs, scales, and scats and the sax player is repeating them behind her. They're jamming and the living room floor is full of dancing black folk.

I see Tim and Carla sitting at the table talking. Carla has her head resting on one of her hands and she's smiling as Tim talks to her about something. I'm pleased with the scene and don't bother them.

I bob to the good time the family is having. I see Bennie Junior standing by the food table. I don't see his date anywhere, so I venture over to talk to him.

"B.J., what's up man?" I give him some dap.

"Aw man! This is great! Aunt Louise and your dad have it going on like a muhfucka!" B.J. is smiling big. I can tell he's up to something. "Say man," he says as he moves a little closer to me and wraps his arm around my shoulder, "what you think of my woman Phyllis?"

"She's okay," I say. "A little old for my taste, though."

B.J. lets his crazy laugh fly. "Oooh cuz, you too much, man!"

"What happened to the other chick who was your age and had her own place?"

"Man, Stephanie found out about her before I could break things off. One night, not too long after she came home from having the baby, she followed me over to Tawanna's and smashed all her car windows in. Tawanna called the police and filed charges on Steph and left me high and dry. She won't even talk to me."

"Damn. See B.J., you need to slow your roll, man. Slow your roll with chickenheads like Steph."

"Aw cuz, I am. I put Stephanie's crazy ass out. Ain't seen her in almost five weeks."

"How's the baby?"

"She had a girl. Ugliest baby I've ever witnessed! Looked like the ass of a monkey. Man, I'm glad I followed your advice and didn't adopt that one. Ain't no way people would've believed that was my kid. I'm an Alston and Alstons don't produce no ugly kids, you know what I'm sayin' cuz?"

"So, you and Phyllis getting along?"

"Yeah. She's sweet. We're living together off of Polk Street. My job is going good and Dad finally has a room he can convert into whatever he wants."

"So this is serious between you and Phyllis?"

"I don't know about all that, but it works for both of us. Living together with no formal plans ain't for everybody. I mean, I like her, but we haven't gotten to any critical points in our relationship yet. It's just what works for both of us right now. She ain't complaining, see?"

There's a tap on my shoulder. It's Carla. I look past her and notice Tim is gone from the kitchen table.

"Where's Adrian?" she asks.

"In the back, lying down."

"Is she okay? Is she sick?"

"No. She just got a little emotional from the scene with my parents, is all."

Carla shakes her head. "That was so beautiful. I wanted to tell you that," she croons. "A Boston grand is nothing to take lightly. Your mother really loves your father, that's for sure."

"For real, those things cost an arm and a leg," B.J. adds. He looks at Carla and smiles.

Carla smiles cordially at B.J. and looks back at me.

"I'm about to leave, so let me go tell Adrian." Carla hugs me and walks down the hall.

"Man, she's fine," B.J. says. He's staring down the hall at Carla. "Where'd you find her?"

"She's Adrian's maid of honor. They know each other from way back. Back when Adrian was in hair school."

Tim comes over. He has his jacket in his hand. "Say man, I'm about to be out."

"You not staying for the New Year's countdown?" Bennie Junior asks.

"Naw, home slice. I'm sleepy and I have to catch a plane in the morning to go see my mom in Austin."

"Well, all right, cool breeze." We grip each other. I excuse myself from Bennie Junior to walk Tim to the door.

"You sure you and Carla Perrone aren't going home together?" I whisper with a grin.

Tim looks at me and smiles. "Actually, she's coming over for a drink, but I'm not interested in her like that. It's something different about this sister. She's like a homegirl. Somebody you've known since birth."

"Yeah right," I joke. "A fetus friend."

"Seriously. I would be surprised my damn self if I end up boning her tonight."

"Well, you two be careful driving to your house. And watch out for these crazies, there are a lot of drunk drivers out tonight."

"All right. Hey, kiss Adrian for me and tell her I said happy New Year."

Carla comes down the hall with her coat and scarf. Judging from her crimson face, she's upset.

"You okay?" I ask.

"Yeah, I had trouble finding my coat." She smiles. "It fell on the other side of the bed on the floor. I couldn't find it at first. I paid a lot of money for it to be losing it, you know."

"Sorry about the trouble," I say to her.

Tim breaks the silence. "I'll call you when I get back from Austin, man." He daps me again and follows Carla out the door.

Inside, the music has been turned back on and everybody has a soul train line going. I join in the fun until it's time to do the count-down. Mom and Pops grab wineglasses and noisemakers and begin passing them around. I head to the back to get Adrian. She's sitting up when I open the door.

"You feeling any better?"

"Not really. Are they getting ready to do the countdown?"

"Yeah, you coming?"

She stands up and slides on her shoes. "Did Carla leave?" she asks.

"Yes," I say proudly. "She left with Tim."

Adrian shoots me a quick uncomfortable look. "How could you let her leave with Tim? Greg, I told you . . ."

"They're just bonding before the wedding." I'm grinning, but I can tell Adrian doesn't see the humor in my joke.

"Greg, that's not funny. Tim could fall in love with her, and she's not prepared for that. Don't you get it? Tim could really get his feel-ings hurt. Carla could, too. I don't have time to be dealing with a maid of honor going through emotional distress over a man at my wedding."

I walk in and pull her against me. She allows me to hold her, but I can tell she's not into the mood of the evening. "Adrian, what's the matter? I didn't think there was any harm in introducing Carla to Tim, baby."

"I know." She sighs. "It's just that Carla is important to me. We're close. Tim is important to me, too. I don't want either of them hurt."

"Well, I'll tell Tim to leave her alone if that's what you want."

"Good." Adrian releases herself from my grip and grabs my hand. "I'd really appreciate that." She pulls me down the hallway and into the living room. Her mood goes from solemn to happy in a matter of seconds. The countdown has already begun. All the guests are surrounding the piano with glasses held high. Pops is in the middle, looking at his watch.

"SEVEN! . . . SIX! . . . FIVE! . . . FOUR! . . . THREE! . . . TWO! . . . ONE! HAPPY NEW YEARRRRR!!!!"

Everybody begins hugging each other and toasting each other, clinking their glasses together. Uncle Bennie starts in a drunk chorus of "Auld Lang Syne." I'm smiling at everyone, but I'm feeling confused. I didn't think Adrian would take my suggestion literally. I can't believe she actually wants me to tell Tim to stop seeing Carla. They aren't even romantically involved. They just met each other, and it seems harmless.

Adrian grabs my waist and looks at me. "Well, aren't you going to kiss me and wish me a happy new year?"

I look at her. She's holding me close and staring into my eyes. "Happy New Year," I say dryly as I lean in and peck her lips.

As I pull back she grabs my head and kisses me passionately. She presses her breast against me and I can tell she wants to get busy. Adrian has this sly way of rubbing her hard nipples against my torso when she's horny. "Now I'm ready to go home," she whispers. She licks her lips, and I know what that means.

As soon as everyone stops singing, I go get our coats. Several other guests are leaving, so I don't feel bad.

Jamal and Freedom, and Aretha and her date agree to hang around and help my parents clean up. Adrian bids everyone good-bye and we head to the car. She strokes me all the way home and I can barely get out of the car when we pull up in her parking lot. I have a hard-on and Willie is bulging against my lower torso. I carry her into the apartment and up the stairs. Before I can get her in the bed good, we go at it. Needless to say, the buttons on my shirt all get snapped off and the lamp next to her bed gets cracked when Adrian's foot knocks it off the stand. By the next morning, I don't have a problem calling

Tim and asking him to leave Carla alone. When he gets back from his trip, that will be the first thing on my agenda.

Adrian and I spent the rest of New Year's Day butt naked in the bed, like Adam and Eve. Adrian is some kind of woman and I can't believe I was actually on the verge of being mad at her. If I'm lucky, Tim and Carla will have fallen out on their own before I get a chance to talk to him.

## 18

GO TO PICK Tim up at Love Field airport. He's all smiles when he gets off the plane and walks into the terminal. He looks well rested and ready to get back into the swing of things.

"How was Austin?" I ask as we grip, do a brother hug, and head to the baggage claim.

"Man, it was all that! Moms made homemade everything! She sent you back two pies, half a carrot cake, and a peach cobbler."

"I'll have to call her and tell her thanks. What else did you do?"

"To be honest, the entire time I was there, I thought about Carla. We even talked a few times. I gave her the number before I left."

I clear my throat. Tim admitting that he's been thinking about a woman is heavy stuff. I can't remember the last time he even talked about thinking about a woman seriously. This may be a good sign. "She's definitely all that," he continues. "We have a lot in common and I have a good time when I talk to her."

"What did you two end up doing New Year's after you left my parents' house?"

"Nothing really. We sat at my place, drank wine, and talked about everything under the sun. We made omelettes together and did more talking. As a matter of fact, she slept in my bed and I slept on the couch."

"The couch? Tim, you know that is unlike you, man."

"Surprised me too. I hadn't slept on a couch since college." He laughs. "But it's the truth. She slept in one of my T-shirts, in my bed."

"So she was the one who brought you to the airport?"

"Yeah."

"Are you thinking about seeing her on a more consistent basis?"

"Right now, Carla and I are just enjoying ourselves. I don't feel pressure to perform with her. I can be Tim Johnson without all the materialistic things. . . ."

Tim is really tripping. I've never seen him like this before. Normally, he would be bragging about how he had Carla climbing the walls, begging for more of his turbo-engine sex injector. He would be talking about how she slid out of her panties and became his love slave for several hours. This is unlike him to be talking about a woman the way he's talking about Carla. In a respectful way! It's like talking to Will Smith about Jada Pinkett, almost revolting and intriguing at the same time.

I don't know what to do. Adrian made me promise a second time to tell Tim to stop seeing Carla. Of course, she was on top of me butt naked at the time. But now, I'm not sure if it's a good idea. Tim looks happy and it's good to hear him talk about a woman in this fashion.

The last time Tim talked about a woman like he talks about Carla was two years ago, with a woman named Nedra Rollins. She was a loan officer at a mortgage company. Tim met her at the mall and he swore up and down she was the one. I thought she was, too. She was nice, good-hearted, had no children, was career-oriented, and had a body that just wouldn't say no. Tim did everything he could to make her happy, and she seemed receptive—until she went on vacation to Kansas and never returned. No letter, no phone call . . . nothing. Six months later, she appeared in *Hustler* magazine as "The Tantalizing Texas Tornado." Ass out. Tim was crushed, but he hid his feelings and embarrassment so deep that now he swears on his father's grave that he never dated a woman named Nedra Rollins.

"We're supposed to go to a concert Valentine's weekend," he says.

I snap out of my daze. "What concert?"

"D'Angelo, Maxwell, Dionne Farris, and Lauryn Hill are doing a Love Thang tour."

"Damn, that's a tight-ass line-up. I didn't know they were coming to Dallas."

Tim laughs. "They're not coming to Dallas—the concert is in Baltimore, on the thirteenth of February. She has some friends there, so we're flying up."

"Tim, you don't do things like that with anybody."

He picks up his bag from the conveyor belt and we head to the airport exit. "Carla isn't just anybody. She's a good woman friend to have. I ain't trying to marry her, if that's what you're getting at."

"Shit, you might as well be."

"Uh-uhn dawg. This player will never be tied down."

"You keep on, your ass is going to be cemented down."

We both laugh.

"So, how's everything going with the wedding?"

"Cool. Everyone has been paid except the priestess, the caterer, and the photographer."

"Adrian is really on her stuff, then."

"Yeah. She has an amazing business sense. She's also doing a damn good job on the house. Looks like some really rich people will be living there."

"Man, with your combined incomes, you'll be living like Babyface and Tracy Edmonds." Tim laughs.

"Shit, more like Florida and James Evans, with the way Adrian spends money."

We both crack up.

Tim looks over at me. "Did I ever tell you that Adrian is a good woman? I admire her. She's . . . she's classic. You've got a good woman, Greg."

"Thanks man."

We load the car and head back to Tim's place. When he arrives, there's an envelope nestled between the door and the jamb. He takes it out and opens it up. It's a card with a dinner reservation on it.

"This is Carla, I bet." He smiles.

"Where are the reservations?"

"At Brother Soul's."

"That's the new soul-food place on Northwest Highway. I read in the paper it's expensive. The cheapest plate was seventeen dollars."

"Yeah, this is Carla," he says, looking at the handwriting.

"So you're going?"

"I can't wait to see her. This will be the perfect meeting place. Carla has class. I like that in a woman."

I help Tim carry his luggage in. I don't linger, because his dinner date is tonight and I'm sure he needs to get ready. Tim usually takes about an hour and a half on the average to get ready for any date or event.

One time, I made the mistake of coming to his place before we went to a Mavericks game. Tip-off was at eight. It was six-twenty when I made it to Tim's. I was trying to beat traffic. When Tim opened his door, he had a toothbrush in his mouth, but he wasn't dressed. It was cool because I figured he'd take twenty minutes, tops. Then I heard him go to the back and turn on the shower.

"Tim man, what are you doing?" I yelled from the couch.

Tim came into the den with a towel in his hand. "I got to take a shower," he said.

"Well hurry up, man."

"Let me shave and as soon as I finish, I'll hop in the shower. It'll only take a few minutes," he assured me.

Needless to say, by the time Cinderfella was ready, it was seven-forty and we still had thirty minutes of traffic to sit through. I was pissed the entire time. On top of that, the Mavericks lost to the sorry Minnesota Timberwolves. But that's Pretty Boy Tim for you.

At any rate, I give him dap and head out. I've decided not say anything to Adrian. Hopefully, she will assume that I told Tim to stop seeing Carla. I don't understand what the big deal is, anyway. I know Adrian and Carla are friends, but Carla is a grown woman and I don't see why she needs Adrian to watch over her. As a matter of fact, Carla seems more assertive than my girl. She can handle Tim, and she doesn't seem like the type to let any man treat her like shit. She has a tough interior surrounded by a fire that has a certain sex appeal. There are a lot of women in Dallas who could learn from her. Especially my sister. Speaking of which, I need to stop by Shreese's house and pick up the draft of the program for the wedding.

My sister is a design layout executive for one of the largest advertising firms in the United States. The company has a small branch in Dallas. She's the main reason Jamal has gotten so many of his graphics in different commercials and print ads. She selects the artwork for every campaign that comes through the door.

Shreese was an art history major at the University of Texas at Austin. She's smart. Way smarter than her big brother. She was on the dean's list every year, she was in *Who's Who in American Universities,* and she won the Dallas Museum of Art academic achievement award two years in a row. She has a lot of book sense, but no common sense whatsoever. None. All she did was go to church and study. She has a gift for painting. She even sold three pieces when she was in high school. One of the pieces hangs in the black arts building downtown. She designed the program for the wedding, and I need to go pick it up.

Her car is in the parking lot. I look around for the gray Mercedes owned by Pastor Dixon and see no sign of it. Shreese opens the door almost as soon as I knock.

"Hey Greg, come on in."

She's still in her pajamas. I look at my watch. It's ten-fifteen A.M. I look around and notice the apartment is devoid of the usual loud Kirk Franklin playing on the stereo. No holy water out on the entrance panel. No Bible nearby. "I thought you spent Saturday mornings cleaning your house, singing joyful songs, and getting your Sunday School lesson together."

"I don't feel like it." Shreese looks at me and her lips begin to quiver.

"What's wrong with you?"

Tears begin to run down her face. "Ulan is seeing another woman and he . . . he . . ."

"Did he hurt you?" I ask.

"He left town with all the money I had saved." She begins sobbing heavily.

I sit on the couch next to her. "How much did he take?"

"A little over twenty-five thousand."

"Hell, Shreese! What were you thinking?"

"He said he'd use part of the money to help fund the new sanctuary, and the other half as a down payment on a home for him and me. We were going to have a prayer closet and everything."

"When did you give him the money?"

"New Year's."

"That was two weeks ago! Why didn't you call me?!"

She's crying a river now. "Up until now, I . . . I . . . I thought he was out of town looking . . . at . . . at laaaand!"

I sit back on the couch, stiff as a board. All I want to do is find this motherfucker and beat him into a pulp.

"Do you know where he went?"

"He told me he was going to Arkansas."

"How did you find out he wasn't there? Did you try to call him?"

"No. When I called the church this morning to get the number, they were looking for him. He supposedly got money from several of the women at the church. It was on the news this morning. Now the police are looking for him." She wipes her eyes. "Gregory, please don't tell Mom and Dad."

"Shreese, I'm not going to have to tell them. Uncle Bennie will beat me to it if it was on the news." I grin, trying to cheer her up.

She continues to cry. "I can't believe God let this happen to me! I trusted Ulan with my soul."

What my mother said about soul needs pops back into my head.

"Shreese, God didn't let this happen to you. You have to be more careful, that's all. Ulan wasn't looking for virtue, he was looking for a nice woman with money."

"No, Greg! I prayed for a man like Ulan. A man of God! A Christian man!"

"There are still plenty of brothers in the church who would love to take care of you and eventually marry you. A good man doesn't have to be a preacher. There are plenty of men at Mount Cannon—"

"No, I'm not going back to that church!"

"Shreese, don't let one bad incident affect your faith. You've grown up in the church, and those people need you." I rub her shoulder. "What about the other women who are going through the same thing? They need your strength." I can't believe I'm saying this to my sister. I never thought I would be telling Nina Shreese Alston to go to church and have faith. Miss "Nearer, My God, to Thee," herself.

She sits staring at the picture of Jesus on her wall. His brownish-blond hair and blue eyes are settled neatly on the calming face that's been painted on him. I look away from the picture and take a deep breath. *Maybe I have been listening to Jamal Bilal too much,* I think. *But everybody should know by now that Jesus is a black man.*

"Greg, you don't hardly ever go to church and look how well you're doing."

"Shreese, I count my blessings every day. Me not going to church on a consistent basis has nothing to do with my faith."

"Then why don't you go?"

"Because church has never made me stronger. Listening to a man with the same needs as mine has never made me feel any better. Especially a man like Dixon."

"Then what has?"

"What has what?"

"Made you stronger and able to live such a good life even though you sin?"

I shrug. "I guess just living and learning from other people's mistakes. I try to do right by everybody, no matter who they are. We all sin, and I don't have an answer for you why I do it. I suppose it's because I'm a human being and mistakes are just a part of growing and realizing how much we do need God in our lives."

"You still need a family to worship with to help you get closer to God. A solid group of believers."

"Look, we could talk about this all day. I have ups and downs just like anyone who goes to church every day, so that should tell you about physical foundations versus spiritual foundations. People have to find strength in themselves to do well in life. You can't pray for no one to do that for you."

"But prayer brought Mom back."

"Prayer got her here, but she came back on her own."

"I don't see what you're saying. Prayer is the moving force behind miracles."

"Shreese, I know that, but people make decisions for themselves. God and prayer protect us. Now, this is just my opinion, but I even prayed for Louise to come home, just like you did, but still it took me calling her and telling her about a wedding for her to come."

Shreese's eyes light up. "Greg, you prayed for Mom to come home? Really?"

"Well, quiet as it's kept, yes I did pray for her to come home, because I believe that prayer works. But Shreese, sometimes prayer isn't enough. You have to have action to go with it."

"You mean works."

"Huh?"

"Works. Prayer without works is dead. James two and seventeen. It's in the Bible."

"So you see what I'm talking about."

"Yes, and it's really the same thing." Shreese shakes her head at me.

"Now what?"

Shreese smiles slightly for the first time since I came over. "I always thought you never went to church because you were a male. Boys don't go to church often." She sniffs. "Neither do their fathers."

"No, I just never believed church could do anything for me that I couldn't do for myself, but what I do and how I live my life is not for everybody. I still have a relationship with God and that relationship is allowing me to help you in your time of need."

"I don't know what I would do if I didn't have Jesus," Shreese proclaims.

"Well, he better help you figure out how you're going to get back on your feet," I joke. "Do you have money for your rent and car note?"

"No. I don't get paid until next Friday."

"I'll give you the money to cover your bills for the next three months. Don't worry about paying it back, just get on your feet and promise me, if Dixon comes back around, you will call me."

"See how Jesus works," she says sarcastically. "You save me, but still have hatred in your heart. Greg, I'm sure he's doing good things with that money."

"Don't start, Shreese." I laugh. I'm glad to see she can still joke after all this. My sister always could see the lighter side of things.

She shifts on the couch and looks across the room at nothing in particular. "I'm going to have to move home until I can get some money saved back up."

"I'm sure Pops won't mind. He'd love to have you home again."

"I feel so stupid. I should have known Ulan was the devil."

"Yeah, and I would love to be the one to knock the hell out of him."

"Well, he's long gone now. Sister Meadows called and said that he ran off with one of the choir members. She was one of those young, loose sopranos."

"God will deal with Ulan in his own time," I say.

Shreese gets up and goes to the back. She returns with the draft of the wedding program and hands it to me. It's a cream two-fold. On the back is a scanned color photo of me and Adrian.

"Hey, I like this," I say as I admire the layout.

"I thought it was a good idea, too."

I get up to leave. Shreese looks comfortable on the couch, and I suspect she will spend the rest of the day inside. "You need anything, baby girl?"

"No."

"Call me if you need anything, I mean that. You have Adrian's number, don't you?"

"Yes."

As I walk to the door, Shreese calls my name. "Greg?"

"What's up?"

"I'm sorry for not listening to you. You saw through Pastor Dixon all along and I wouldn't listen."

"That's what big brothers are for. I'm just glad you're okay, that's the important thing."

"I'm worried. I don't know what I'm going to do." Tears begin to fall from my sister's face again.

"Hey, doesn't Genesis say something about 'Do not worry'?"

Shreese laughs through her tears. "No, dummy. It's in the book of Matthew."

"Well, read it and don't sweat this. God will see you through, but you have to make some changes. Remember, faith without works . . . well, you know. Sometimes bad things happen to really good people."

She smiles and gets up to lock the door. I hug my sister when she walks up to me. It's an awkward moment for both of us. I hardly ever hug her.

When we were little we hugged all the time; then, when I entered high school, I showed my affection for her by making her laugh any way I could or making her mad. Picking her up and spinning her around, giving her a wedgie, licking my fingers and touching her face, anything that disgusted her but made her giggle.

Now she's a woman, and I'm afraid to touch my own sister. She's as stiff as I am, but I'm glad that we're hugging, even if it's only for a crisis situation.

## 19

ADRIAN HAS BEEN busy these last few weeks. The wedding is next month, and I'm beginning to feel more anxious about getting it over with. Adrian has been at her wits' end and taking me with her. I've been trying to get her to relax, but even my efforts go unnoticed. One day she had me out all day looking for a set of earrings for the maid of honor.

We haven't been spending as much time together as I hoped, either. As a matter of fact, we haven't spent any quality time together like we used to. She's either coming by to pick something up or dropping it off. I guess the closer the wedding gets, the less we'll see of each other. It's cool, though, because it has given me more time to spend with Mom and Pops.

They were really torn by what happened to Shreese, but she told them she gave him only $800 instead of $25,000. I guess lying is Shreese's first step to recovery.

I also convinced Adrian to let my sister house-sit our new home in Winnetka Heights until after the wedding. That way, Shreese won't have to let Mom and Pops find out the total truth about her financial situation. Adrian owns her two-bedroom town house, so Shreese will move in and rent it after the wedding.

Louise never said much to Shreese after everything was explained to her. She just looked at my sister and said, "I hope you've gotten some wisdom from this. There will be problems no matter where you go or who you're with."

When Shreese called me and told me about that talk, she said she was glad Mom didn't fuss like she'd thought she would. She said Pops did all the fussing about the money. I told her it was probably because Louise didn't raise us. Pops cussed for hours on end about Ulan Dixon and his crooked-ass ways. The last time I went by there, he was still talking about it.

Speaking of going by the house, Louise has done a lot of redecorating. She had new carpet installed, and she removed some of the pictures from the walls. They turned my old room into an entertainment room, and now the Boston grand sits boldly in the living room giving the house a fresh, classic appearance. Pops plays every day and he's even written some new tunes. I don't know what's going on between him and Louise, but it's obvious that whatever it is, it's good for both of them. I don't want to go as far as to say they've been doing the nasty or bumping uglies, but it sure seems that way.

Today, when I walk in the front door, they are in the back bedroom with the door closed. I make as much noise as I can to let them know I'm there, but ten minutes still pass before either of them comes out. Pops is first. He has on a pair of old jeans and a T-shirt. He goes straight to the kitchen and grabs an apple before joining me in the den. I assume they've been getting busy, because I head straight to the fridge after good sex too.

"Hey, what you know good?" he says as he sits next to me.

"Nothing. I was just coming by to see what you two were up to."

"Oh, I've been in bed most of the morning. It's still a little too chilly to be doing much else."

I hear the bedroom door open, and Louise comes into the den, smiling. She's humming a tune I've heard Dinah Washington sing, but I can't recall the name of it. She's wearing a dressing gown that flows to the ground. It actually looks like something Versace would create.

"Good morning, Mom."

"Well, well, this is a nice surprise." She leans in and kisses me on the cheek. "What brings you to this neck of the woods?"

"Nothing, I was just stopping by to visit. Did I interrupt something?"

"Son, you always interrupting something," Pops says.

"Adolphus, stop." Mom laughs.

I watch them laugh and make goo-goo eyes at each other. Looks like they worked out some things . . . *worked them way out.*

"How's Shreese holding up?" Pops asks.

"She's good. She's been helping Adrian out a lot on the wedding."

"Did that Dixon guy ever show up again?"

"Not that I know of. Shreese said someone called her not too long ago, but no number or name came up on her Caller ID."

"I bet that was him," Mom says. "Men are prone to doing things like that."

"And women ain't?" Pops says. "Women invented harassment."

"Well, it goes for both, but you rarely hear of stories where women did men wrong, because men don't talk about things like that as openly as women do."

"It's an ego thing," I say.

"I just hope Shreese doesn't get caught up with that nigga again. Otherwise I'm gon' kill him *and* her," Pops says.

"She's never had a boyfriend until now, has she?" Mom asks.

Me and Pops both shake our heads. "One boy tried to court her when we were in school together. His name was Earl, and he was churchy like she was."

"Really?" Mom says, interested.

"Yeah, he would walk her to class and carry her books. I don't know why she didn't like him. Shreese has always been particular."

"What about you?" Mom asks.

"Me? I'm choosy, but not too choosy."

"What made you decide on Adrian, then?"

"She was fun. From the time I met her, she was adventurous and full of energy. I like that in a woman."

"So your other women weren't like that?" Mom asks.

"Cheryl was," Pops interrupts. "Cheryl Coleman was a nice girl."

"Pops, Cheryl was a fatal attraction."

"She was not. That girl had her head on straight, she had a good education, and she loved children."

"There you go with that again." I laugh. "When are you going to give it up?"

Louise looks at both of us. "Give what up?"

"Pops is on this grandchildren kick. He can't wait for me or Reese to have kids so he can be a granddaddy."

Mom looks over at Pops. "Oh really?"

"Gregory, I'm getting old. I ain't going to tell you no more. Shit, at the rate you two are going, I'll be dust before it happens anyway. Besides, what's wrong with wanting a grandchild?"

"Adolphus, children cost money," Louise says.

"This boy makes enough money. Gregory makes too much money, if you ask me."

"Pops, it's more to it than that," I say.

"Greg, it's no use. Adolphus will just have to get over it."

"Aw woman," Pops says as he bites his apple. "Greg is just being selfish."

We all laugh at Pops.

He can be a real character sometimes. He got on this whole grandchildren issue after I turned twenty-six. We were leaving a restaurant, and this old man and a small child walked out ahead of us. Ever since then, Pops has been wanting grandkids. But I'm not having it. I know I'm not ready. Hell, I've been through too much to bring a kid into the world. Although once I'm married it won't be a problem. Adrian will be a good mother, and I know our children will have a good foundation to be raised on. Solid as a rock.

I end up taking a nap on the couch, and when I wake up, Mom and Pops are locked up in the bedroom again. This time, I can hear the bed squeaking and it gives me butterflies that make me want to sneak up to the door and listen to my parents getting busy. Instead, I grab my keys and leave without saying a word.

## 20

CALL TIM FROM Adrian's place. She hasn't made it home yet, and I'm cooking dinner for her tonight. We're having baked smothered chicken served with corn, hot rolls, and string beans. Mom gave me the recipe and so far, everything is going okay. Tim and Carla are leaving tomorrow for Baltimore and I want to holla at him before he leaves.

A female voice answers. "Hello?"

"Is Tim there?"

"Sure, hold on."

"Yeah. It's Tim."

"Since when do you let a woman answer your phone?"

"Oh, that was just Carla. She can answer my phone anytime."

"Sounds like you're on lockdown, if you ask me."

"Greg, I'm still the same Tim. Mack Daddy Supreme!"

Carla laughs in the background and I can hear her say, "You are so funny."

I laugh on the phone. "Still the same Tim, huh?"

Tim sucks his teeth. "Man, she's tripping. Anyway, what's up?"

"I was just calling to chat with you before your trip to Baltimore."

"We're leaving in the morning. We won't be back until Tuesday."

"Tuesday? I thought this was a weekend excursion."

"Well, Carla hasn't seen her family since she moved here, so we're going to spend a day in D.C."

"You know what meeting the family means, don't you?"

"Come on, Greg. This whole trip is innocent. Honestly, Carla and I have a lot of fun together. She's the ideal woman, but I have to maintain my player status, bro. I will always be a player. Always." Tim puts me on hold, and seconds later he comes back. "Say, Greg, can I call you back?"

"Nigga, whatever. Carla has your ass hemmed up tight." I laugh. "Yeah, you can call me back later. I'm at Adrian's."

"Look who's talking about being whipped, Mr. I'm-in-the-kitchen," he teases.

"I'll talk to you later, Tim."

"Yo, Greg?"

"What's up?

"Remember. I'm tha man!" Tim leaves me hanging. I shake my head and hang up on my end. Just as I do, Adrian walks through the door. She looks tired.

"Long day, baby?"

"Yes. My sisters came to the shop today."

"How are they doing?"

"Tired and trifling. Both of them" is Adrian's response.

She goes upstairs and changes into a pink lounging outfit, then comes into the kitchen where I am.

"Whatever you're cooking, it smells good."

"It's smothered chicken."

"I didn't know you had cooking skills." She smiles.

"My mom gave me the recipe, and I decided it was time to surprise you with a li'l somethin' somethin'."

"Well, bring it on then, big daddy." Adrian giggles.

"So, how did it go with your sisters?"

She exhales a deep breath. "They came up to the shop today to get their hair done. Angel wanted her hair cut like mine. As soon as I cut it, she started bitching that I took too much off the top. She always does that."

"Does what?"

"Comes to the shop to get her hair done, and then after it's finished, she complains."

"What about Alanya?"

"Alanya never knows what the fuck she wants done, and she brought those bad-ass kids in the shop with her. I don't know why she doesn't make Daniel keep them when she has to get her hair done."

"She and Daniel still together?"

"Off and on. All I know is, if both of my sisters never step foot in my shop again it would be fine with me."

I give Adrian a hug.

At first she's stiff in my arms; then she loosens up.

"Greg, I'm sorry. I didn't mean to come home and bring all this down on you."

"No, it's okay," I say, holding her. "That's what I'm here for. The good times and the not-so-good."

"Thanks. I wish Carla were here so I could talk to her."

"You can't talk to me?" I ask.

"Well . . . Carla knows my sisters a lot better than you do. It's just easier to talk about them with her." Adrian looks away. "It's a girl thing."

"Oh."

"I can't believe she's been going out with Tim. That was the shocker."

"I guess we both rubbed off on her." I laugh. "Made her get back into the dating scene."

"I guess we did," Adrian says quietly.

The timer on the stove rings and I rush to take the rolls out of the oven. Adrian finishes setting the table while I make our plates.

When we finish dinner, I'm ready to take Adrian upstairs and make love to her. I'm always like that after a good meal. Most brothers are. That's the best way to end a night and get some good, old-fashioned sleep. And the best way to start the morning off is having sex, too. Adrian is usually down with sex after a good meal, but tonight she falls asleep as soon as her head hits the pillow. To be honest, I think she's just not in the mood. She's been out of it lately. Here I am, lying in bed, ready to serve my woman penis on a gold platter, and she's asleep! Women don't know what they're missing half the time. They just don't know.

## 21

THIS IS THE first Saturday in a long time that I've had to be at work. Adrian woke up this morning ready for some action. At first I tried to play it off because I wanted some last night, but beggars can't be choosers and when she placed her wet crotch on my back and kissed me on my neck, I had to go ahead and make her happy. I know a whole lot of brothers who go through shit like this on a daily basis, so I'm lucky not to have to. What she got from me this morning still wasn't half as good as what she could have received last night.

She left for the salon early because she wanted to fit additional customers in to make some extra money.

Tim and Phil are already at the office when I get there. Their cars are parked side by side. The few people who are present look tired. Everyone's dressed in blue jeans, sneakers, and T-shirts. A few folks have their children with them.

On the way to my office, I see Phil in one of the meeting rooms with other members of the finance department. I don't see Simone. She's head of the department and I assumed she would be present. Phil nods, and I wave back as I pass by.

My office has a totally different feel to it on a Saturday. It's quiet and I don't have a million messages on my phone waiting to be answered like I have during the workweek. Data Tech is moving into the beginning of another fiscal year and everybody has end-of-the-year reports to do. My biggest plan is to have the database division partially virtual by the summer. That way, when we're not working on presentation demonstrations, we can all communicate via laptops, cellular phones, and pagers. It's long overdue, in my opinion. With all the money the teams helped me bring in last year, I'm sure we will be accommodated. But for right now, I have got to finish my report and get down to the copier room. Eric comes into my office and Jamal is with him. They both have serious looks on their faces. I'm wondering what Jamal is doing here in the first place, since he works from home.

"J, man, what brings you this way?"

"I was on my way to drop some layouts over at the Crescent Center. I saw your car pull in, so I stopped by. Glad I did."

"Greg, you got a minute?" Eric sits in the chair nearest my desk.

"Sure, Eric. I need a break anyway. What's up?"

"Man, did you know Simone left?"

"She left the company?"

"Turned in her resignation last week and never came to clean out her desk or nothing."

"Damn. I guess that scene between her and Phil at D and B's restaurant forced her to go. What did Phil have to say?"

"Phil is tripping. He's been talking about it ever since he found out."

"I saw him in the meeting on my way in. I'll talk to him about it later."

"Yeah, they're trying to get all the reports together. Simone wasn't the most organized person, from what they tell me."

"Damn. Pressure is a motha."

"But get this. Just so happens that LaShawn did dabble with the lesbian vibe," Jamal says.

"How do you know?"

"One of her classmates works with my girl, Freedom. They all went to high school together."

"What did the classmate say?"

He shrugs. "She just said that LaShawn dabbled after the relationship with her boyfriend went bad and she came up pregnant. After that, she was involved with another woman for about two years."

"So she really is gay?"

"No. That relationship went down the drain. LaShawn went into counseling and ever since then, she's been single and celibate."

"Damn, that's crazy."

"That's what I was thinking. Our people need to quit running around here doing all this crazy, out-of-nature, off-the-wall behavior. Black people aren't supposed to be gay, especially the sisters."

I laugh. "J, you know as well as I do that homosexuality has existed for millions of years. Early Greeks practiced."

"Yeah, after Greece took over Egypt. Man, wasn't nothing like that going on in Africa."

"Then why is it mentioned in the Bible?"

Jamal pauses. "Greg, the Bible has been rewritten a thousand times over. We all know the story of King . . . I mean Queen James."

"I read that somewhere," Eric chimes in. "There were gay people in Africa."

"Whatever, Eric. Don't get me started," Jamal snaps.

"J, man, stop the madness. I'm not saying that being gay is something that should be acceptable, but it's obviously something not to be ignored. I was looking on the Internet earlier this week. I saw gay ski clubs, credit cards for gay people, restaurants, you name it. I didn't even know that shit was out there like that."

"That's a shame. It doesn't make sense to me, either. And some of them have the audacity to say they were born that way. How can you be born gay?" Jamal asks.

I shrug.

"See, if these brothers and sisters understood their true nature as the original man and woman, then they wouldn't want to be doing all that homo-whatever jive."

"Did you see on one of those talk shows when they were talking about the chemical in the brain that gay people have?" Eric asks.

I laugh. "No, but I saw the fight between a man and a transvestite who had impregnated a woman but was going to take the baby to his male lover."

Jamal points at us. "Man, you two better quit watching all that dead television. That's another form of brainwashing that our people have got to get rid of. The only thing I watch is the Discovery Channel, BET, CNN, and reruns of *Good Times*."

"*Good Times!?!* Man, that was real blaxploitation at its grandest." I laugh. "How can you try to check us about watching *Jerry Springer* and you're watching *Good Times*? They never got out of the projects, and that's something to be pissed about."

"Man, *Good Times* is classic Negro television," Jamal argues. "Especially the episode when J.J. painted Ned the Wino as Jesus. That shit was dope!" We're both laughing when Phil walks in.

"Shit, what did I miss?" he asks.

Jamal sits on the edge of my desk. "This brother is trying to criticize me for watching *Good Times*."

"Phil, don't listen to him." I laugh. "The conversation wasn't even about all that."

"Oh. So, what was the conversation about?"

"Simone and LaShawn," I answer.

"Ain't that some shit?" Phil asks. "I would have never thought LaShawn Denton has bumped uglies with another woman."

"She's young," I said, speaking in her defense. "She was probably hoodwinked into sleeping with another woman. Maybe she was curious. Some of the people running around here that are gay were tricked into being gay. LaShawn could be a primary example."

"I don't know," Phil says. "From what her old classmate said, LaShawn was a full-fledged member of the Titty Bumpers Club. She didn't need convincing."

"Phil, you are one ignorant brother," Jamal says. "I can't believe you would say something like that about a perfectly straight sister."

I'm laughing. Phil says some wild shit for him to be twenty-eight.

You would think someone that age would be pretty stable, but Phil is buck wild. "Phil, that was messed up, what you said."

"Hey, I call it like I see it. A titty bumper is a titty bumper." Phil looks out the window and checks his watch. "What are y'all doing for lunch?"

"I don't know, but I'm hungry already," Eric says.

"I don't have any plans," I add.

Jamal gets up from my desk. "Me either. Why don't we go to Jo Mama's?"

"Cool, I'll meet you two in the parking lot in an hour." Phil leaves and heads back to the meeting room.

"Phil needs some serious help," I say. I'm still grinning from his titty remark.

"That's the main reason why our people can't rise today," Jamal says. "I'll see you in an hour, G. Peace out." Jamal gives me dap and heads out.

I go back to working on my report without much thought to the conversation. I think that whole situation with LaShawn is bad. It really seems like she experimented with being a lesbian. On the one hand, she tried it out and is now sure that she's not gay. On the other hand, she had to try it out to be sure.

That reminds me of an incident that happened when I was young. I remember when I was little and Louise would always try and get me to eat black-eyed peas. I hated them. Especially the purple hull. I always thought they looked like alien roaches. I'd never eaten them because they looked so nasty. So, one day she says to me, "How do you know you don't like them if you've never tried them?" I was still arguing my because-they-look-nasty point of view. Then, one day when I was in the kitchen alone, there stood a big pot full of black-eyed peas. I looked around the kitchen to make sure no one was watching and I got a spoon and dipped it in. At first my hand was shaking so bad that the peas rolled off the spoon and back into the pot. I had to dip again. On the second try, the peas were plentiful on the spoon. I closed my eyes and shoved the spoon in my mouth. By the time I finished chewing, I was hooked on black-eyed peas and have been ever since. Mom would put bacon, salt jowl, and green leaves in hers. They're perfectly seasoned straight from the pot.

My whole point being, should that same rule apply with people's sexuality? Where does the curiosity come from? That's what I don't understand. I've never been even remotely attracted to a brother and it kills me to know that there are some brothers out in the world who can look at me and think, *I bet he's a good fuck.* And to know there are women who look at me and think nothing sexual about me. See, women excite me in ways unimaginable and there is nothing I like better than to be up in there, if you know what I mean. But when did the rules of life have exceptions?

Okay, I've gone too far in my thinking. Let me digress and finish this report so I can go to lunch. I feel real sorry for those who have to deal with skeletons in the closet. Those like LaShawn and Simone.

## 22

TWO WEEKS LEFT and I will be a married man. Mom and Pops are excited. Pops tried on his tuxedo yesterday and Mom has been bragging ever since about how handsome he looked. They've been spending a lot of time together. I think Louise is going to stay here and not go back to Paris. She's been doing some performances in Dallas, and some of her CDs are on sale at small record stores in the U.S., finally. I picked up two copies the other day at Mr. Blues record store. She had given me copies, but I went to purchase some to support her.

Pops called me this morning. He said he has something very important to talk to me about. I think that's what it is. I privately hope that's what the talk will be about. I would love to have Louise back in Dallas and back in our lives.

He's sitting outside when I drive up. His car is gone, so I assume Louise is out and about. Pops is dressed nice. He has on some black slacks with a brown, orange, and off-white knit sweater. He reminds me of Bill Cosby.

"Hey Pops, you looking good," I say. I sit next to him on the porch steps.

"Your mama got this for me. I'm sharp, ain't I?"

"The sharpest man in D-town. So what's up?"

"I want to talk to you about some decisions I've made."

*He's going to let Mom stay in the house,* I'm thinking. "What kind of decisions?" I ask.

"After you're married, I'm going back to France with Louise."

*What?!* "Pops, you can't go back to France. What about me and Shreese? What about the house?"

Pops is looking at me like my response has surprised him. "Greg, you and Shreese are grown. You're adults. I've spent my entire life raising you. Now it's my turn to live. What did you expect?"

"But in Paris? Pops, you've spent your life waiting on Mom. And now, out of nowhere, here she comes and you let her take you away. Why don't you make her stay here? Why has she come and changed everything?"

"Greg, me and your mama had a dream together, long before you and Shreese were thought of. We were both supposed to go to Paris, and I decided to stay, and honestly, I can't really say I know why I said no. Even though I said I didn't want you kids on the road, up all hours of the night and spending time with people you barely knew, I knew from the beginning that raising you two and living our dreams was possible. But fear gripped me when the opportunity came. I caved in, saying I wanted more for you and that you kids needed stability, when I let your stability walk out the door. I've never been stable."

"Pops, you *are* stable—"

"Not in here." Pops points to his heart. "I am a musician, son, always have been. A man who makes money under the stars in city after city and enjoys doing it, and now I miss it. Louise has a spot for me in her band and I've told her yes. Gregory, can't you understand that?"

I shake my head. "No. I can't understand having a hypocritical mother or a weak man for a father."

"Boy, you better watch what you sayin' and how you say it. I ain't too old to pop you in your jaw and take you to the yard like a man." Pops takes a deep breath. "When you and Adrian start your new life together, you won't have time for me anymore. Shreese is in church all the time, and if she needs anything, I know you will be here for her."

I sit quiet.

"I've made arrangements to keep the house and rent it out—"

"Pops, this is our house! How can you just up and leave it for a total stranger to move into?"

"Greg, memories can never be erased from the mind and heart. Besides, you just bought your first home. What good is this big house going to do me living in it alone?"

"I just don't think this is right and I can't support what you're doing."

"Well, son, I'm your father and I'm grown. I just wanted you to know, I don't need your damn support." Pops gets up and goes inside, slamming the door behind him.

I jump in my car and head over to Jamal's crib as fast as I can. He's the only one who can help me understand this bullshit. Maybe all this time, Louise has been planning on coming back and getting my father. Next time I see her, I'm going to tell her exactly what she needs to hear: that she's a no-good piece of half trash, who never wanted to be a mother.

When I pull up to Jamal's, I have run the speech to my mother over and over in my mind. Jamal opens the door and lets me in. He's burning Yellow Rose incense and as I inhale the sweet fragrance, I begin to feel calmer.

"Damn G, what's wrong with you?"

I sit on the black leather sofa in the den. "Pops just told me that he's moving to France with Louise."

"For real? Man, that's cool." He takes heed of the frustration showing on my face. "Or maybe it's not so cool."

"All this time, she's been planning this. All those years she's been calling him long distance, sweet-talking the shit out of him! Now, all of a sudden, she comes home, gives him some pussy, and he thinks he's ready to move back to France with her."

Jamal sits across from me in a matching black leather chair. He sits quietly and looks at the floor.

I'm still venting. "Dallas is his home. He can't just up and leave. His family is here."

"Greg, when I was at your parents' house for New Year's, I really saw love between the both of them. Man, that's your soil and water."

"Jamal, my mother left a long time ago. She gave up that right. Now she's come back to take Pops like he don't have shit going on for him here."

"Greg, you are a grown man. Let your pops have a little fun for a change. Let him live. You want him to sit over in that house and rot while waiting for you to have kids?"

"You don't understand, Jamal."

"What I understand, brother, besides the fact that it's really not your decision to make, is that this is none of your business, and when two people love like your parents love, then there's nothing you can do."

"She doesn't love him."

"How do you know?"

"Man, Louise is a user. She uses people, then walks away. She used us to make Pops stay in Dallas, and now she's using her money to take him with her."

"Do you think your dad is that naive, man?"

"I know Louise can't do no wrong in his eyes."

"That's his wife, brother."

"J, my pops didn't start doing all this crazy shit till she came back. He was fine until she came."

"Last week you were loving your old lady to death. She is your mother and if your pops and your mother can still be in love after that long a separation—in love like two rabbits in spring—then I say it's all good."

"Then why can't she stay here? All of her family is here."

"Bro, what your parents are doing is about the heart and making a living doing what they love to do, using wisdom, experience, and natural skills. We all know that a jazz musician can't make a decent living in this country. Your folks can't do what they love and pay bills in America."

"I just don't want to see them—I mean, him—leave," I admit.

"Greg, I think you need to think about what you're saying. You may have a valid point, but the bottom line is that they can do what they want to do. They don't need your approval, and they damn sure don't need your disapproval."

I get up and go to the kitchen to get a drink of water. While I'm there, I call home and check my messages. There's one message from Tim. He sounds upset, but I can't deal with him right now. He probably found a scratch on his hundred-and-fifty-dollar loafers. I'll call him later; right now, I just need to chill.

Jamal goes into his study to finish working on a sketch he's doing for Pepsi. I lie on his couch and take a nap.

When I wake up, it's almost nine o'clock. The house is dark, except for the dimmed light where I am and the light on in the study. Jamal is still working on the sketch. I get up to go take a piss.

The doorbell rings and I hear Jamal greet Eric as he opens the door. I bet Jamal called him and told him everything. *See, that's why you can't trust niggas with your business!* I think. I wash my hands and come back into the den. I dap Eric. He's holding a beer.

"Hey, Greg man, what's going on?"

"Aw, you know, the usual," I say lazily.

"I came by to see if you guys wanted to hang out a little. You know, get some fresh air."

I look at Jamal. I know he put Eric up to this. Eric with his no-acting ass sounds like a commercial. "You fools think you're slick," I say. "This is one of those things you do when somebody is all down and shit. Y'all ain't slick, you know."

"Well then, play along. Your ass running around here like somebody has died isn't good for the energy in my house." Jamal grins.

"So, let's go." Eric raises up.

I get up and stretch. "Where are we going?"

Eric shrugs. "I don't know, you have any ideas?"

"Before we go, I want to go see the new house," Jamal argues. "You promised me last year I would get to see it and I'm still waiting."

"All right. Come on, I'll drive," I say.

We leave out and just as we get to the car, I think about Tim again. With the way he was sounding, I may need to go pick him up, too.

"Damn," I say as I unlock the door.

"What is it? You forget something?" Jamal asks.

"I meant to call Tim. Forget it, I'll call him from the bar."

We pile into my ride and head over to the new house in Winnetka Heights. Hanging with the fellas feels good and it clears my thinking. I've thought a lot about what Pops was saying, but I still don't like how this has been done. I feel like Louise crept into our lives and now is creeping out with valuable goods. When we get to the house, Shreese's car is out front, but the house appears dark inside. I take the guys around to the back and open the sliding patio door.

"You guys wait here, let me make sure Shreese is dressed." I go to the back and knock on her bedroom door. There's no answer. I peek inside the room and all of her things are gone. I guess she moved over to Adrian's place early, and I assume she's in Adrian's car, since it's larger. I guess Adrian is out and about with Louise. I close the door and head back into the living room. Eric and Jamal have come inside.

"Greg, Shreese has been living it up over here," Eric says.

"Why?"

"Her panties are laying on the kitchen table." He points.

I go over to the table and pick up the gold and black bikini-cut panties from the table. I smile. These are Adrian's panties. She's been in the house naked, I think. I imagine her walking around our new home naked, the same way she did at my place, but I don't know why she would leave her panties lying around like this. I begin to feel nervous all of a sudden.

"Your sister got it like that?" Jamal asks. "I thought she was . . ."

"Jamal, chill out man," I say, annoyed.

The guys follow me down to the washroom and I show them the

lower deck of the house. When we come upstairs, I turn on the lights and show them the living room, den, and front bathroom. Adrian has nicely decorated the place and each room has a theme. As we walk down the hall, Jamal and Eric are voicing their impressions of the house. I show them the room where Shreese was staying. Jamal really digs this room because there's a huge mask from Kenya hanging on the wall. It's one of the masks Louise bought as a gift. The room is decorated in different shades of brown and cream with a zebra-fur piece laid across the bed. We get through the next bedroom and bathroom quickly. We turn the corner to the master bedroom and I'm immediately alarmed. I hear a voice coming from the other side. Jamal and Eric stop in their tracks also.

"I hear someone in there," Eric whispers.

"Hold up," I whisper back. We all edge closer to the door. The voice we hear is actually moaning. It sounds like pleasure moans.

"Is that Shreese?" Jamal asks, under his breath.

"Yeah, and I bet she's with Dixon," I say. I clench my fist, trying to keep my cool. Heat rises inside of me as I listen to my sister. Fucking the pastor in me and Adrian's king-sized bed.

The voice on the other side gets louder. "Oooh, you feel so good! Yes! Yes! Yes! Right there! Ooooooh!"

"Who is Dixon?" Eric asks.

"The church pastor," I answer. My hands are sweating. I'm about to go bust his naked ass.

"The pastor!?!" Eric and Jamal say together.

"Will you two shut the fuck up!?"

Before they can answer, I burst into the room. At first, all I can see is two bodies beneath the white sheets. The late-winter moonlight is sharp and I feel like a burglar the way my shadow stretches across the ivory carpet. Shreese is lying up near the headboard, spread-eagled, and Dixon is underneath the sheets, a mere silhouette, but I know it's Dixon because the body frame is small like his.

I flick on the light and instinctively dash to the bed and grab the pastor, who is still under the sheet with his head buried between my sister's legs. We begin to struggle like wrestlers. He's stronger than I thought.

"Motherfucker, get off of me!" the voice from under the sheet cries out. I loosen my grip just enough for the pastor's head to come out.

"WHAT THE FUCK!????" It's Jamal, and he's stepped all the way inside the room. I can hear his voice, but it sounds distant. Heat is rising all over me.

I grab the pastor and hold him as I look at my sister. Beads damp with rising moisture appear on my forehead. At first, her face confuses me. It doesn't look the same. Shreese's name doesn't fit the face or the body, but "Adrian" would be perfect for the honey-colored face that's looking at me now. Guilty as a kid in a cookie factory. The woman in the bed being fucked is my fiancée, Adrian Jenkins. And dangling from her neck on a gold chain is the engagement ring that just yesterday she wore proudly on her finger. It hangs loosely as the light flickers against the diamonds and stray starlight flashes across the room's darkness every two seconds.

"Shit, Greg!" she yells as she pulls the bedspread up against her body.

I can see the back of the head of the person I thought was the pastor. I let the sheet go so he can come all the way up and be exposed. I'm ready to punch this motherfucker as soon as he turns around and looks at me. As I stand near the bed, shit is happening so fast that my heartbeat seems to be taking over every ounce of my being. He's one of them light-skinned curly-hair motherfuckers. Not Ulan Dixon. He doesn't have too much of a body, but it's firm. When he turns around and looks at us, all I hear is Eric's Heineken bottle hit the hardwood floor in the hallway. Shards of glass hit the walls and beer fizzles loudly, then subsides. The curly-hair nigga isn't a nigga at all. It's a woman about as tall as Shreese, but it's not my sister. It's Carla. Carla Perrone, the maid of honor. I step back from the bed and push her away from me. She catches her balance and stares at me, breathing as hard as I am. I look at her, still trying to make sure this whole picture is right and these people are really who I think they are.

"Adrian" is all I can fix my lips to say.

Carla leaps over the bed and trots quickly into the bathroom. She's holding her breasts like she has an armful of eggs. I notice one of her nipples sticking out, still erect and hard. She looks back at Adrian. "I told you to tell him!" she says before slamming the door, still ranting and raving on the other side.

"Greg, can I talk to you?" Adrian asks. Her facial expression holds nothing that remotely shows me she's sorry for this scene. I don't even see an ounce of regret on her pitiful, beautiful face!

I can't say anything. I hear Eric's footsteps retreat calmly down the hall and out the door. Jamal is leaning against the wall. I can only see him from my side view and I can't tell if he's paying attention or not.

"Talk to me about what?" I said. "I ought to kill you!" I lunge at Adrian, but Jamal is on me before my feet leave the floor, where my knee takes a hurtful thump.

We fall against the edge of the bed and I'm squirming like a madman trying to get to Adrian so I can get my hands on her. I want to squeeze the life out of her and I can feel the heat in my face and the sweat on my back and I envision me beating her down. Jamal has his arm around my waist and the other is pulling my pants. The belt loop he's gripping snaps and I get a little closer to grabbing Adrian's foot. My hands grab her ankle and squeeze it tightly. She screams and struggles free by kicking one good time. Her foot catches me in the lip and I can taste the warm blood oozing over my teeth as I continue to try and grab her. She's crouched on the bed like a runaway slave. I look at her and I see for the first time that she never loved me at all. It's in her eyes, and she's not afraid of what I want to do to her. Actually her eyes seem to dare me to put my hands on her and this makes me struggle harder. I grab her foot again, this time clawing my fingers into her skin. She yells out in pain and I can feel her skin break. This time Jamal hooks his forearm around my neck and pulls on me. I feel my breath being restricted, so I give in to Jamal's hold on me; otherwise I'm sure he'd choke me to death. When I release Adrian's foot, I notice tears streaming down her face. They were probably there all along and I didn't notice them at first. Jamal grabs me up and pulls me away from the bed.

"Greg, let's go man! Let's go!" He pulls forcefully. I hold my head in my hands and walk with him. I feel like the life has been sucked out of me. I turned around one more time and stare at Adrian in the bed. She's still crying. Still huddled in the bed like a child. I have no mercy for her.

"HOW COULD YOU DO THIS TO ME, SLUT?! AFTER EVERYTHING THAT I'VE DONE FOR YOU AND ME!!! FOR US!!!" I feel myself losing what little sanity I still have. "Don't let me see you on the street, Adrian Jenkins! Don't let me see you ever!"

Jamal has a tight grip on my arm, but I don't resist. I kick the wall on the way out, creating a large gash in the freshly painted Sheetrock. My face is still hot and all I want to do is hit something else. As we walk through the moonlit living room, I knock several pictures off the wall, including the double-signatured Jacob Lawrence original, sending them crashing to their untimely deaths.

Jamal grabs my keys off the counter and we leave out the patio door, the way we entered. I slam it so hard, the glass cracks. I never turn around to lock it. Eric is sitting quietly in the backseat waiting for us. I forgot briefly that he's with us. I get in on the passenger side and Jamal drives this time. We end up driving around the city for an hour before any words are said.

"Where in the fuck are we going?" I finally ask.

Jamal continues to keep his eyes on the road. "Wherever."

"I thought we were going to the bar." I let the window down, and a cold burst of winter air hits me in the face. "Let's go to the motherfucking bar!"

Jamal glances at Eric in the rearview mirror. He points to the Sherman on ramp. "Exit here and get on Greenville. Rudy's Tavern is down the street."

When we get to Rudy's the bar is packed. The waitress takes our drink orders and brings them over to us. Jamal and Eric sit like scorned children. Quiet. Waiting on me to say something. I sit looking around the bar. I can't concentrate on the different faces in the crowd like I normally do. I really don't want to. Don't have the strength to. All the women look like undercover lesbians. Even the ones who are snuggled up against their men. Jamal's voice rings from across the table.

"Yo Greg, man, I'm sorry that shit happened to you."

I can't say anything to him. I just shake my head. Eric is still quiet.

"I would have never thought in a million years that Adrian was like that." He takes another drink of his beer.

I still can't say anything. A lot is running through my mind, but it's all jumbled. Clouded. The only thing I can decipher is that I should have called Tim. This is probably what he was upset about. A woman comes over to the table. She's brown-skinned, short, and has medium-length hair. She's smiling at us. "You three look like you're not having a good time," she says. Her voice is friendly and high-pitched.

"Queen, I really don't want to be rude, but now is not the time," Jamal answers.

"Oh." She gets an attitude. "Well, I'm sorry for the interruption. Excuse the hell outa me." She switches around and walks away, back into the crowd. I shake my head.

"Women ain't nothing but bitches," I mumble.

"They can do some trifling shit," Eric adds. It's the first thing he's said all night. I'm actually shocked that he finally said something. Seems like he's taking this a lot harder than I am.

I gulp my beer. "Eric, you all right man?" I ask. "You ran out of the bedroom pretty fast."

"I had never seen nothing like that before. I would have never thought Adrian . . ."

"Man, none of us did," Jamal adds.

"Well, I for one am not going to sit and mope all night about this shit. I have a wedding to cancel, a suit to take back, a house to sell, and parents to tell." I drink the rest of my beer. "FUCK ADRIAN JENKINS!!" I yell.

Several people look over at our table and start cheering. Jamal shakes his head in disappointment, but says nothing. Eric finishes his beer off and orders another round for the table. This time, I order a vodka straight.

Before the night is over, Jamal is the only one with his faculties remaining. Eric stumbles to the car and I'm carried out by two bouncers and laid across the hood of my Accord.

I'm crying and depressed like a fool. My speech is slurred and I want to go home. Jamal manages to get me and Eric in the car. He takes us back to his house, where we crash. I'm numb as I play the scene over and over in my mind of Adrian and Carla. My stomach begins to turn. I think about how satisfied Adrian sounded. I think about having to tell everyone what happened. The picture returns to my head. Carla was my competition. A woman took my woman. Damn! My lips exude air in heaves. I feel myself being quickly dragged somewhere, but it's too late, I throw up in the hall.

"Aw hell, Greg! Couldn't you wait until I got your drunk ass into the bathroom? I figured you were gon' pull some shit like this!" It's Jamal and he's wiping his shirt. "This shit stinks too!"

I'm thinking an apology, but my lips only quiver and close up. He leans me up against the wall and goes to his room. He comes out with a new shirt on. "Get your ass in the bathroom!" he yells at me. I start laughing and crawling down the hallway as I sing, "IIIII've got a riiiiiiight toooooooo siiiiiiing the bluuuuuuuuuuuues."

Jamal hoists me back into his arms and drags me to the bathroom. He leans me against the floor and removes my shirt. I fall over and Jamal leaves me bare-chested, leaning against the toilet.

"Keep your ass in here and don't come out until you're finished," Jamal says.

"Aw Jaaay maaan, I love you," I say. "You my dawww-aough!" Before I can get my slurred words out, I throw up again, this time on myself. Jamal laughs and closes the door. "Maybe this shit will teach you a lesson, brother. Alcohol is not the solution."

I pass out seconds later.

THE NEXT MORNING, I can't even open my eyes. The sunlight hitting my face from the bathroom window feels like lasers. I try to move but my stomach muscles feel like I've been doing situps for days. My throat is burning, my clothes are soiled, and my breath smells like the crack of a horse's ass.

I can hear someone in the kitchen. I assume it's Jamal. I look around and notice one of my hands is lodged in the toilet. Wet.

Soaking in my own vomit. I remove it slowly and flush. I feel like I've hit rock bottom. As I get up to wash my hands and face, I hear a knock on the bathroom door. I try to say something but can't. My throat is on fire. Eric peeps in and stares at me from the hallway. "You all right, bro?" he asks. I shake my head as I lift some water to my mouth and rinse. "You hit the alcohol pretty hard last night. We didn't think you'd wake up today."

"Man, I feel like shit," I say as I look at myself in the mirror. Bloodshot eyes. Crusty, dry, bloodied lip. Soiled shirt.

"Looks like you messed Jamal's bathroom up. Damn near remodeled it." Eric winces at the sight. "A little more vomit on the wall and I wouldn't know where I was." Eric laughs, trying to cheer me up.

I look around and see the dried upchuck on the floor, in the tub, and on the toilet seat. I'm trying to figure out where did it all come from; then visions from last night begin to reappear. Vaguely, I can see us at the bar, laughing and turning women away. Cussing them out.

"Adrian called over here looking for you."

The name strikes a nerve as I go further into my aching brain to think about last night. Adrian and Carla. Wrapped together like lovers. Making love. They were loving each other. I lean on the sink and hold my head down.

Jamal joins Eric at the door. "Breakfast is ready. . . ." He comes in and pats my back. "Greg man, you gon' be all right?"

"This shit is fucked up," I croak.

"Fuck her, man. She ain't worth it."

"She was my fiancée, man. How can I just take that attitude? I was in love with her."

"Greg, your girl was a lying, two-faced lesbian. Ill-natured," Jamal says calmly. "You're going to have to get over her."

"Shit."

"Hey Greg," Eric interrupts, "she's no good for you. Who knows where she's been and who she's been with?"

I feel my eyes water, but I hold on to the tears. I can't get the picture of Adrian out of my head. Images of me killing her. Strangling her. Loving . . . the bitch. My stomach begins to ache as I try to hold back the tears.

"Greg, take a shower, clean yourself up," Jamal says. "I have some sweats you can borrow."

"Take all the time you need, man," Eric's voice rings in.

Jamal leads me to the other guest bathroom in his house. I turn the shower on and the steam immediately releases the stress from my face and arms. I begin to look forward to having the water against me, like an old friend. I forget about last night and begin to think about tomorrow. I also begin to think about how I will make it through all this. How I will cope. I think about having to tell my family. The different attitudes about Adrian that they all had. I think again. I'll wait before I tell them. A couple of days to let my anger die down. A couple of days to be a hurt brother trying to bounce back.

## 23

I T'S BEEN FOUR days since I found Adrian and Carla in bed together. Adrian has only called once since it happened, but fuck her! I don't want to hear her voice or see her face! I've finally decided to tell my family that the wedding has been called off. They are on their way over now.

At first I couldn't even say it. To think the woman you are in love with is bisexual is not the most entertaining of thoughts. Especially for a man, because sometimes we wake up in the morning just to make a woman's day.

Women can handle shit like this because they talk about it and read about it all the time. Men, on the other hand, are different. We may joke about those kinds of situations, but to actually know your woman cares more about another woman than about a man is unreal. Real men don't talk about men sleeping with men, or women sleeping with women. We consider women like Adrian as women who can't handle a good, strong, sexually active man. She's weak and lacking, in our minds.

That situation with her and Carla would have been fine if I was

Phil. See, Phil is crazy. He probably would have jumped in the bed and yelled, "Don't stop on my account!"

But since I'm not like Phil, things are different. Women like Carla and Adrian are different, is all. Unacceptable. We don't picture their kind as wives. Asking a woman to marry you is a big step for a man, and the last thing he wants to know is that somebody else is getting what he considers is his pussy. No matter who's getting it!

Jamal, Eric, and Tim have been supportive like the brothers I never had. Tim was trying to call me and tell me what he knew. He said Carla told him everything one night when he was expressing his feelings to her. He had grown fond of her and was ready to commit. He said before he could even set his lips to say what he had to say to her, Carla came right out and told him she didn't like men and she could only be his friend. She said she was flattered and all, but life had dealt her too many blows to deal with another man ever. That's when he asked her about her relationship with Adrian. Carla told him everything.

Adrian and Carla go back as far as fourteen years. They've been lovers off and on, but Adrian could never decide what side of the fence she wanted to walk on. Carla became frustrated and moved out of the city. After that, they would see each other every now and then, but Adrian wanted to keep her relationship with Carla a secret, so she introduced Carla to LaShawn. Those two dated for two years. It turned out Carla was too demanding and she wanted LaShawn to have another baby, but LaShawn wasn't willing. Carla put so much pressure on LaShawn that she eventually suffered a mild breakdown and had to go into therapy. Carla relocated to her hometown of D.C., and was out of the picture right around the time I met Adrian. I guess she was going through her I-love-men stage then. Anyway, Carla told Tim, she came back because she loved Adrian and wanted Adrian with her. Carla still wanted children, so Adrian's plans with me changed for the worst. Adrian obviously still was weak behind Carla, so I became just a well-off sperm donor to her. Adrian was planning to marry me, have my child, and leave me to be with another woman. That way, she could get alimony and child support from me. Ain't that a bitch? And on top of that, she probably would have gotten the house because you know the court system don't care about a brother. When I told Tim what happened he was real upset about the whole situation. The sad part is that none of us had a clue that Adrian was bisexual.

A whole lot of shit fell into place after that explanation. I mean, things like why her parents treated me like royalty. They were happy to see their baby girl with a man. Her choosing to always ride me when we were having sex and her fetish with Nia Long, *who* I pray to God isn't a lesbian because I still have hopes that we'll meet one day! And all the gay friends she had should have been another clue. Like I said, I have nothing against a person being gay as long as I know about it.

Being in the closet hurts more people than just the person hiding in that motherfucker. But it's over and now comes the toughest part. Telling my family.

The doorbell rings and I'm still trying to clean this pigpen of an apartment. I drop some clothes on the floor and answer anyway.

When Louise and Shreese walk in, they immediately started criticizing my place.

"Gregory Alston, I know your daddy raised you better than this!" Louise says.

Shreese looks at me. "Boy, what is wrong with you? This place is a mess."

"Come in and sit down," I say dryly.

"Where? Son, this place looks like World War One." Louise bends down and picks up the clothes I left on the floor two days ago. She takes them to the bathroom. She hasn't even taken her coat off. Pops comes in quietly. I guess he's still mad at me. Shreese sits next to Pops on the couch. She's looking at me. Concern rises on her face, but she stays quiet. Louise comes back into the living room long enough to take off her coat and put her purse down. She immediately walks into the kitchen and begins cleaning.

"Mom, I really need to talk to you about something. Do you mind?"

"Gregory, whatever you got to say, you can say over running water. I can see that something is wrong, but this kitchen is dirty."

I let her comment slide. To argue over where I want her to be when I break the news is trivial compared to the reaction. I just hope she doesn't break any of my plates or glasses when I say what I have to say.

"First of all, I want to thank all of you for coming."

"You'd do it for us." Shreese smiles.

"I want to tell you that Adrian and I have broken our engagement."

Louise never looks up from the dishwater she is running. Pops looks at me in surprise. Shreese is the only person able to talk. "Oh my God, what happened?"

"I caught Adrian in the new house having sex with someone." A lump of butterflies fills my stomach.

"Lord have mercy. I should have followed my first instincts about that girl," Shreese says.

"What do you mean, 'caught her in the house having sex with someone'?" Pops asks. "Did you ask her why she was with someone else?"

I can see now that Pops isn't taking this as lightly as Louise or Shreese. "No, I left her there and haven't talked to her since."

"Well, it serves her right. The Lord don't like ugly." Shreese sucks her teeth and leans back onto the sofa.

I look in the kitchen and Louise is still washing the dishes. She looks at me and her eyes tell me she understands.

"When did this happen?" It's Pops, and he is still looking surprised.

"Friday night."

"Who was the man? Was he one of your friends?" he asked.

I paused for a second. "No, Pops. I'd never seen this man before."

"Hmph," Louise says. She looks up and tries to pass it off with a cough.

"Lord have mercy," Shreese repeats herself. "So what about the wedding stuff?"

"Jamal and Eric are handling the cancellations of everything. Some of the finances I will have to take as a loss. I haven't talked to Adrian, so I don't know what she's going to do on her end."

"What about the house, son?" Louise asks from the kitchen.

"I'm keeping it. The mortgage payments are in my name and it's high time I quit renting anyway."

"Gregory, I'm so sorry about all this," Shreese says.

"Son, you sure you two can't work this out?" Pops says. "People make mistakes."

"Adolphus, you can't forget nothing like that. Adrian should have thought about all that before she climbed into bed with somebody other than Gregory. There is nothing to be worked out," Louise states.

"Mom is right, Daddy. The damage has been done and the Lord has to handle the rest."

"I guess so, but this is the craziest shit I've heard since Miles Davis put out *Bitches' Brew,*" Pops mumbles. "Well son, are you going to be okay?"

"Yeah, I just have some thinking I need to do."

"And some cleaning too," Shreese says. She raises from the couch with her coat in her hand. "If you need anything, call me. I have an emergency meeting at the church. We got a new pastor."

"Is he married?" Pops asks.

"Yes, Daddy."

"Good," he says.

Shreese comes over and gives me a hug. This time, we both feel comfortable. She goes over, kisses Louise, and heads out the door. Pops flicks on the television and watches the news.

I go to my bedroom and start cleaning up. There are hints of Adrian's presence everywhere. Her clothes, perfumes, things she bought me over the years, her jewelry, and, under my bathroom cabinet, her feminine goods. I feel violated. Like a brother who's gotten beat down by the police before he's sent to jail. The phone rings, but I don't answer it.

I hear the water turn off and Louise picks up the phone in the kitchen. "Gregory, this is Freedom on the phone. She says Jamal is on his way over with the boxes. Do you want to talk to her?" she calls out to me.

"No, tell her thanks," I answer. I gather Adrian's things and stack them on my bed. As soon as Jamal gets here, I'm packing them up and sending them to her. Hopefully she'll have sense enough to get her shit out of the house too.

Pops comes to the back. "Gregory, I have to go back over to the house and take care of some business. Can you bring your mother home for me?"

I look at Pops, and for the first time in a long time, I can see what he means by he has a lot of living to do. He still stands like a newly built building. His hands are strong and his legs are sturdy. I used to be teased when I was younger for having a father who was so much older than everyone else's in my class, but he has withstood the test of time. Maybe time held still for him and Mom . . . to be honest, I don't know, but I see that he's still as sturdy as he was when Louise left.

"Yeah, I can drop her off," I say.

"And Gregory, you get over Adrian and move on. You still got grandkids to produce for me, you understand." He smiles. His eyes still twinkle.

"I understand, Pops." I give him some dap and he pats me on the back before he leaves out of the room. I hear him say some things to Mom and then he leaves out of the apartment. She's in the front busying herself with cleaning my place up. I'm actually relieved she's here. Otherwise, I'd still be carrying on like a depressed snail. She flicks the television off and turns on my stereo.

Music has gotten our family through some hard times, and now I can appreciate the value of why people write lyrics and why they work so hard at getting their songs to have the emotional feeling that songs should have. Surprisingly enough, she put on my Donny Hathaway CD. I used to listen to him in high school. Uncle Bennie turned me on to him. I dig his daughter Lalah Hathaway, too. Her first CD is definitely the lick. As Donny's voice and piano playing fills the quiet spaces in the apartment, I think about my days in high school, when life was much more simple. I had dedicated his version of "For All We Know" to this girl named Rita Jackson. She was older than me, but I had a crush on her that some thought would never end. I wonder what happened to Rita. Mom's selection of music was perfect. She just so happened to pick one of the only CDs I have that

Adrian never heard. There are fourteen in all she never heard. She didn't care for Donny Hathaway, and I never tried to force him on her. Mom must know something I don't know. Mothers are like that. They can always say or do the perfect thing at the most appropriate time.

As I think about my mother, I suppose Pops will be happy with her. He hasn't been to France in years and I suppose letting him go, with my support, would make him happy. Shit, I may need to join them! After Friday night, I feel like Dallas has just caved in on me. Nah, Pops was right, I'm a grown man now and I don't need him as much as I used to.

The doorbell rings and Mom lets Jamal in. They greet each other. He's carrying two well-packed grocery sacks. I help by taking one and carrying it to the kitchen.

"Freedom and her sisters cooked up enough food to get you through the next two weeks, my brother." He smiles.

"Good," Louise says. "I'm glad, because it's going to take him two weeks to get this apartment cleaned."

I help Jamal get the boxes and as soon as I get them in my room I begin to pack Adrian's things. We spend the rest of the day cleaning, munching on the food Freedom sent, and packing boxes. My lease is up in one week. This will be the last week in my apartment.

Jamal leaves after we get Adrian's boxes packed. Mom puts on her coat and grabs her purse and we head out on our way back to the house. Once we're on the freeway, I begin to talk to her. "Mom, I know you're taking Pops back to France with you."

"What do you have to say about it?" she asks.

"At first I wasn't excited about it. I was against it and I felt like you had come back to split the family up again."

"What else?"

"Pops means a lot to me, you both do. I just wasn't prepared for this kind of separation again."

"So what caused your change of heart? Why aren't you fighting this anymore?"

"It was the look in Pops's eyes when he told me he was going back with you. At first I ignored it, but it was such a familiar look. The same look he had the day we were at the airport. He . . . I don't know, he just looked so young and full of energy when he looked at you."

"There's a lot in your daddy's eyes that was there long before you were born, Gregory. Your father and I shared a lot before you and Nina came." Louise smiles and closes her eyes. "Adolphus is the only man in this whole world that I love and will always love."

"I know."

"It's like a song you can't get out of your head because you fancy it so much and you hope you never wake up one day and can't remember it."

"I guess love is good when you know it's the love that makes a three-thousand-mile distance seem like it's right next door."

Louise takes a long look out the window before speaking again. "That's right, son, and with your daddy and me it was just that simple. Thank you for finally seeing that."

"For what it's worth, I hope you two are happy over there, and I will always be here rooting for you."

Louise notices my attempt to appear happy for her, but I can't fool her. I envy what she and my father have. I don't think I will ever be able to get back on my feet and be in love like that. "Child, don't let this mess with Adrian get the best of you. I can assure you, she will be back. Women like her always feel the need to explain themselves and their actions."

"What do you mean?"

"Gregory, that girl had more tragic flaws than just getting caught in bed with some woman."

"How did you know it was a woman? Who told you? I never said it was a woman."

"Well, *was* it a woman?"

I keep my eyes on the road. "Yeah. It was Carla Perrone, the maid of honor."

Louise sucks her teeth. "The one Tim left with at the New Year's party? I figured as much."

"How did you know?"

Louise laughs. It's one of those laughs mothers do when they know that they know what they know. "Child, I have seen it all my travels.

I can spot one of those rascals a mile away. But to tell you the truth, I thought something was funny with Adrian and I couldn't put my finger on it, until I heard her and Carla arguing in the room the night of the New Year's party. Them two rascals was going at it about Carla leaving with your friend Tim."

"They're called lesbians," I say to correct her.

"Rascals. Lesbians. Thrill seekers, you name it. I can spot them a mile away. The woman who wrote the lyrics to one of my songs is a lesbian, and we've been friends a long time. I've seen her bring famous jazz and soul singers around, who I never thought in a million years were like that. Adrian may be your first rascal, but she won't be your last. You just have to be real careful, Gregory. Sleeping with folks is serious and deadly business. It always has been. AIDS didn't start nothing new but awareness."

"Oh yes she will be my last," I say emphatically. "I'm doing police checks from here on out."

We laugh together.

"You think a woman's sexual orientation is on a police report? You 'bout as bad as that sister of yours. Maybe me and 'Dolphus need to stay right here and help you two along into your old age."

"No, we'll be fine." I chuckle. "Speaking of which, have you found anyone to rent the house to yet?"

"No, but we aren't leaving until the first of April. Why?"

"I was thinking Shreese could stay in the house. That way all of the family stuff can stay where it is. She can stay in Winnetka Heights with me until you leave."

"I don't mind. Your daddy could definitely quit worrying about that piano if she did move in, but we'll see. I have to talk to him first."

We exit off the freeway into the neighborhood and I pull to a halt in front of the house. Mom kisses me and hugs me tightly.

"Stay strong, Gregory. Troubles don't last always."

"Okay." I hug her back and watch her get out of the car. She waves to me as I pull out of the driveway and head back to my place. I dread going to work tomorrow, but I have to.

When I get back to my place there is a note on my door. It's

Adrian's handwriting. I zip my jacket to keep the nip of the air away from my body. I open the letter and read:

*Gregory,*

*I just wanted to tell you that I apologize for what happened. I wanted to tell you about my past in the beginning, but I was in denial about who I was and what I wanted. I had sincere intentions going into our relationship, but by the end I knew I couldn't pretend with you any longer and I planned to tell you, but you found out the hard way. This doesn't mean I never loved you, because I did. It's just that loving a woman is secure for me. It's total understanding all the time, and I need that. Because you found out, I have finally told my parents that I am a lesbian, and finally I am proud of it. I know you don't want to see me again and I know this has cost you money, time, public opinion, and probably the question of knowing what a real woman is. I know you know. I came to you, you didn't come to me, so don't doubt your own feelings and instincts. I will not take anything from the house except my belongings. The furniture and decor are yours if you want them. If not, call me and I will send you the receipts.*

    *Adrian*

I crumple the letter up in my hands and toss it across the parking lot. The wind blows it behind the wheel of a car, where it's wavering when I walk away. I grab my keys from my pocket and head to my apartment. "Bitch" is all I can say as I go inside. Tomorrow will be a new day for me. I'm going back to work to face the world.

## 24

THE OFFICE IS quiet today. Everyone seems extra quiet and they all have these comforting smiles on their faces as if a great loss has occurred. Sympathy for me, the brokenhearted bachelor. I'm assuming it's because Eric and Tim let everyone know that my wedding has been canceled. I'm calm about it. As a matter of fact, I'm glad everyone knows. The quicker they know, the quicker I can move on with my life. My secretary, Dorothy, hands me my phone messages from the past two days.

"We missed you, Greg." She smiles.

"Thanks, Dorothy," I say warmly.

"You know we got some new employees this week?"

"No I didn't," I say. "I suppose you're going to tell me about them?"

"You know I will, but not right now. You have a lot of catching up to do."

"You're right, Dorothy."

"Greg, are you going to be okay? I mean, I know you don't want to talk about the breakoff, but if you need to I'm here."

"I know, but I've got some good people supporting me. Thanks anyway." I head to my office. When I get inside, I leave the door open. I don't want people to think I'm taking this as bad as I am. See, being a man is a hard job. How a man handles a crisis says a lot about his character. By leaving my office door open the third day after my crisis (two days don't count because Saturday and Sunday were week-end days), I show that I'm strong and able to bounce back. I know the brothers have my back on this one. It's plain and simple, a man who dwells on the loss of a woman for too long is not going to be the same in the eyes of his fellow brothers. They treat him differently after that. As long as Jamal keeps quiet about how I cried like a bitch the night I found out and got sloppy drunk, I may be moved into the Real Man Hall of Fame.

It's hard for me to deal with what happened. These past few days, I've just put it in my mind that my fiancée was killed in an accident. That makes more sense. I miss holding Adrian. I miss her laugh and her kisses. I can't believe she chooses to give all that to a woman. Women can't appreciate women sexually! What ever happened to missing strong hands, a deep voice, and penetration? I look on my desk and notice that one of the guys has removed all the pictures of Adrian. It's good to have thoughtful friends around. Seeing Adrian anyplace other than my mind would really piss me off right about now.

There are several folders on my desk and I'm tempted to assign them out to my group members, but I need something to keep me busy, so I start working. There's a knock on my door. I look up and Tim is standing at the door with a woman. I stand up.

"What's up, my man?" I say smiling.

He walks in with the woman. "Hey G." He grins. "Welcome back."

"Thanks."

"How you holding up?"

"Like a champion, man. Thanks for the help this weekend."

We give each other dap.

"No problem. Anytime. I wanted to introduce you to our new head of finance, Lisa Carter."

The woman smiles and extends her hand to me. Her most noticeable feature is her hazel eyes against her dark skin. "Hi, Mr. Alston. It's nice to meet you."

I take her hand and return the favor. "Welcome aboard."

"Lisa has a master's in finance. She was able to jump right in and get all the paperwork cleared up in no time," Tim adds.

"That's good. It's good to know we have some people in the workforce who are self-motivated."

"Thanks. Maybe we-all can do lunch sometime," she suggests. She smiles again and leaves the office. Tim watches her walk down the hall.

He looks at me, smiling, back to his old self. "So what do you think?"

"What do you mean, what do I think?"

"She's beautiful. She's a beautiful sister, man, didn't you notice?"

I pull back from my desk. "Tim, I just got out of a fucked-up situation. What makes you think I want to go into another one? For all we know, Lisa could be an ax murderer. Shit, with my luck, she probably is." I laugh.

"I don't think so. All I can say is, consider getting to know her."

Just as Tim finishes his sentence, Phillip comes running into my office with his small portable television. "Where's a plug!? Where's a plug?!"

"Damn, Phil, if I didn't know you, I'd be calling 911 right now to report a theft," Tim says, laughing. I point to the empty socket near my desk. Phil runs over and places the television on my desk. "Greg, you got to see this shit, man!"

I look over at Tim. I know they told Phil that Adrian was in bed with another man, and I'm hoping he hasn't found out the truth. Phil is one brother in my crew who would not be able to handle what really went down. When he flips the television on, the picture has not faded in, but a newscaster's voice can be clearly heard.

"We are standing at the Lew Sterrett Justice Center in downtown Dallas, where the members of Mount Cannon Baptist Church are assembled. . . ." The picture begins to fade in. A news reporter is standing in front of a building with several black people standing around her. They are all holding Bibles and dressed up in fashionable church attire. To my surprise the person standing right next to the reporter, about to be interviewed, is my sister, Shreese. I turn the volume up to hear what the newscaster is saying.

"Live on the scene where Reverend Ulan Dixon has just been brought in from Madison, Wisconsin, where he was captured this morning. He was taken into custody along with his eighteen-year-old girlfriend, whose name has not been released at this time. Here we have with us one of the Mount Cannon Baptist Church members who had money taken from her by Reverend Dixon. Her name is Shreese Alston." The news reporter turns to my sister, who has a serious look on her face. I do notice she's wearing her hair down and she has lip gloss on. Phil lets out a long whistle. "Greg, your sister is fine-looking."

"Phil, she's off limits," Tim says loudly.

"Shhh man, chill out."

"Ms. Alston, why are you here today?" the reporter asks.

"I'm here because Pastor Dixon took money from me along with some of the other church members assembled here today and we want to see him get what he deserves," Shreese answered. "We want justice!"

"Ma'am, how much money did he take from you?"

"I don't want to disclose the amount. But it was my life savings."

"What do you hope to get from this protest today?"

"I want Ulan Dixon to know that playing with God's people is not the answer. Romans twelve and nineteen reads, 'Vengeance is mine; I will repay, saith the Lord,' and vengeance is now upon the head of Ulan Dixon!" Several members of the church begin to clap and cheer. Phil is laughing and Tim is shaking his head. The phone rings on my desk and I know it's one of my parents. "I'll leave this in here for you to watch," Phil says.

"Let me know what else happens," Tim asks. They both leave as I pick up the line. "Hello?"

"Hey Gregory Bean! This is your Uncle Bennie!"

"Oh, hey Unc," I say, surprised.

"I was sitting up here watching *The Price Is Right* and the news interrupted the show. Have you seen your sister on here talking about that preacher boyfriend of hers?"

"Yeah, I'm looking at it now, Uncle Bennie."

"Oh you is? Well, good. Your mama should be calling shortly."

Uncle Bennie hangs up quickly. In a matter of seconds, my phone rings again. I pick up.

"This is Greg."

"Gregory, your sister is on television." It's my mother, and she sounds disturbed by what Shreese is doing on television. "Why is she on television singing church songs and cursing the devil?"

"I know. I'm watching her."

"Gregory, what is going on with Shreese and this church? Why is she carrying on like this?"

"Like what? Shreese has been like this since she was twelve. Haven't you noticed?"

"No I didn't notice! Shreese never talked about her church life to me. Not once did she give me any indication that she had become some Bible-thumpin', finger-pointin' holy roller. Did that Ulan Dixon man do this to her?"

"Mom, Shreese began going to church praying for you to come home. I don't know why she never told you about her life, but it's extreme and it stemmed from you leaving."

"So this is my fault." Louise sniffs into the phone. "I never meant to—"

"Mom, Shreese has done this herself. At some point she probably realized that Pastor Dixon wasn't any good, but she's a woman."

"But Gregory, I just wish someone would have told me. I didn't like the way she treated you when that man was around and I didn't like the way she treated Adrian with her comments, but I was too busy trying not to interfere in your lives because I'd been gone. I ignored being her mother."

"The church has been her mother for sixteen years, don't you understand that?"

Mom sniffles and her voice begins to quiver. "I didn't mean to do this to my kids. Lord knows I wanted what was best for you."

"Mom, don't cry. We just have some issues to work through, that's all. Shreese will be okay. I will look after her. I can handle it."

"No Gregory! You spend your life dating all kinds of women and end up engaged to a lesbian, your sister gets used and abused by a no-good pastor, and your father didn't play his piano until I returned. I did all of this! I made these things happen!" She's sobbing heavily.

I lean over my desk and turn the television off. "Mom, at some point we had to take the blame for hindering ourselves. At some point in each of our lives, we were responsible for our actions and they no longer had anything to do with you. What has happened to me, Shreese, and Pops became our fault a long time ago."

Louise is still crying. She's crying like I've never imagined her cry before.

As I sit and hold the phone, realizing how hurt my mother is, I begin to see the hurt she has carried and hidden all these years. I understand her hurt. I also feel guilty. She hurt before any of us and now, we must help repair her life as well as our own.

## 25

THREE YEARS HAVE passed since my parents moved to France. They call every Thursday to talk to me and Shreese. Before they left, we got a chance to sit down as a family and have a long heart-to-heart about anything and everything. Mom admitted to the family how much she regretted leaving, and me, Pops, and Shreese comforted her. On my thirtieth birthday two months ago, my parents released their first CD together. The title is *Wishful Thinking*. They are blowing up over there, and I'm glad for them. I spent my birthday listening to the CD and thinking about how proud of my parents I have become. I didn't mind spending my birthday alone. We are led to believe we have to party or be with the person or persons we love to celebrate our existence on this planet. In a way I did party, because I spent my birthday with someone I love. Me.

Shreese did move into the house on Rivermoon Drive. She's still in the church, but she doesn't attend Mount Cannon any longer. After the scene with the news people, she and Louise spent some time together, and ever since, my sister has been a different woman. She goes to a small church near the house in the old neighborhood.

I've visited with her several times and I liked it. It's a big change from what she was used to. The members are nice and they have a professional counselor on staff, who Shreese has sessions with three times a month. She's come a long way.

She will turn twenty-seven soon and I'm proud of her. She's met a nice group of sisters from her job. They are all in a reading club together called Page Turners. They read everything from Tina McElroy Ansa to Connie Briscoe to E. Lynn Harris. She was shocked when she read one of E. Lynn's books, but she said it helped her understand and not get involved with the private lives of others. It was funny, because Shreese didn't burn the book like she has so many others in her heyday. She was the reason my *Message to the Blackman* got roasted when I was in college. Her favorite phrase now is "That's between them and their God." She says it all the time, whenever some kind of conflict occurs that doesn't involve her. She's also been reading a lot of self-help books from black women like Pearl Cleage, Iyanla Vanzant, and Gwendolyn Goldsby Grant. The ladies from her job took her out to her first club set and she still talks about the good time she had. It's good to see her enjoying all of life's offerings. She even bought some secular music. I laughed because it was all dated. Stuff like Gladys Knight and the Pips, the Temptations, Natalie Cole, and George Benson. Sometimes, she will sing the songs and if you've ever heard Carmen McRae or Oleta Adams sing seventies soul music, then you've heard my sister in there somewhere. It's a nice flavor. By the way, Ulan Dixon went from Lew Sterrett jail to Huntsville Prison, where I heard that he was doing a minimum of twenty years. He's still ministering.

As for my homeboys, they're all holding their own. After his experience with Carla, Tim stopped dating altogether. He went back to school to get his Ph.D., in business finance. He plans to open his own business. He wants to be a financial counselor to people who have trouble with money management. He no longer professes to be the Supreme Mack Daddy, either. He says women have soured him. He's taken a "vacation away from the poo-nanny," as he put it. He hasn't dated a woman since Carla. The incident left him mad at every woman in the world. To top it off, one of his many women from back in the day called him up and announced that she was pregnant by him. Tim denied it at first, but once the baby was born, there was no way he could deny the child. He still took a blood test, but we all told him he wasted his money because the chocolate little girl he carries pictures of and pays child support for is his spitting image. Don't get me wrong, Tim still plays the field, but he's a lot slower getting to home plate than he used to be. And yup, he's still the Supreme Mack Daddy, whether he believes it or not.

Jamal and Freedom married and now are expecting their first set of twins, which will make three. Their first child, Jobari, is one year old, and he is already trying to say big words like "Kwanzaa" and "Caucasoid." It's fun to see him morph into a mini version of his father. Jamal is making more money than ever, and Freedom has opted to stay home and teach the kids. They've become my closest family since Mom and Pops left. I eat dinner over there almost every Sunday and Tuesday. I even baby-sit Jobari when J and Freedom want to get out of the house.

Eric is leaving Data Tech at the end of this year. He got a job teaching finance at the University of Maryland. We've already planned to send him out in style. I'm going to miss him. The coolest white boy I know. He is taking his girl, Darcell McElroy, with him. Yes, she's the Indian-Thai chick he brought to the New Year's party a few years ago. They've been together three years and are expecting their first little one, but no plans to marry anytime soon. See, he's just like a stereotypical brother! I'm just kidding. Eric wants to marry her after they move. He said he'll let us know. So when I know, you'll know.

Phillip is still with the company and still dating anything and everything he can get his hands on. I don't know if this brother is ever going to change. His Christmas gift to himself last year was a gold tooth with the initial "P" in the middle of it. No surprise to the rest of us. He also purchased a Sony Playstation. We all get together every Sunday now and play like teenage boys with no life. Right now, Phil is getting ready to buy his first home. It's in the suburbs and that's going to be a treat, hearing the stories of Phil in the 'burbs. He's going to be like a fish out of water.

As for me, I'm doing good. The house is holding up great and I enjoy coming home to the quiet and the peace. I even enjoy mowing my own lawn. I'm still working at Data Tech and have been upped two notches as executive over the entire database division. This has put me in a position to expose the communities to what Data Tech does. Through some heavy numbers crunching with my bosses, I was able to donate all of our old computers and software to the black arts building downtown and to one of the cultural centers in the heavily populated Hispanic area in Dallas. I go to the cultural center on weekends now and spend my free time with the kids. Although our office never went virtual, we did get everyone pagers and laptops, so we can pretty much come and go as we please. Jamal and I are working on an after-school project for young black males, but it's so hard to get them motivated about anything. Hopefully, our idea about a classical study in music lyric writing will go over well. We got it set up with some major hip-hop artists and others in the music business, so I think it will be successful.

I know you're waiting to hear about my love life, right? Well, Lisa Carter and I dated for about five months, but I broke it off because I wasn't ready to commit to her the way she needed me to. We're still friends and she's still at Data Tech. We never had sex or anything, and she was down with that. I don't know what kind of experiences she's been through with men, but she stated up front that sleeping together was not an option, and that was cool with me. I never could bring myself to go to that level, even after five months. As a matter of fact, I haven't slept with anyone since Adrian. It was hard at first, until I realized that my love and bedside manner isn't for every woman I meet, I don't care how special she appears to be. I've gambled with my dick and my heart long enough. Now it's time to gamble with my mind; that way the stakes may be high but I will always come out a winner.

I've dated other women off and on, but sometimes it gets scary knowing what I've been through. I don't know whether or not some of these sisters are coming or going.

I'd even met this one sister I thought I could really vibe with, turned out to be a palm reader by profession. She said she made good money, but when she read my palm, she read me wrong. She said I was a doctor with lots of money and three kids. I politely took my palm and my wallet and got the hell out of her past life. Then there was this sister Tina, who criticized everything I said. Whatever I liked, she took the opposite opinion. I don't think her self-esteem was up to par or something, because when I broke it off with her, she wrote me a seven-page letter apologizing and talking about her broken childhood.

Now, a woman has to be on point with me. Any slight idea that she is something other than what I think she should be and she is out the door. Others came and went but at this point, I'm just trying to be the best man I can be. I'm looking for a woman who's responsible. A woman who is honest and who can solve her problems and not just talk about them all the time. I want a woman who gets along with her family. That's the problem with a whole lot of black folk, if you really want to break it down to a science. Family just has no value anymore when picking out a mate. It's important to me and I want it to be important to my woman. That should have been a warning sign to me when I saw how Adrian treated her mother. But I was concentrating on something else. My next woman also needs to be assertive, spiritual, a thinker, and most of all, a one-man woman. One-man and *one-man-only* woman! Some of you may be looking for a person with variety, but it's not for me. Since I've been hanging with Jamal and his family, I've learned a lot about roles and responsibility. I realized that maybe I was a bit anxious with Adrian and I never paid any attention to what she wanted. I think it's important for a man and woman each to stay in his or her own space until it's time to move to higher ground as a couple. I'm learning to be more patient with myself. Women are women, and some are so out of touch with themselves that I worry about the future of black America and strong black families. Women don't want to raise their children; they don't want to cook or clean. All they seem to want nowadays is independence with no responsibilities. They want to brag about how they are living without the assistance of a man. Yet they scratch and claw at one another with no thought to the damage they do to themselves. I want a woman in my life. I know I can't live without one. We need each other. God meant for me to have a help-mate, and once I get myself together, a strong woman will come my way and she won't mind staying at home, with or without me. I'm willing to raise children, cook, and clean and I want someone who is willing to do the same.

And to be honest, if I could do it all over again with Adrian Jenkins as a straight woman, then I would. I would have fought a man for her. I miss her. I miss her smile, her laughter, the way she felt at night . . . I miss all of that. She was a good woman and her being gay didn't make her any less. But what man can compete with a woman's love for another woman? I remember telling Jamal one night that my mother was the kind of woman who used people, then left. I never associated the same with Adrian, but in many ways they are alike. Strong. Strong-willed. Women with wings. Kind of like my mother leaving us didn't make her any less of a mother after all those years. She still had that mother instinct, just like Adrian still knew how to make a man feel like a man and nothing less. That's a reality I had to come into during my depression.

I just wish I hadn't been the one Adrian chose to shit on. That shit was fucked up. Like I told my sister, sometimes bad things happen to really good people. Life is a motherfucker and it's a game you have to play to win. Make decisions wisely. Pray. Anticipate. And that's what I'm doing now, playing to win! Forget everything else! Now I'm back on track and ready for the next love.

# A Thought from Adrian

HEY. I KNOW I'm probably the last person you want to hear from after I took Greg through so much. His mother said I would return with the need to explain and I guess she was right. She never liked me anyway. She knew about me even though she never said anything, she knew. I could see it in her eyes the first time we met.

I have been gay, or at least thought I was gay, since I was seventeen. I was never raped, molested, or promiscuous as a child. I don't believe in the chemical-in-the-brain theory either. It's just a preference for me. Plain and simple. I've always found women very attractive. Always. When I was an adolescent, my mother caught me leafing through a *Playboy* magazine and she whipped me. I hated her after that, and I guess I rebelled by speeding up the process. I stopped wearing dresses and started hanging out on the gay side of town. Stuff like that. After I graduated high school and enrolled in beauty college I began to explore the club scene. Some girlfriends and I went to a hair show in Chicago, and that's where I met Carla. She was a model for one of the hairdressers. We were immediately attracted to one another. She introduced herself and invited me to her hotel room later that night. We were supposed to go out, but one thing led to another and we ended up in bed together. Confirmation for me at nineteen years of age. Carla was the first woman I slept with in a sexual way. She was very aggressive and I liked that at first, but she was so obvious and butch at the time that she wasn't good for my in-the-closet image. I tried to fight it and keep my desires for women on the down-low, but working in the beauty-shop industry only made it worse. Once I opened my shop, I had to go deep cover because my parents were on me to settle. Get married. Have babies. I broke down and told them about my sexual preference and they've been in denial ever since. Now that Greg is out of my life, they don't even speak to me. Took back their house keys.

Thinking back on my experience with Greg, if I hadn't allowed Carla back into my life, I would have still married him. I did love Greg, because he made me feel wanted. He cared about me and cared for me. But Carla makes me feel safe, and I knew I couldn't have the best of both worlds for too long.

I saw Gregory about two years ago. He was with a woman. Pretty. Hazel eyes against dark skin. She saw me, but she didn't know who I was. She wasn't gay, either. We know our own. I wonder if he's still with her. They made a cute couple and I was glad to see him back on his feet. I heard that he had given up on women altogether. Or was that Tim Johnson I heard about?

Anyway, the sisters at the shop still can't believe what happened and talk about it to this day. Arnelle, the nail tech, was the only one who left. I guess she thought she would catch my gayness from hanging around the shop with me. I'm getting ready to open a shop in Atlanta. It's a more progressive city for the life I live. Progressive. I like that word.

One of Carla's guy friends just graduated from hair school and he will run the shop here while she and I go and start up my new salon in the A-T-L. I'm planning for the move to be a permanent one. Dallas is no longer a place I can call home sweet home.

Every now and then, I think about Greg. He was special. I also think about Kevin, Jason, Cedric, Vincent, and Zavier. All that time

I wasted when I could have been happy with Carla. It's amazing how much of other people's time we waste when we don't follow our hearts and be true to ourselves. When Greg told me why his mother left, I thought, *Good for her! A woman not afraid to follow her heart!* I should have taken the initiative a long time ago. I think people spend too much time weighing the costs, which only leads to confusion, self-denial, lies, broken egos, and broken hearts. Maybe one day, it won't be necessary to pretend. Folks will be the best human beings they can be without all the drama. Maybe then we can *all* exhale, right Terry? Shit, now that *would* be something.

# About the Author

A native of Dallas, Texas, CAMIKA SPENCER holds a degree in radio and television broadcasting from East Texas State University. She is currently working on her second novel, *Cubicles*.

If you would like to write to the author, the address is:

c/o Camika Spencer
P.O. Box 41062
Dallas, TX 75241